# Hook

A MEG GILLIS CRIME NOVEL

## C. J. Songer

SCRIBNER

SCRIBNER
1230 Avenue of the Americas
New York, NY 10020

This book is a work of fiction. Names, characters, places, and incidents
either are products of the author's imagination or are used fictitiously.
Any resemblance to actual events or locales or persons, living or dead,
is entirely coincidental.

SCRIBNER and design are trademarks of
Macmillan Library Reference USA, Inc., used under license by
Simon & Schuster, the publisher of this work.

Designed by Colin Joh
Text set in Janson

Manufactured in the United States of America

1  3  5  7  9  10  8  6  4  2

Library of Congress Cataloging-in-Publication Data
Songer, C. J.
Hook: a Meg Gillis crime novel/by C. J. Songer.
        p.   cm.
        I. Title.
PS3569.065393H66   1999
813'.54—dc21      99–27490
        CIP

ISBN 0-684-85043-5

*"We sleep safely in our beds because rough men stand ready in the night to visit violence on our behalf."*
—Attributed to George Orwell


It's a hard job visiting violence,
and it's harder still not to bring it back home.
This is for the rough men and women who are making the effort—
from me and the rest of the people who love them.

# Hook

# 7

"So her husband slapped her around some?" I asked. "This guy, what's-his-name, De la Peña?"

We were sitting at our desks in the office, leaning back in the roll-away chairs, and maybe I had that look in my eye. Mike knows me fairly well—Michael Johnson, my partner.

"Yeah, some," he said. He was playing it down, talking past me to the wall, and I've known *him* a long time, too.

"Bad?"

"Pretty bad."

"She call anybody?"

He looked at me, grim.

"She called *me*, Meg."

Mike's an ex-cop. So am I, actually, so I can't hold it against him, both of us being that little bit stupid. You tend to feel more responsible when you're the one getting the phone call.

"Mike," I said gently, "she's got to go in to Beverly PD."

"She says De la Peña's got pull, back in Argentina."

"Then she should be grateful she's here," I said. "Make it official, get those pictures of her bruises on file."

He was trying to find words, not something usual for Mike, at least not with me.

Finally he shrugged.

9

"Look, babe, I tried."

We've all tried. That's the hell of it, really. People have their reasons why they won't call the cops, and you come to understand every one of them. You hate it, but you understand. Bones heal. People promise. Victims feel shame. And some things *are* worse than a police investigation rummaging through your life—like a guy who has the clout to reach out to your homeland and destroy what you might have left there.

"So who's going to give De la Peña the divorce papers?" I said. "And the restraining order, right? Are you getting Francine?"

Francine's a process server we met a few years ago out at the River. Parker Dam, skiing. She was there with an LAPD guy but thought Mike looked better, and she was looking pretty good herself at the time. She runs her own service now, branching out.

"Nah," Mike was saying, "she's out of town. I was thinking I'd get someone else from her office—Olson, maybe."

Maybe. He wasn't meeting my eyes, and it was 4:05. Friday afternoon's not the prime time to reach people when you haven't even picked up a phone. I stared at the pen holder, made up my mind.

"I'll do it."

"*You?*"

You'd have thought I was offering to murder the guy.

"How big is he?"

"Big," Mike said, "but that isn't it."

"What's his build?"

"Meg—"

"I'll drop the papers on him tonight at the restaurant, Mike. Quick in, quicker out, before he even knows it's coming."

"He'll see you."

"So I'll wear a disguise," I said lightly. "Who am I, anyway? I'm just the messenger. He won't do anything with people around."

"I can't let you do it," Mike said.

"Can't" and "let" is an interesting combination. In all the years I've known Mike, thirteen, fourteen years now, he's never really said that to me before. We've always operated on the assumption that I was a pretty darned competent female and he was a reasonably competent male, and between us we had almost everything covered. I could trust him to watch *my* back, and he trusted me to watch his. Respect. Out on the street that's not a small word, but we'd been off the street for a couple of years.

"You don't think I can do it?"

"Babe," he said in a placating tone, like "Hey, little sweetness," like I was one of his ladies. I stared at him levelly over the desks.

"You don't think I can do it, Mike?"

He held up his hands. "It's not that," he said. "It's, just, y'know—Reilly."

I *do* know Reilly. Joe Reilly, Sergeant Reilly, of the Beverly Hills PD. I've been seeing him for about six months.

"He won't like it, Meg."

Mike knows so much.

"He's working tonight," I said. "Are *you* going to tell him?"

"It's in Beverly Hills."

"What is?" The answer was written all over his face. "The restaurant is?"

"They're meeting at Chaven's."

Hell and damnation. The odds were much greater, then, that Reilly'd find out. In his own city. If something went wrong.

"So you can't do it," Mike said. "I'll get somebody else."

Mike has his own code of ethics, which is maybe not much, but it serves him, gets us both by. He was lying through his teeth this time, though, I could tell—he wouldn't get anyone else. He was planning to go out and serve the papers himself, and if he ended up in a confrontation with this abusive husband, that would suit him just fine. I could do it better and cleaner, and we both knew it, but he was my honorable friend, so excessively male.

"She can't change the restaurant?"

"That isn't the point, Meg."

I knew what the point was for *him*. It was that he wasn't going to mix me up with the man in my life, whether he likes him or not, whether he needs me or not. Mike draws his line in the sand and stands by it. I draw my own lines, though. Draw my conclusions.

"Where's this gal now?"

"She's at a girlfriend's, at her bungalow. She's been there since this morning, when she . . . managed to get away. De la Peña doesn't know where she is."

Hiding out. That was good. She'd had that much gumption then, the right kind of smarts. Enough to get a lawyer, too.

"You've got the papers on you?"

"Out in the car."

Not enough gumption to serve them herself. Enough to call Mike, though, turn the problem over to him. He'd gone out of here like a man on a mission, come back like a man on a stove. He hadn't wanted to tell me about it, but these days I pry a lot more than I used to. He was lifting his coffee cup casually, draining it, and his left hand still doesn't close like it should, but he doesn't like me to notice, so mostly I don't.

We run a small home security business on the fringes of Beverly Hills. John Gill Security Corporation, that's us—Michael Johnson, Meg Gillis, the people who bring you those rotating cameras and computer relays so that you can feel safe behind your burglarproof walls. We set everything up, oversee installation, and then we connect you to a private guard company, your choice, because they're the ones who actually respond to any alarms. We vet them, if you like, to make sure they're okay. Keep tabs. In return, we get a lump sum and a small monthly fee.

Mike does the bulk of the selling because, frankly, he's good at it. He likes people, likes to mix, so he can fit in most places, hold his own. And he's very competent-looking, has that sheen of toughness from his years in the uniform so he comes across as capable, physical, with a

"Who, me? Naah, I'm just one of the guys" kind of quality that appeals to tycoons.

Also to females.

Including, obviously, this Sylvia de la Peña.

I hadn't heard of her before today, but that isn't unusual—Mike doesn't tell me about his married affairs. I'm sort of his notion of a virgin. A nice girl, you know. Not someone to point out your adulteries to.

We've been friends for a fairly long time.

And for all that Mike's thick, which he frequently is, and for all that his morals aren't what most mothers like, he's okay for his kind of guy, he's good people. He's forgetful and casual and very self-centered, but he's loyal to the absolute bone if he knows you; if he thinks that you need him, he's yours.

His hand doesn't close right because he tore it up helping *me* out six months ago. Ended up in a Palm Springs hospital trying to get me back with the living, so, really, I could do him a favor tonight. I'd just have to be more persuasive.

Even if Reilly hadn't been working, I think I'd have gone.

Because Mike was going to help this girl anyway.

And I couldn't let him do it alone.

# 2

My name's Margaret Gillis, although I generally go by Meg. That's what my dad used to call me in his easier days, so that's what I kept. My real name is actually Mary Margaret, but other than Reilly, who tends to unearth things, there aren't many people who know it. I buried "Mary Margaret" about ten miles deep before I went through the Academy because it's tough enough being a female cop, without being the one with the Catholic girl name.

We feed on the same John Wayne notions that the men do, you know. That spirit of the Duke standing tall, narrowed eyes against the sunset, holding the bad guys back by sheer force of will and the coiled threat of the Peacemaker that a good man always has at his side.

There's no Jill Wayne, though. Women have to adapt. When I was very new, I came around a corner into the wrong end of a Colt. The guy was saying "Die, bitch," which leaves you no time, so I just kept on moving, one leg up in a sweep, falling hard on the other, and I caught him square in the groin as the revolver went off and the bullet zanged where my face would have been. Fortunate that I wasn't just standing there tall. Fortunate, too, that I knew something about scrapping so I wasted no time coming out of the dirt to take this guy all the way down. That'll pump you up some, the adrenaline and the other cops coming up to congratulate you, pounding on you, telling you you did fine—but the truth is, I should have been more careful. The next guy might not be talking first, and there's no particular privilege to being dead. I try to learn from things like that, try to learn from the people around me. Try not to learn everything by personal experience, which is frequently harder than you'd think. This situation with Sylvia de la Peña was a big case in point.

I got home that day about five-thirty. Checked in with Mike, and we were still on a go. People *do* change their minds, but Sylvia hadn't. Mike was at the bungalow with her, holding her hand, of course, so that might have helped.

I called Joshua next because I wanted to be sure he was going to be safely home for the evening, not likely to be coming by. Josh is my stepson, twelve years old. Charlie's boy. He lives about a mile away with his mom.

The thing is that I helped Charlie raise him when he was little, and so we have kind of a bond. Charlie's my husband—used to be, that is; he died several years ago, shot on the job. Josh was nine. He had a tough time dealing with his dad being suddenly dead, and I guess I did, too. It's hard to lose the whole family at once, all the normal routines. Anyway, I worked out a deal with his mom to keep paying child support in return for visitation, so Josh mostly comes over every other weekend, and he and I do stuff, usually with Mike or with some of his friends from school, unless, of course, it's baseball season. Then everyone's schedules go on hold while we revolve around midweek practices, back-to-back games, and weekend-long tournaments, as well as those minor things like school and homework. Caroline and I try to be civil, to do what's best in the long run for Josh. I respect her for that, at least. And it's convenient for all of us that I have a rearrangeable work calendar so that I can get to some of the midweek games, and he can come home with me afterwards while she goes out and does things. A person has to have a life.

It's worked out pretty well, all things considered, although it might be a little too easy for Josh to hop on his bike and come over whenever he's fussed at his mom. He's been doing that a lot lately—I guess twelve is the age for it. I try to be careful with that, too, try to have common sense about it. No point in encouraging problems. On the other hand, it doesn't hurt to have an outlet.

It was important that he wasn't feeling fussed-out and moveable *that* night, however, so I called with some feeble question about his practice schedule. I could probably still have worked around him wanting to come over, but I didn't think he needed to see me leaving the house in disguise. I always changed at the station when he was little. Caroline sounded positively cordial, and Josh was spending the night at a friend's so that deck was cleared. Systems on Go.

I almost called Reilly.

I kind of wanted to, for the connection, I think, just to hear him. Had my fingers on the phone buttons, ready to press.

Mike wasn't wrong though. Reilly wouldn't like it, and he wouldn't like it for a number of reasons, one of them being that it was happenng in his territory. Cops get possessive about that. You wouldn't think it would matter, a quarter-mile one way or the other, but it does. "If you're going to get drunk, don't do it in *my* district," and so on. I couldn't change the restaurant, though. It had to be Chaven's in Beverly Hills because that's where Sylvia had told De la Peña she'd meet him. You lose the element of surprise if you call back making other arrangements. People get suspicious, and I didn't really want this soon-to-be-ex-husband on his guard—not if he was as large as Mike thought he was, or as violent.

It was stupid to fret. There was nothing I could have said to Reilly anyway, so I don't know why the sound of his voice would have made any difference. I was just feeling restless, I guess. Antsy. Starting to prime.

I used to be like this doing the job—gearing up for it mentally, or getting mental, depends how you see it. Pacing. Talking the moves. Standing how many times in the made-over bathroom, not even a real locker room, dressed in my costume, uniform, whichever it was, staring into the fly-speckled mirror over the sink.

I always worked outside of the shadow, but just enough near it, you know? Where I could dive in for cover. I wasn't part of the Brotherhood, being a female, but I was tolerated for the most part—like an annex, a semi-auxiliary. I used to have Mike and Dave and two or three others I could count on for backup, and this time, there was no one. Mike was sitting with Sylvia, and this serving-the-papers ought to be nothing, I was pretty sure that it would be, intended to make it that way, but I kept thinking of Charlie, my used-to-be-husband, what he'd have to say.

He'd think I should call someone.

Domestic stuff is the worst, always has been. Hazardous. I could say what I wanted to about this guy not making trouble in front of a roomful of strangers, but people get carried away. They get on that emotional hook and forget about consequences or that anyone's watching. See a target, try to hit it—that kind of thing. He might reserve his anger for his property, his wife, but you can never be sure, because people get crazy. And I'm a female, you know. The distinctions blur. It's always best to have someone else there.

I could hear Charlie saying it.

There was just nobody, really, that I *could* call. I was private now, a civilian. Once more removed.

I dug both hands into the makeup bag on the bathroom counter—my bathroom counter, not the sink at the station. Sorted through the old stuff. Mascara and liner, shadow, tattoos. It's all how you wear it, and it doesn't take much, actually, as long as you fit what people expect. Chaven's was a Beverly Hills restaurant, so I couldn't be too extreme, but I managed a fashionable face.

Pouted my lips at the mirror and I was almost a stranger. Sultry. Hard. I needed the black dress I used to wear, the one with the spaghetti straps and no back to speak of. Charlie had liked it a lot—had liked *me* a lot, made up like this. I had his ghost on my shoulder as it always is, approving, disapproving, and the ghost was saying, *"Hey, baby, come on."* Nuzzling me, arching my neck. Tightening my nipples. He should have loved me better when he had the chance, I guess. Should have stayed home.

17

Charlie died three years ago. Almost an accident. I quit the department shortly after that, cut all the connections.

All except Mike.

And now, of course, Reilly.

I threw on extra lipstick, glossed my mouth, and steadied into the work. Pulled back into planning, strategy, how to get in and out, what to say if I was stopped, if there was a nosy maître d'. If De la Peña had a bodyguard.

I snaked a sheath dress off a hanger from the back of the spare-room closet and skinnied into it. It was tighter than I remembered, and quite a bit lower, so I stuck on dangly earrings to draw up the focus and covered the whole thing with a black see-through shirt wrapped loosely around. That made me a call girl rather than a streetwalker, so maybe they'd let me into the restaurant. Four-inch heels. Thin-strapped leatherette purse.

I checked myself once more in the bathroom mirror, and the stranger smiled knowingly back at me. A high-tech smile, hard and glossy. Smug. "Not a stranger," she was saying, "you've been here before," and I had been, God help me, too many times.

I thought of Reilly again, quickly—what he'd think if he saw me, tricked out, dressed for speed. He hadn't known me before, when I was doing cop work, I mean, and that makes a difference, always matters, I think.

I stretched, arched my shoulders, and the image arched back.

It was me in the mirror.

Dressed for trouble.

To kill.

He wouldn't know me like this, but Mike did, Charlie did. The ghost on my shoulder.

*"Hey, baby, come on."*

It was just for the night. Just serving some papers.

Hazards come all kinds of ways.

# 3

Chaven's is in one of the brick buildings off Rodeo Drive in Beverly Hills. They have valet parking, but I'd already left my car around the corner. I wanted to know where it was if I needed a quick exit, so I'd gotten there early enough to cruise until I found a car pulling out from one of the street spaces. The space was metered, of course, but I had some change, and I'd just have to hope that De la Peña wasn't late or that Beverly wasn't working its traffic division overtime tonight.

I could see right away that I was underdressed for the crowd. There were a lot of expensive women in silks and bluff businessmen in suits, uncles and daddies, expansive with their Friday-night drinks, their little women on show. There were some younger men, too, thin, pointed types, who were there to show themselves eager as they listened to the bosses, their little women on hold or at home. I smiled at one as I passed and he thought about smiling back until he remembered the Boss with the Capital and why he was there. I turned my painted face and took a small corner table away from the bar so I could have a good view of the door.

I had about twenty minutes till De la Peña was due. That was cutting it close, but it had taken longer than I'd thought to find a parking space, and then, too, I hadn't wanted to be sitting there waiting too long or too obviously, in case anyone else got ideas. Or in case Beverly

Vice was doing a sweep tonight, because that would just about do me. I wouldn't have to wonder what Reilly thought then.

The waitress brought me a lemon twist with some soda and gave me a sisterly smile. I'd been watching a dark man across the room, but he didn't have a mustache and he looked more Middle Eastern than Argentine. Iranian, probably.

"That's Mr. Kashoggi," the waitress said.

I wondered if she steered a lot of girls right, and if the house got a cut. "I'm waiting for someone." I smiled at her to make it nicer.

"Sure, honey," she said, "but you don't want to wait all night."

She was right. I didn't. My nerves were getting that pre-action glow and I was feeling good finally, wanting it. I hadn't done this for a long, long time. This was a cakewalk compared to some things I've done, a stroll in the park. I lifted my drink to her, toasted, and laughed. "No, not all night," I said.

She thought I meant something else, I guess, and went away smiling, shaking her head. I turned my attention back to the room. They had it set up so you had to pass through the bar to get to the dining part where the maître d' took names, and it looked to me as if, reservations or not, the wait was at least forty minutes. Management had made it easy for people to flop into overstuffed chairs in the bar while they waited, and there were a half-dozen leggy waitresses taking the drink orders, so I'd think the restaurant made a nice profit on the delay. It's not that I have a particular interest in restaurant economics, you understand, but it looked like a good scam to me. It also improved my chances of hitting De la Peña cleanly, because unless he owned the place or something, they'd be making him wait in the bar, too, and it would be a lot easier to drop the papers on him and be gone from the bar than it would be from the dining room. Closer to the door, for one thing. More people milling, for another. You always look for the cover.

The bar was filling up. Friday night. That was good and bad because it meant that I wasn't as noticeable, but also that more people were eyeing my table as a place to be sitting. I examined my freshly-pressed-on nails and ignored a three-piece suit who was bearing down on me from the left. De la Peña was late.

Three-piece stopped, a pouter-bellied little bantam, maybe my height, maybe less. He'd been drinking, it smelled like, and was weaving a little. "You saving this seat?"

New York City accent. Queens?

"Yes, I am," I said.

He already had his hand on the back of the chair. "Yeah?" I could have brushed him off, I guess, but two people are less conspicuous than one. I let my eyes roll up from his belt buckle without lifting my head, and smiled at him through my lashes. "Well . . . I'm just waiting for a friend."

It was an open invitation, and he didn't lose any time pulling out the chair. "So'm I, honey. What're you drinking?"

"A Joan Collins."

He didn't know what a Joan Collins was, and he didn't care, he was impressing me by getting the waitress back fast, hey, pronto. A take-charge kind of guy. "Another martini for me, and the lady'll have—"

"What you brought me before," I told the waitress. Her eyes thought I could do better than this, and she was probably right, but I stretched delicately and tapped an enameled nail idly against the side of my glass. Mr. Kashoggi had found other company and Rudolph de la Peña had just walked through the door.

"What's your name?" three-piece robin was saying.

"Sylvia." I gave him a brilliant smile and watched De la Peña making his way to the dining room. He didn't seem to have any friends here, nobody stopping him to chat. Nobody coming in, in front or behind him, looking over the crowd. I ducked my head back towards the suit. "Do *you* have a name?"

"Art. Artie Minklow." There was a diamond flashing on his left pinkie finger, no wedding ring, and Artie was making sure that I noticed. De la Peña had reached the maître d', was hearing about the wait. I watched for money changing hands, but he just shrugged and turned unhurriedly back towards the bar. He was a big guy, all right. Older than I would have thought, in his early fifties. A very elegant suit that he wore with an easy grace, matador-like. I wondered how he looked when he was slapping the ladies. Artie was clearing his throat.

"What line of work are you in, Artie?"

He leaned back, chest expanded. "Investments," he said grandly, and it was too much to pass by.

"Really? Religious clothing?"

"No, no. Investments." And then Artie realized that I was twitting him, coy. Wasn't thinking he liked it. "I'm a broker," he said very stiffly.

I didn't want him going away in a huff. De la Peña was finding a table by himself across the room, and I needed cover for a few more minutes. I put my hand on his arm. "I'm sorry," I coaxed, "I was just having fun. Don't you like to have fun, Art?"

This was more in his line. He was wary, though, not so sure now that he wanted to have fun with *me*. "Yeah."

I laughed at him lightly, stroking the suit cloth. Crinkled my nose at him, twinkled my eyes. "Do you live around here?"

"I'm staying over to the Wilshire," he said. "Got a nice little room there." He didn't really mean "little" and we both understood that. I was seeming receptive and he was making his mind up, easing again. Artie'd played *this* game before. De la Peña had ordered a drink and was looking around while he waited, not checking his watch. He seemed very calm about it—was Sylvia usually late? I leaned in to Artie before De la Peña's attention got to our table.

"Do you come here a lot, Art?"

"Yeah, when I'm in town. They know me here. It's a nice place to eat, meet some company. I'm out to L.A. right now to check on our offices."

A big wheel.

"So you live in New York City?"

"Yeah. Jackson Heights."

Just about right.

"Do you fly out here often?"

Artie'd gotten his mind made, was blinking at me, ready to clinch things. "Yeah, I do, yeah. Three, four times a year. Got to keep an eye on the branches, y'know. And it gives me a chance to look up old friends."

I could be an old friend, I could maybe even have my own key, but De la Peña had a drink now and was settled, and it was time to move on. "Artie," I said sincerely, "you've been a tremendous help. My date's here, though, and he'll be upset that I'm sitting with you. That large guy over there. Don't get up. Thanks for everything."

"Hey," he said, "hey."

"No, really, he's got a bad temper. I shouldn't have let you talk to me, but you just seemed so nice. Thanks."

I was standing and smiling apologetically, but I thought maybe he was getting the notion of liberating me from the Life, so I kept on going. The waitress was closing in with our drinks and I threw her a "Thanks, honey" and a twenty as I passed. She saw me making for bigger game, and she'd stall Artie for me with the bill; I wasn't planning to be long with De la Peña. The leatherette purse swung from my shoulder and the Colt was a comforting weight.

"Rudy?" I said, stopping abruptly, right next to him. "Rudolph de la Peña, isn't it?"

He looked up from his glass, and he was still, very still.

"I'm De la Peña," he said.

"*Rudolph* de la Peña?" I had to be sure, have him give me the name. I stood over him at the table, right leg extended to show the short skirt, all the wares underneath it, left hand on my hip to emphasize line. I was feeling good, yes, I was, everything working, everything clicking. This guy might be big but he wouldn't be trouble, I could feel it way deep in my bones. I just had to drop the papers to get the thing done—quick in, quicker out—and I might have been dancing. I pouted my lips at him for the effect, and he *liked* the effect, his eyes fixed on me, narrowing.

"Yes," he said slowly, "I am Rudolfo de la Peña."

I smiled at him then, wide open and glossy, a cobra engulfing her prey. "Your wife wants you to have these." I snapped open the purse, slapped the papers down onto the table in front of him, right there by his drink hand, touching his sleeve. "Consider yourself served, Mr. de la Peña."

I was back out of reach in case he went ugly, my feet already pointed and moving, turning, in fact, for the door. This had been so damn easy, a piece of cake, a damn cakewalk. There was just nothing to this at all.

"So you're Margaret Gillis," he said.

# 4

I fell out of a two-story window once—well, the truth is, I was pushed—and when you're hitting the ground, the lungs kind of collapse like an accordion does, squeezing all of the air up and out through your throat in one massive wheeze. It's hell's own job pulling the accordion open again, and that's how I felt at that moment. I was in the act of turning, walking, aimed for the door, and suddenly my lungs suctioned shut.

"Excuse me?"

"Margaret Gillis."

He said it "Mar-ga-re-ta."

His eyes were still on me appreciatively, more than that, but I was safe behind my high-tech mask of paint. Safe except that he knew my name.

Knew who I was.

He wasn't making any moves, wasn't getting up or ugly, just sitting there calmly, ignoring the papers and sipping his liqueur. Watching me over the edge of the glass, amused. He set the drink deliberately back down on the table, holding my eyes. No red-faced shouts, no threats, no surprise. Why wasn't he surprised?

"You were expecting me?"

"Not you specifically—although I'm delighted. Would you care for a drink?"

Urbane, sophisticated. Not much like a man who has murderous rages.

I shifted my balance, still aimed. "Those are divorce papers."

"Yes," he said, and stuffed them into his jacket pocket without looking at them. He smiled, a warm, charming smile, the mustache lifting away from his cheeks. "Won't you join me for a cocktail? Since it seems I shall be dining alone."

"No," I said baldly. Why wasn't the damn man surprised?

"Your friend is coming after you."

I threw a harassed look over my shoulder: Artie was deciding to interfere. Christ in heaven, I should have been halfway to the car by now. De la Peña was rising, so I pivoted left, but he'd gotten between me and the door. There were people clustered at the next table, standing around discussing their seats, and Artie was coming from the back of the room—I was as trapped as if De la Peña had planned this. I smiled at him coolly. "He thinks you're my pimp."

There was a faint Spanish hauteur about him as he paused, as he took in the notion and was offended by it, and I wondered again what sort of man he was.

"I shall send him away then," he said.

I could still have outstepped him, could have played him off against Artie and worked my way out and maybe I should have, but the truth is I'd been caught since he first said my name. I didn't think he wanted to hurt me, I thought he wanted to talk. About Sylvia, probably, and I had a few questions along those lines myself. Like why he'd been expecting someone with divorce papers tonight. And why he didn't seem to care.

Artie was with us, unsure of himself and belligerent with it. Liquor always talks louder. "Is this guy bothering you, Sylvia?"

"Sylvia?" De la Peña said, looking suddenly at me. And then, "Sylvia is my *wife*." He might have been a Spanish grandee, all haughty angles and wealth, but Artie Minklow came from scrappy New York City stock.

"You come on," he said to me.

"Artie, I can't. Really, it's okay."

"Sit down," De la Peña said very sternly to me, and then to Artie, "You have made a mistake."

"Not me, mister. It's not *me* who's making. I know a couple a the guys on the Vice Squad here and I'm telling you—"

Great. What I needed. Beverly Vice.

"Artie," I said hastily, "you've got it all wrong," and I threw myself into Harmless Little Woman mode. I pressed in closer to him, and put my hand appealingly on his arm. "It was from one of those books, you know? Rudy and I have been, well, having some problems lately, and they said to spice it up." I gestured at my outfit. "Like a pickup, you know?"

He did know. Artie turned red. I wondered what games he and the missus got up to back in New York.

"I'm sorry," I said. "I was just going to sit there until he came in, but I was getting a little nervous by myself and you seemed so nice."

"You should not have done it." De la Peña was still being the outraged don, disapproving and rigid, and he was reminding me forcefully for some reason of Reilly.

"I know," I said meekly. There was an awkward pause before Artie coughed.

"Guess I'll get back then," he said very tightly.

"Thank you," I said. "Really."

"Yeah."

He wasn't going to stay at the bar to try his luck again, I guess, not after this, because he forged a fairly direct path to the door. I was left facing De la Peña.

"Won't you sit down?" He moved to pull out an armchair for me and I thought of Reilly again. Christ Almighty, how this evening had gone.

"I'm not staying," I said.

"I only want to know where Sylvia is."

"I don't know." It was true, too. Mike hadn't told me because I hadn't asked. Probably if I mentioned "girlfriend" and "bungalow," De la Peña could figure it out, but I wasn't going to do that. None of my business.

"People are staring."

They were. The next table over had finally sorted its seats out, and there were curious glances because we were still standing. Or maybe they'd heard the stuff I'd told Artie, maybe they were hoping that the sex games would start.

I had two choices right then, as I saw it. De la Peña was waiting like a courteous lion, not going to sit until I did, and he might be no trouble if I turned to walk out, might just stay there and watch me make my way through the crowd. But he had Reilly's broad shoulders, and his sizeable chest and that indefinable aura of power. Someone used to command. A man who can focus and get what he's after.

"You played soccer."

"Some time ago. Sylvia told you?"

There were undertones of unconscious pride, masculine pleasure. The womenfolk naturally talking about him. She hadn't told me, though, she'd told Mike. A "national hero" were the words Mike had used—a popular player who'd made good in the leagues. International cups. He could probably outrun me.

"You just want to talk?"

"A few minutes," he said, "of your time."

I sank into an overstuffed chair, not the one he'd pulled out. Stared bleakly at him until he sat down.

"I don't want a drink," I said.

"No." He seemed saddened, resigned—much older, suddenly. No spark at all.

"What the hell *is* this?" I said.

"This?"

"This whole set-up," I said roughly. "This 'encounter' at Chaven's— is this how you rich get your kicks?"

"I am getting no kicks," but he was, it was coming right back, that look in his eyes, the lift of his mustache. The damn man was smiling again.

At me.

As if I were a prize or some get with no mouth.

"You beat up your wife," I said savagely.

"Never." He seemed genuinely startled, taken aback.

"I saw the marks."

Well, I hadn't, exactly, Mike had, but Mike knows what he's seeing.

"There were no marks when she left. On my honor." He was earnest, perplexing, but I don't take people's honor.

"She was battered all over," I said.

"You cannot think *I*—" He could tell that I did. He was silent a moment then, one finger tracing the rim of his glass. Finally he lifted his head. "This changes everything."

It didn't change a dime.

"She hasn't been to the cops," I said. "I think you can probably still work something out."

"No."

"Get some counseling. Learn some control."

He said something in Spanish that I didn't catch, but his hand was clenched on the liqueur glass, knuckles dead white and flaring. I slid to the back of my chair.

"So I am a monster." He wasn't speaking to me, but the glass couldn't answer.

"We all do stupid things," I said.

"We think we are young." He looked at me then, remote, not quite seeing. "I should have stayed with my first wife."

The things people say. "Look, Mr. de la Peña—"

"You have been married?"

I have been, you know.

"When someone comes, so interested and alive, and they remind you, too well, of what you were, what you could be—yes, then, men are foolish."

I smiled at him tightly, not my day for confession. "Women, too, Mr. de la Peña."

"Yes? Yes, I suppose."

"Absolutely," I said. "You work it out or divorce them, you don't slap them around."

"I have not touched her," he said. Finito. The end. I was looking at him and I was prone to believe him, not something easy for me. It was the way he was sitting, though, the strength of his eyes.

"Mr. de la Peña, she's saying it's you. She got Mike to take pictures."

"Pictures?"

For protection, Mike had said, in case De la Peña denied it—and he *was* denying it, wasn't he? So it had been a smart thing to do. But I was looking at the man across the table, adding him up, the whole situation.

"How old is your wife?"

"Sylvia? She is twenty-three."

And he was what? At least fifty? Talk to me of young love.

"Some trophy," I said.

"Trophy?"

I looked at the diamond on his elegant finger. Two carats, maybe, I'm no good at that, but sparkling for sure in a platinum setting. Put another slant on her not wanting to go to the cops.

Because call me stupid—and sometimes I am—but I can see that an envelope of black-and-blue photos makes better deals at the divorce table than it does at the police station, particularly if your husband's a national hero.

A *wealthy* national hero.

High-stakes divorces. Not everything clear.

"How'd you know who I was?"

That snapped him back, he was smiling again. Two can play any game.

"You've been having her followed," I said.

It wasn't really a question. Private eyes are a dime a dozen in L.A., and I hoped he'd had the sense to hire a good one, not scrimp on those pennies. "Check with your PI, Mr. de la Peña. Maybe he got pictures of her leaving your house this morning—some proof she was fine when she went."

"I will do that." He reached out his hand, open-palmed. "Thank you, Ms. Gillis. Mar-ga-re-ta."

I couldn't touch him. I had fake nails and a painted-on face so it should have been safe, but it wasn't—he knew more than my name. He had a fire warming his eyes, and a secret amusement, and a wife who was about to divorce him.

"You seem very calm about it," I said.

Remarkably calm.

He was still again, staring down at his outstretched hand. Then he shrugged, a Latin shrug. "You cannot fight the wind."

"Sure, you can," I said strongly. "You just build higher walls. Put a roof on 'em. Gild it. You telling me you haven't thought of that?"

He raised his eyes, smiling. "But then you are a jailer. Always checking that the doors are locked."

Right.

"That would be hell," I said.

"Yes."

"You had her followed anyway."

"To know," he said simply.

"I'm sorry."

I was then, really was. Maybe he was better than the average liar, maybe he was playing all over my sympathies. It's possible, you know—I've been taken before. Maybe the truth was that he beat his wife up in private and counted on money to stop her, but I was liking him, more than a little, and I didn't know Sylvia at all.

The situation wasn't mine to judge, of course. I was the messenger.

"Mr. de la Peña," I said, leaning in to him as I rose, "maybe you ought to just pay what she's asking. Maybe it's not worth it to keep her."

"It isn't," he said. He was smiling at me, a rueful, charming smile. "You won't stay for dinner?"

There was warmth in his eyes, and knowledge, experience. "I can't," I said, and almost wished that I could.

# 5

It was odd, you know. The night was disturbing. I found myself wanting to tell Reilly about it, to get his reaction.

Didn't seem like a plan.

I couldn't think, and I couldn't go home, so I ended up at the office, stripping the nails off while I sat there, chucking them at the wastebasket under my desk. Unscrewed the dangly earrings, made little piles of them on the In tray. I always have another set of clothes in the back—earthquake ready or too many nights as a cop—but I was edgy and fretting and there was no one to see me, so I didn't bother to change.

What was I going to tell Mike? "Met your wife-beater, babe, and I think you've been had"? He'd seen the bruises; hell, he took the pictures—he wasn't going to think she was wrong.

I'd promised to call him by ten to let him know it was done, that I was okay. Gave me maybe an hour. He was at the bungalow, safeguarding Sylvia, and there was a variety of things I could hear myself saying, but nothing that warned him without warning *her*; nothing that answered the question of which one was lying—Sylvia or Rudolfo.

I wasn't the jury.

It wasn't my problem.

The rich can do each other however they want to, and why should it matter to me?

Because Mike was with her.

I threw my shoe at his desk. Tried mantras and rosaries.

Finally, I dialed the phone.

"Yeah, I did it," I said.

"You okay?"

I wasn't okay. Everything *wasn't* just fine. "This guy knew my name, Mike."

"Who—De la Peña?"

"He is also," I said, "pretty goddamn convincing. Swears he didn't hit her. Never touched her."

"Meg—"

"She have any other boyfriends, Mike?"

"Hey," he said. Macho time. Who'd want someone else when they could have Mike, right? Or I guess she was such a nice girl.

"You haven't seen the bruises," he was saying fiercely, sternly, "*and* you don't know her. She's not anything like that."

I fingered the pen on my desk.

"He was expecting the papers, Mike."

"No way."

"Not a whiff of surprise, babe—he didn't even look at 'em. Stuffed 'em into his jacket and asked me to stay for a drink."

"Jesus." He whistled. "A cool enough bastard."

Yeah, very cool. The kind to be flaming and hitting? Maybe. I remembered his hand, clenched on the glass.

"You want to ask Sylvia how he'd have known?"

"Well, he's got bucks," Mike said, which was partly an answer. "Somebody in the lawyer's office probably tipped him."

Or his PI'd reported it.

"Ask her anyway, Mike. And I hope you're being discreet, by the way—he's been having you followed."

"Me?"

"You and/or Sylvia. I don't know for how long. You spending the night there?"

"We'll see how it goes," he said. "Maybe. You know."

I knew. He'd be there till morning. Sylvia's bruises must have healed very quickly. I chucked the pen at the door.

"Let me rephrase it, Mike—you want to give me the address?"

"Why?"

He's not always quick.

"So if De la Peña comes calling, I'll have something to tell him," I said. "What d'you think?"

He was laughing, then, touched. Finally with it. "You're *not* gonna sit out on me, Meg."

I would have. I would have parked myself across the street all night, staring at the bungalow door. I'd been thinking about it, seriously considering it, I couldn't say why. The same reasons that drove me to the restaurant, I guess, and Mike's a big boy. You can't guard everybody forever.

"You call me tomorrow," I said.

"Yeah, sure, Meg, I will. Let you know how it's going."

He wouldn't. He'd forget, was already forgetting. Had that vague ifish note in his voice, and hey, it was a weekend, he'd just helped a lady, what the hell was the matter with *me*?

"Watch your back, buddy," I said, and hung up.

There's a bottle of V.O. in a box in the storeroom. I don't normally drink it, don't drink much at all, but I couldn't go home, couldn't sit there and worry, so I poured a major amount of it into my coffee cup and turned out the lights, flipped the radio on. Watched the headlights slice through the half-open miniblinds as cars turned the corner, while I listened to someone sing "Rockin' My Baby," "Who's Cryin' Now? Whose Heart Is Breaking?" and "I've Had My Share of Those Blues."

I probably was planning to stay. There's a couch by the window or I could curl up on the floor, so it didn't really matter how much I drank or how late it was—it beat going home where anyone could find me, beat having to answer a lot of damn questions or just flat out lying. Beat having to unlock those doors. The night had turned odd and disturbing, *De la Peña'd* disturbed me. I lifted the mug and toasted his eyes. To you, Rudolfo, you Latin philosopher. Maybe it just isn't worth it to keep her. "It isn't," he'd said. "You won't stay for dinner?" That personal, knowing-me smile.

V.O.'s very smooth. It tingles your tongue. I had nowhere I had to be going so I gulped some more down. Set up the cup for a refill, didn't screw back the top, just let it lie there. Energy wasted, you know?

I wondered then if *he* was still drinking.

Wondered if Mike was all right.

Dredged down deep and dirty into memory-river, into talking to ghosts, into arguing things. I tend to recycle. Tend to obsess. Alcohol lowers the dams, gets the floodwaters rolling, and it's not that it's useful, but it sweeps me along.

I wasn't expecting the phone. I was a little bit hazy and I wasn't quite sure of the time. Late. After eleven. It rang, kept on ringing, and we have a machine, but I was thinking, I guess, it was Mike. It was very shrill in the office, one bright red eye blinking. I scooped the receiver up off the base, said into it, "What?"

There was a moment of silence. A male voice, very deep.

"You're still there."

Not Mike. Not Michael at all.

My Nemesis-Man. I tried to sound welcoming.

"Hello, Reilly," I said.

"You all right?"

I must have gotten the tone wrong. "Yeah, sure," I said lightly. "I'm just, you know, finishing things."

Kind of a pause. "I've been calling your house," he said slowly. "Starting to worry. This is pretty late for you, isn't it?" and he was right, it was late and he was being too casual. "Mike still there, too?"

"No," I said, not quite thinking, just reacting, to the hour, to his tone, the way he feels about Mike. Then I heard his voice change:

"You're there by *yourself*?" Kind of sharp, very focused, and I know how this works, for Christ's sake, the cop mind: she's alone, she's my woman, there'll be somebody lurking.

"I'll come by then," he said. "I'm leaving now anyway."

"Reilly, I'm fine."

"Well, *I'm* not," he said easily, "so you can take care of me. I'll see you in five." Then he hung up, he was gone, not giving me time to disagree or deny him, and Christ, he'd be less than five minutes, the station's only a few blocks away, and I was still decked out in makeup, still dressed like a B-picture queen. I stumbled going around the desk, stubbed myself on the foot of the couch in the half-light, the dark, and I couldn't even find the damn light switch. The radio was cranking out "Your Cheatin' Heart," and I could hear Michael laughing, but it wasn't so funny, it was Reilly coming to see me, and me like a rabbit, panic clutching the heart in my chest. Headlights came blinding through, and I froze, half-crouched because it couldn't be him, it *wasn't* him, not already, and what the hell was I going to say? The lights drifted past.

It's perspective, you know, the rabbit perspective. I wouldn't have noticed the car otherwise.

It was a dark Ford Torino, standard design, not remarkable, parked at the end of the lot. It hadn't been there when I got to the office, but there are film people upstairs, independent producers, and they keep some odd hours when they've got something going. I didn't know if they had now or not.

What I'd seen was a flicker of movement when the headlights swept by, like the driver's door starting to open, someone changing his mind.

No interior light coming on.

I'm not a stickler for things—you can blow out a fuse and I won't report you, forget to get lightbulbs, and, hey, man, it happens.

Or you can yank out that fuse so no one'll see you, which comes under "Premeditation—Felonious Intent."

It's dark in that particular corner, streetlamps blocked by the overhang, not an innocent place to be parking when you could have the whole lot, all thirty spaces. Most people go for the center. I had two fingers on the miniblinds, barely parting them, enough to see better without declaring my interest, crouched off to one side of the window.

Door cracking open?

Not. No visible shadow inside, just a blackness, a feeling. Born probably of late night and the note in Reilly's voice: "You're there by *yourself*?" I've been lots of places myself. It doesn't help to be hanging with cops who remind me.

Something moved, shimmered in the dark behind the windshield— a scope, a barrel catching light?

I had the .45 in my purse somewhere under my desk, and an oiled knife in a drawer. I just hadn't thought to tape up a weapon by the window—remiss of me, actually. I'd have to address that.

Something crashed in the back, made a loud bumping noise.

There's an alley behind us, trash cans and Dumpsters. It sounded like one of the Dumpsters had rolled, thumping into the wall. Or like someone had been standing on one of the cans, tried to balance, and fell. The storerooms all have small windows, six feet from the ground.

More lights coming by.

I was focused on the Torino, trying to see, but the angle was wrong. The headlights passed quickly, someone driving too fast, like a maniac, really, for so narrow a street, and where are the cops when you need them? Slow it down, bud, way down.

Not a driver who listened.

There might have been a movement in the Torino, I couldn't tell. Nothing else from the storeroom, no tinkling of glass, but with the radio playing, I wouldn't have heard the faint scritch of a cutter. It was time to decide: go for the Colt or keep my eye on the four-door. I couldn't do both and check out the storeroom, which was starting to get to priority level, so I scrunched myself down to the floor, scrabbled wormlike across to my desk in the damn tight-knit sheath, eating dust from the rug and my mascara flakes starting to shed. Hell of a night. Reilly'd probably walk in and I'd shoot him, which stopped my hand for a second on the leatherette purse. How long had it been? Three minutes? Four?

I was one goddamn lunatic.

I threw myself towards the window, clutching the purse, coming up off the floor in a two-scissor lunge. The Ford was still there, still backed into the corner. There was a truck coming in, though, a shape and an engine that had to be Reilly's, and I flailed for the light switch, connected, flipped it up, flipped it down, the lights flashing wildly, slashing through the miniblinds like lightning bolts, semaphores, something to warn him.

The Ford's engine revved, that squeal-screeching sound of trans-mission in gear, and its high beams came up, twin spotlights, seeking out and then pinning Reilly's damn El Camino. I was yanking the office door, trying to get there and the Ford went straight at him, gun-ning up, barely missing. It swerved on two tires, overcorrected, caught the pavement again and then launched, jumped the sidewalk. The left rear tire hit the curb as it landed, and it shimmied around in a pull-the-wheel war dance, a suspension-swayed dip-and-a-curtsy, before shooting off. It skidded straight towards the corner, revved again, hauled around it, and then it was gone.

I was shaking, you know. Trying to get to Reilly, but he was already coming to me. He'd slammed the El Camino more or less into park, away from the entrance but not quite in a spot, and he was rounding the front of the truck very quickly with his hand at his waist coming out with his off-duty piece. Reached out, grabbed me to him, swept me up with the one arm, holding me hard. I was hanging on to *him* pretty tightly myself.

"The office," I said.

I'd forgotten what I looked like, I honestly had, until we were in, had the door locked behind us. His free hand reached out for the light switch and everything came on, devastatingly bright. "You all right?" Urgent, concerned, in that sharp tone of voice, and then, "Jesus Christ," he said, stopping. Taking in my dress, what remained of my paint. It was more than awful, the look on his face—something like shock, loss of faith.

"I'm sorry," I rushed. "God, Reilly, I'm sorry. It's not—it isn't—"

Not very coherent, and I was a chattering lunatic fool, flagrante delicto, self-convicted, and meanwhile, the back unsecured. I pulled against him, tried to loosen his hold but he wasn't releasing at all then—he'd tightened.

A reflex.

I tried to speak calmly, maybe a little bit breathless.

"I have to check the storeroom. It sounded like someone was trying to break in."

"I'll do it." He'd found himself, closed himself down. Had a level set to his mouth, to his eyes, very banked, very guarded. He put me aside, moved fluidly past me, and I felt like a witch, a betraying Delilah while he eased through the hallway to check out the back. The radio was singing "It's a Cold Night in Hell," and I'd say that it was, you know— likely to be.

# 6

There is a God. I figured it out a couple of years ago. It was a revelation for me, and not entirely a welcome one, but ever since then the universe has made perfect sense. This is a God with an oblique sense of humor.

You didn't get it? Just wait a bit and the punch line will come back around.

Sometimes attached to a *real* punch, you know.

Solar plexus or lower.

I thumbed the damn radio off and went back to stand by the side of the window, to stare through the miniblinds at the parking lot. Kept seeing the look on Reilly's face.

Felt the movement finally behind me.

"It's clear," Reilly said. He wasn't precisely lounging in the doorway to the storeroom, but he had a shoulder against the left side of the frame, was propped there watching me, his face unrevealing. "Anything else out front?"

There was nothing else there, just his El Camino skewed sideways and my lone little car sitting under the light. "I don't think so."

"So what's going on?"

He meant more than "What's with the car out of nowhere?" He meant the clothes I was wearing, meant my not being me. There are ways to tell truth, but I was fresh out of them.

"I was doing a favor for Mike."

He was nodding, expressionless.

"What was the favor?"

"It was just a thing," I said. "I was serving divorce papers for a friend of his."

"Like that?"

His eyes were very deliberately not on the dress, and what was I supposed to say? "Hell, no, I went home and changed"?

"Reilly—"

"Who's the friend?"

"Sylvia," and then I couldn't think of her last name, it just went away from me, got lost in the way he was standing there, looking.

"Sylvia?" he said sharply.

The way De la Peña had said it: "Sylvia? Sylvia is my *wife*."

"Yeah," I said numbly, "Sylvia."

Reilly shifted abruptly, was still.

"All right, we'll try it like this," he said very coolly. "Where's Mike?"

*Holed up with Sylvia.*

I didn't say that out loud, I'm pretty sure that I didn't, but I must have looked bleak or something, torn, like I just wouldn't tell him, because he swore suddenly, vivid and angry, and then he had my arm in a hamhold, had stripped the Colt out of my hand, and was moving me forcibly the few steps to the couch.

"Sit there," he said. Command mode, crisply distinct. He wasn't even looking to see if I did it—he was stuffing my gun into his pocket, was over by my desk, by Mike's desk, surveying the contents, noting the mug and my shoes and the bottle of hooch. Swinging around.

"Was that him just leaving?"

Leaving?

"No," I said, "he's with Sylvia."

Reilly's very controlled, very large. Menacing, maybe, if you're in that frame of mind, and I'm not sure that I wasn't. Spacing the words through his teeth:

"Who's-the-guy-in-the-car-Meg?"

Oh.

"I don't know," I said lamely, "I didn't even see him till I was looking for you. I was trying to warn you, flashing the lights, in case it was an ambush or . . ." I ran out of words. He was staring at me tight-eyed.

"You drunk?"

God.

"No," I said.

"No?"

Maybe I was. I didn't know *what* I was, exactly. Trembling, though. Starting to lose it.

"You saw the car, Reilly—"

"I saw you," he said flatly, "coming out with a weapon."

"He was trying to *ram* you."

"He was trying to leave."

Fleeing me, he meant.

Drunk ex-cop with a gun.

I hadn't been out there waving it around.

"It wasn't—" I said hotly, "it's not—" but I didn't know what it *was* anymore. "He was watching the office, Reilly. He was sitting there in the dark, he didn't have any lights on—"

"So?"

So I didn't know now. He seemed so normal, Reilly did, so pissed off and hard-edged and physically there.

And me just so wrong.

I could see it from his point of view, yes, I could, the cop in me flinching. If there'd been shots fired—if *I'd* fired or if Reilly had, trying to protect me when the Torino came revving. With me in this dress and, yeah, okay, maybe a little bit drunk and not quite coherent, trying to explain it to the Beverly cops who would come—God, what a mess.

It hadn't happened that way, though. It wouldn't have, but I could see all the doubt in his eyes.

"Don't," I said.

"Don't what?"

"Don't do this," I wanted to say, and "Don't hate me," and maybe somewhere in there, "Don't expect quite so much," but I was tongue-tied and twisted, still down in deep river. "Just *don't*," I said, shaking.

"I'm supposed to accept this?"

I didn't know anymore.

"No," I said.

He drew sort of a breath, thought several things that he just wasn't saying while the silence ticked by. Flicked his eyes at my outfit finally, spoke very curtly: "You have something else to put on?"

I had the sweatsuit in the storeroom. It was a long way past him to change. The sheath dress wasn't much to step out of, and the sweatsuit wasn't much to pull on. No kind of armor. I fumbled around with the sweatpants, trying to hurry, and it was cold in the damn, dim store-room, hanging on to the shelves.

When I came out, Reilly was standing in front of our map of the city, a three-foot blowup on the wall by my desk. His back wasn't looking any easier, but he heard me, turned around. Nodded slightly when he saw the sweatsuit, left his eyes on my face. I probably should have taken that extra minute to scrub off the makeup, but it was too late to duck into the bathroom and do it.

He'd put the cap on the bottle.

I'd had speeches worked up in my mind while I was undressing, quick things that I was all ready to step out and tell him. I don't muscle in on *his* stuff, you know what I mean? Don't sweep in taking over.

But he was standing there tired, waiting for me—angry and bent but determined to sort it. He'd worked a long day already. Had fretted himself some trying to find me, I knew that he had. I hadn't wanted to see it before, but Reilly's a part of my life these days. Looks for me, thinks of me. Expects me to know it.

I'd been doing him much more than wrong.

"I'm sorry," I said. Went for him blindly before he could turn me away. "It was stupid," I said as I buried myself, felt his arms come around me, "it was godawful stupid, but I knew you were working and I thought it wouldn't matter. It wasn't much, really, just serving divorce papers, but Mike would have plastered the guy or started a fight and I couldn't let him do it, okay? I just couldn't."

Not very coherent, but he was still holding on.

"What was the dress?"

"It was cover," I said. "A disguise."

"His idea?"

Reilly thinks that Mike leads me.

"He didn't even want me to do it," I said. "He knew you'd be pissed."

He breathed out over my hair. "*Some* sense," he said, and I probably would have pulled away then, but he had me in sort of a lock.

"Think you want to tell me the details, Meg?"

I didn't.

I don't really know why.

I used to tell Charlie everything after a job, every damn twist and line—how the guy had jogged left or pumped right or whatever he'd done, and I'd still come around him, how bitching it was.

I didn't want to tell Reilly.

He was angry, you know. Trying to contain it, to be some sort of reasonable, but ticked at me, ticked at Mike, so I couldn't just *say* it, couldn't pour the thing out. He wouldn't see it the way Charlie had, wouldn't be right alongside with me, feeling it.

He was . . . possessive. That was the word. *His* woman doing it. What he didn't approve of.

Didn't matter how well.

"Meg?"

I had to do something, though, had to respond—he was getting that edge on again.

"Yeah, sure," I said. "I just have to sit down."

He let me go as far as the couch, all of three feet away. Listened without much expression while I gave him the facts: I went, I saw, I delivered the papers. I didn't tell him everything, maybe—sort of skipped over Artie, and I didn't give him each little specific on De la Peña, not the part at the end where he'd asked me to stay. It wasn't important stuff, really, but it would be guaranteed to be rubbing him wrong.

Not that everything wasn't already.

He'd settled himself onto the corner of my desk while I talked, pushing the trays back, the calendar, and he looked quite formidable, looked like a jury, a bulked-up kind of jury, wanting a few things explained.

"You sat and you *talked* to this guy?"

"It's a public place, Reilly. It was perfectly safe." I didn't mean to sound so defensive.

"He follow you out?"

As if I'd never done anything, you know? Never been anywhere. I just looked at him. He stared unrelentingly back.

"Anyone else could have followed you here?"

He was thinking "black Ford Torino," and so was I, then. It couldn't have tailed me because I would have seen it, but De la Peña's PI might have guessed where I'd land. Here or at home, you know—creature of habit. Looking for me to hook up with Mike, and from Mike then to Sylvia. It was possible, I couldn't say no. Pretty far-fetched, though. Exotic revenge.

Unless you remembered the hand on the glass and the jealousy factors, the way people get. Kind of like us, less than reasonable, eh?

"Reilly," I said, "the world doesn't turn around *me*. There's a film office upstairs, all kinds of stuff there—TVs, VCRs. Maybe this guy was scouting a burglary or something, and you scared him off coming in."

He had a thumb kind of rubbing the underside of his jaw, that stone-stubborn look on his face. He couldn't be wrong, but *I* was—already condemned. And what was he looking for—crying and sorry? "Please, Reilly, forgive me for putting myself out there, forgive me for making a choice on my own"?

"It isn't that big a deal," I said.

"Yeah? You do this a lot?"

On the nights I'm not with him, he meant. When he's not there to see.

"You know I don't."

"I don't know anything," he said curtly. "What's with the drinking?"

Because the night had turned odd and disturbing. Because sometimes I swirl like a whirlpool going down.

Memory-river.

I used to go to the desert when it threatened to drown me—used to go and shoot guns and get drunk and get well. That's what we did, what we all did. Under the stubborn cacti, in the glare of the sun, with the grit of the dirty-white sand like salt in the wounds to burn out the toxins. Charlie knew. Mike knew. A couple of others. Reilly should know it because he was a cop, but I was a woman to him, don't you see? Somebody separate.

"You *tell* me," he said—and it was suddenly there out of nowhere, an impulse, a flash, and it was all I could do to bite down on the words, not to tell him to get the hell gone. Because I hadn't asked him there, had I? It seemed to me that I hadn't. Seemed to me that I'd been trying pretty hard to avoid this, because why else would I not have gone home, where he'd find me? Why else had I been here, drinking alone?

If he'd come by tomorrow, it wouldn't have been much—"Where was I last night? Oh, I was doing a favor for Mike, helped him out with some papers" and that's pretty much the end of it, you know what I mean? "And how was *your* day, dear?" He wouldn't have seen the dress then, wouldn't have seen me, wouldn't have been bent out of shape.

*He's* the one who came over, set everything off.

I couldn't say that to him, though. Couldn't say anything much, so I shrugged.

He moved and I tensed in spite of myself, and then he was still. Focused and hard.

"You missing the streets?"

I wasn't.

I didn't.

I don't know why he was talking.

"No."

"Seems like."

He was wrong.

"Maybe you should sign up again."

"Reilly," I said, "just leave it alone."

"Maybe you need to think about it."

Think about it—*that's* what I needed. It was drink or my demons or wanting to provoke him, I don't know what it was, but I was up then and facing him. "Yeah," I said, "both of us working as cops would be fine. You'd sleep well at night then, wouldn't you?"

"If that's what you wanted."

What *I* wanted? Hot damn. That was a notion.

"I'm not hiring on again," I said, "so there's no point in bringing it up, okay? I don't want to be a cop anymore, and if you'd be honest, you wouldn't like me doing it either."

"Better than a stunt like this on your own."

"There was nothing *to* this," I said. "It was a Beverly Hills restaurant, for Christ's sake, not a South-town ganger bar."

"You shouldn't have done it"—and, God, I was hearing echoes. Reilly and De la Peña even had the same look to the bridge of their noses, the set of their mouths.

"Reilly," I said dangerously, "if I were working, I'd be out on the street. I'd sign up for Vice or whoever would take me and then you could worry about *me* for a while, worry if I'd be coming safe home."

"I wouldn't have to." He was standing to meet me, cracking the words out. "Nobody in his right mind would give you a field job. Communications, maybe—yeah, it might be safe to let you handle the phones."

He was a damn slamming block. "You son-of-a-bitch," I hissed, "you couldn't have done it any better."

"I wouldn't have done it at all."

"Oh, that's right—I forgot, you're a sergeant." I meant it like "cowardly lowlife" and that's how he took it, all right, his mouth a thin line, but he just said very curtly, "Don't forget it again."

Not in *his* town.

I flung myself over to the window, stared hard at the cords, at the blinds. This was the first goddamn fight that we'd had since we'd started, and it was a bad one. Mostly my fault. *All* my fault, if it came right down to it, because I should never have answered the phone.

"You okay to drive?"

I was okay.

"I'll follow you," he said. "To your place, all right?"

He wasn't really asking if I wanted to go there.

"Reilly—"

"We're going to go through it again," he said.

Flat.

Absolute.

It was fair, I guess, that he'd want to. That he didn't want to hang around here. I picked up the purse from the floor by the couch, dug for my keys, and by then he'd come up behind me, had me tight, clipped against him, body to body, mouth by my ear.

"You're drunk," he said roughly, "made up like a whore—is that what Mike gets you?"

"Don't," I said, "Reilly," but he was kissing my neck, sandpaper kisses, holding me aggressively still with his hands, and I don't know why I respond when he's hard like this and angry, but I do—he knows I do.

"You like dressing up?"

I couldn't have told him. Couldn't think with his fingers. "I like *you*," I said. I twisted somehow, and kissed at his chest. Pressed into him, drew him, both hands very tightly. He held me a little away, looking down.

"You're going to tell me," he said, "every last detail. Are we clear on that?"

Maybe we were. Nothing was clear, to tell you the truth, none of the boundaries. He released me abruptly, moved to the door.

"You ready?" and I was, yes, blinking at him, had the keys still clutched in my fingers. He shook his head at me then, laughed as if it was in spite of himself.

"You can put those away," he said softly. "*I'm* driving." A meaningful glint in his eye. Planning to exact his own brand of vengeance, taking his time, but hot for me underneath it, made up and all. Wanted me to know it before we set off, so I could think, maybe. Stew some. Get in a lather.

It was looking to be quite a ride.

# 7

I didn't tell Reilly every last detail. He was all over me anyway, giving me grief, about Mike, about De la Peña, about doing the meet, so there was no point in making it worse. I told him about picking up Artie. He had me pinned mostly naked and it definitely lit him, so I didn't maybe spell out that De la Peña'd been looking, that De la Peña had asked me to stay. I wanted to, a little, to flaunt some, you know, but it wasn't the time. There's a fine line between "Hey, look, I'm attractive" and "Hey, man, I was doing you wrong," and I didn't think Reilly was in the mood to be making distinctions. He was already forgiving me one kind of folly.

We had a good night. Had a very nice weekend. Mike remembered to call me, which stunned me to hell, but he was maybe turning over that new leaf for Sylvia.

They were both fine.

There was nothing more on the black Ford Torino. Reilly checked it out Saturday. No report of a burglary, no hit-and-run, and really, it might just have been a driver fumbling with keys—I hadn't seen enough to be sure. Maybe he saw Reilly pulling in and my office lights flashing, and thought we were carjackers or something, who knows? Ram 'em and run. It happens.

Reilly was working Saturday and Sunday, the swing shift, because his squad is STU, the Special Tactics Unit, and they get real weekends off when the blue moon is rising, but he came by when he was done and stayed over both nights. It was too late, really, for him to go home. We watched some old movies, slept in Sunday morning. Did a few projects. Sorted some things.

It was odd to have him dressing for work in my bedroom. He glanced up at one point, fastening his rig, and caught me there, watching. I couldn't look away. He broke the moment for me casually, continued the movement, shrugged into his windbreaker as if it were nothing.

I gave him a key to the house.

I'd been putting off doing it, I don't know why. The last vestige of freedom, I guess.

He had a key for me, too, to his place.

He'd been carrying it around, apparently, waiting—had it there on his keyring when I gave him mine. It was awkward and stupid, exchanging the things, but Reilly was quietly pleased. Stretched back in the kitchen chair and pulled me onto his lap, dropped a kiss on my hair. Held me for quite a long time.

I love him, you know?

Monday was different.

Mike got to the office early, before me. It's not usual for him, so I wasn't expecting it, but I guess he'd gone home for a shower and change, and then stopped back to see me, fill me in on the weekend. He'd found the black dress on the floor of the storeroom, and had jumped to conclusions which weren't quite false but weren't much of his business, and he was having a great time making racy suggestions when the telephone rang. He was in a high old good humor, so things must have gone well with Sylvia. I picked up the phone unsuspecting.

It was a female voice asking for Michael Johnson. She didn't sound Argentine, but I handed it over and watched his face change, get very serious fast.

"Yeah, sure," he was saying, "you want to tell me what it's about?" and she didn't, apparently. "Okay, fifteen minutes." It was trouble coming, I could feel it. I just didn't know what it was.

"Sylvia?"

"Beverly PD," he said. "Reilly lodge a complaint?" He didn't mean that, exactly, but we were both kind of spooked. Mike's got several people he knows on the force there, but they don't call him like that. It's generally "Hey, buddy, what's doing?" or "Let's you and me skip to the races," and this was clearly a formal invite to the station.

"Not one of your friends?"

He shook his head. "Unless someone's playing a game."

"Should I call Reilly?"

"Jesus, no," he said, "he'd come over and sink me. I'll find out what it is when I get there."

I wasn't okay with it, but it wasn't my choice, and as it turns out, they were wanting me, too. Someone called from the station a long two hours later, requesting my presence. For verification, he said.

It had to be about my serving the papers. If they wanted Mike and then me, then that's what it was. There's nothing illegal about acting as process server, so I went in and shook hands, met Jacoby, detective, let him usher me up to the Bureau and straight on to an interview room. A little more private than sitting out at his desk, he said. That was fine with me, actually, extremely so, because Reilly was working day shift that Monday, down a floor but around, and I figured that least seen the better where I was concerned.

I figured Jacoby was thinking that, too. He was courteous about it, not even a mention, but conscious somehow for a cop who'd just met me, who didn't happen to know I was dating a Beverly Hills sergeant. It's a smallish department and the Bureau is smaller, and police people tend to think everything's their business, particularly who's sleeping with whom. So we smiled at each other very politely and said things like "Yeah, it's a nice day" and "No, thanks, no coffee," and naturally, I didn't mind answering a few questions about Friday, that, yes, I'd met De la Peña at Chaven's, and, yes, I'd given him the divorce papers there.

I was expecting, of course, some kind of trouble—that Sylvia was dragging Mike in somehow, maybe saying that *he* was the person who'd hit her. Or that De la Peña had violated a part of the restraining order, called her, whatever, and she was filing a police report, trying to prove he'd been served.

"Can you tell me what this is about?" I said, and Jacoby *could* tell me.

"Yeah, Mr. de la Peña was found dead this morning, Mrs. Gillis. We're just trying to verify a few things."

"De la Peña." Like an echo, and I had to be sure, have him give me the name. "*Rudolph* de la Peña?"

"Yeah," he said. "The same guy you served. Rudolph."

Rudolfo.

The Argentine Flame.

"You okay, Mrs. Gillis?" and I was, I was fine. I just wished that he'd told me before I came down to the station—before I'd shaken his hand, or was alone in this room with him, with him less than three feet away.

"How'd he die?" I said, and I sounded odd, very hollow, even to me.

"Gunshot wound. Self-inflicted, it looks like. Through the roof of the mouth."

Self-inflicted.

"A *suicide*?"

"It looks that way, yeah."

"But he was Catholic," I said, without thinking.

"Yeah?"

I thought he was. Wasn't he? Spanish Argentine.

Jacoby was watching me, systems alert, and I wasn't handling this right. I was being too much, too involved, for someone who'd only dropped papers. I could see him refiguring.

"Did you know him, Mrs. Gillis?"

Catholics kill themselves. I know that. Just because I get so uptight about things doesn't mean that everyone else does.

Through the roof of the mouth, though, for Christ's sake. Pretty definitive, that. You wouldn't have to worry about spending the rest of your days in a vegetable ward.

Jacoby was waiting.

"No," I said, "no, I didn't know him. When did it happen?"

"Sometime Friday night." Jacoby was a lean man, on the short side, gray toned and pale, with wavy black hair and very dark eyes. Absorbent. Nonreflective. Taking everything in and letting nothing back out. Tar pool eyes—the kind that people get trapped in.

"I gave him the papers around seven-thirty," I said. "He took them okay."

"Did he say anything?"

He'd said quite a bit. Not much of it public.

"He just stuffed them into a pocket. It didn't seem to bother him any."

Jacoby was leaning back in his chair, casually easy, his right thumb and forefinger smoothing each other.

"His wife said that he's been despondent. 'Despairing,' she said."

Did she? I didn't know her. It wasn't my call.

"I understand that you talked to him some."

Mike might have told him that—or the waitress might have mentioned it, if they'd had time to be checking. Or he might just be making it up as he prodded. Those dark eyes waiting, and I couldn't be sure.

"Yeah, I did. For a minute."

"*A few minutes*," he'd said, "*of your time.*"

"What'd you talk about, Mrs. Gillis?"

Men's foolishness. Women's.

"He wanted to know about Sylvia," I said, "if I knew where she was. I said I didn't, and that was basically it."

"Basically?"

This man worked with Reilly. There were a lot of things going on here—what Mike might have said, what the waitress had told them—even the parts that Reilly would know, because I'd said quite a bit Friday night about Sylvia when I was trying to explain to him just why I'd done it. Stressed the "poor, battered woman" to make it seem better, seem less like I did it for Mike.

"Yeah," I said, "basically."

"You didn't talk about anything else?"

He seemed to know that we had. Seemed to know what it was, too. He might look outwardly waffled and mild, but underneath was a confident predator—one who knew all the bolt-holes, had the escape routes.

Mike had been here this morning, talking to him.

And—"His wife said that he's been despondent. 'Despairing.'"

Sylvia, too.

Sylvia with her visible bruises.

"Did his wife tell you he'd beaten her up?"

She had, yes—that slight drop of his eyes. So much for her secret and not wanting to let in the cops. But, then, of course, De la Peña was dead now.

"She had my partner take pictures," I said very coolly. "We discussed that a little at Chaven's."

"You mentioned the pictures?"

I had, yes. And I was quite sure then that he knew that I had, knew it from Mike and/or Sylvia. He just wanted to hear the confirmation from me, have the double-backed check. Housekeeping details to round out the reports. That's all this meeting was for.

Stamp. Next?

Thanks so much for coming.

Because the way things work, here's how it sounds, here's the progression, here's how it suits the logical mind: Meg mentions pictures,

De la Peña's alarmed, feels exposed, kills himself for the shame. A neat enough package.

Stamp.

I don't have a logical mind.

"They weren't 'pictures flagrante,' Jacoby—they were pictures of bruises, not of him in the act. *Anyone* could have done it."

"She's not saying 'Anyone,'" Jacoby observed.

And "Anyone" hadn't gone home to a gun.

Next?

"He denied it," I said, "denied ever hitting her," but they all do, you know? Jacoby didn't have to lean in to remind me.

"Mrs. Gillis," he said, "the man killed himself. Took a Browning .380 and jammed it into his mouth. His gun. His prints. All alone in the house. And now you're telling me that you talked about pictures, which pretty well substantiates what his wife has been saying."

I didn't even know Sylvia. It was totally irrational that I didn't want to be supporting her story. Everything was irrational.

"He wasn't despondent," I said.

"You had, what, five minutes with him, Mrs. Gillis?" He meant it like "Whaddaya—psychic?" and Christ, you know, I had Reilly to consider, his damn reputation here at the station. What I owed and to whom.

What I owed to a dead man.

"He dismissed her, Jacoby. He wasn't despairing. She was a rich man's folly, a goddamn trophy. He wasn't worrying about pictures or scandal or counting the cost—he was coming on to *me*, for Christ's sake, he asked *me* to stay."

I could see Jacoby then, adding the twist: the sergeant's girlfriend enmeshed. Sucked in by her ego, another man's charm. I hadn't saved De la Peña, I'd jettisoned Reilly. Thrown all three of us out of the boat. The black eyes had me, looking me over, and Jacoby'd seen denial before. Fairly kind. Nicely spoken.

"You don't want to be blaming yourself, Mrs. Gillis."

That's what he thought I was doing, I guess, and maybe, you know, he was right.

"No, I won't," I said quietly then.

I let him finish up, ask the rest of the questions, say a few civil things. He walked me downstairs through the mantraps and let me out, and I stood outside by the library for five longish minutes to give him time to get back to the Bureau.

Then I went into the lobby again, to the front desk officer, and asked him to call upstairs for me.

"Yes, ma'am. Who'd you want?"

"Reilly," I said. "Sergeant Reilly. STU."

The five kids playing truant to hang out and smoke were laughing and shoving at the other end of the grass triangle. We were fairly silent at our picnic table because I was about finished talking.

"I thought I should tell you before you heard it around." It was easier not looking at Reilly, so I hadn't been. We were in the small green zone that passes for a neighborhood park near the fire station. Had bought paper-wrapped take-out together and driven over for lunch. We could have gone to a restaurant, I guess, but this way, I could talk out loud without worrying who'd hear it.

"You weren't going to tell me otherwise?"

I think he knew that I wasn't. "No," I said. "It didn't really matter before."

"I might have a different opinion on that."

I was pretty sure that he did have. You get to know somebody a little and you can figure these things out.

You can't undo things, though. Can't be a different person than you are. Somebody else wouldn't have gone out Friday night, wouldn't have had to be sitting there Monday explaining it to Reilly. I had to tell him now, you know. Jacoby knew about it, for all the good it'd done, and the way things work, Lieutenant Abbott would be finding out soon. As soon as Jacoby's report hit his desk, probably, if Jacoby wasn't in briefing him already.

Abbott's the Detective Lieutenant and the temporary head of STU these days. Reilly's boss. His mentor. His training officer from way back when. It's more than being friends, it's Abbott having a stake in Reilly's progress through the department. That makes him not exactly indifferent to how his man spends his nights, and not entirely comfortable that he's been spending them with me. Beverly Hills PD was in on the case those months ago when I first met Reilly, and I'd had the prime spot in Abbott's mind then as a suspect. That was mostly my fault, okay? I don't get on well with lieutenants as a rule, and I was harboring a few suspicions of my own.

The point was that sooner rather than later, Abbott would be spotting my name on this case, Mike's name, and he'd be wanting to discuss it with Reilly. Not formally, but just taking a little walk down the hall, getting some coffee together, and then "What's this with your girlfriend, Joe? Fill me in." That's how it works, and I couldn't have Reilly finding out that way. Have him knowing half of it, and Abbott being surprised and then perturbed or, worse yet, amused, that he didn't know it all. I couldn't set Reilly up to be a bobbingblock in his own department just because I didn't want to tell him.

So I was sitting there at the picnic table, metal bench hard underneath me, letting Reilly grill me, and wishing I'd ordered anything but a steak sandwich for lunch.

"Why do I have the feeling that I'm talking to the air?" Reilly said.

To the wind, I thought, and remembered why else I was there.

"I'm maybe going away for a little while," I said.

"I don't think so."

"A couple of days."

He leaned in across the table. "No."

"I think we could use the time," I said.

"Look at me."

I looked.

"You tell me what's going on, Meg."

It was a different pair of eyes I saw, though—De la Peña's eyes, across a table in a crowded bar. Looking at me, seeing through the disguise—knowing *me*. Not good old Meg, reliable Meg, but Meg-Margareta, who pitted her wits against the wind and the night, who danced and sparkled, glittered in the barlight. "You build higher walls," I'd said, and like an echo, "You cannot fight the wind." How long had I been building walls? How long had Reilly?

"Six months ago," I said carefully, "you brought me a weapon because of who I was. Trying to suit the presents, you said. These days—I don't know, Reilly. These days I keep expecting embroidery hoops."

He was very still.

"I just need a little time to think, that's all."

"All right," he said deliberately, after a moment. "You can think. Don't do it anywhere near Sylvia de la Peña."

He knows me so well.

"Maybe San Francisco." I was watching the pattern I was drawing with my plastic fork on the table.

"I'm serious, Meg."

I'd make sure he got a postcard, then.

His hand was firm over mine, stopping me. "This is my town."

"And you and Jacoby are the cops," I said. "Maybe someday I can answer your phones."

His hold didn't loosen, but there was a definite pause.

"You know I didn't mean that."

I knew. He hadn't meant it, maybe, but he'd said it all the same. And then he'd had me down between the sheets, ruthless and driving, taking control. It was harder to keep it straight, though, with his hand on mine, the thumb playing over, rubbing my skin.

"Mary Margaret," he said strongly, and he's the only one who ever calls me that now, saying it in his nighttime voice, low, deep, reaching, "you *tell* me what's going on."

I could feel the tears prickling, and he wouldn't let go of my hand. "I don't know what's going on," I said, "but I think somebody used me to set him up. That makes it personal for me. Jacoby says there's nothing and you want me to stay home knitting, for Christ's sake, Reilly, but there's something, I swear to God. I mean, you see somebody driving down the street—how do you know they're dirty? They're not dodging you, they're not running, but there's something that says. It's instinct or experience, whatever, but you pull them over and there's something. Or sometimes you're wrong and there's nothing, that one time they're clean, and you can feel them laughing at you all the way back to your car."

"Somebody's laughing?"

"I don't know." I stared down at our hands. "If he'd cut himself. That's crazy, isn't it—but if he'd slit his wrists, I'd accept it."

"Wouldn't use a gun?"

"Not a Browning .380," I said.

He was considering something, weighing it. "I'll talk to Jacoby, see what there is."

"There's nothing, Reilly. He already said so."

"He doesn't have to tell you everything."

"He didn't have to tell me *anything*," I said. "He only did because this is a straight and simple suicide, all the pieces in place, and he figured it didn't matter."

"I'll look anyway."

That was nice. I'd appreciate that.

"You need to eat."

He tends to focus on food around me, I'm not exactly sure why. I'm not anorexic or anything.

"I'll *look*," he said. "Come on."

I'm a rag, you know? I moved my hand under his, pressed the fingers. "Okay."

He still had his thumb rubbing, thoughtful, but he didn't say any more, just let go so that I could eat, so that he could, too. We finished the sandwiches, gristled and chewy, listened to the kids. Didn't say very much. I drove him back to the station, to the parking indention outside of the library.

He wasn't getting out of the car. We watched a couple of people trail along the crosswalk.

"What else?" he said.

There wasn't anything else, that was all, that was it.

"Meg."

He thinks he knows me so well. And it was there again suddenly, that "Go to hell" flash, that "Who the *hell* do you think you are?"—but he knew who the hell he thought he was—he thought he was my man, the one to say "Don't." I'd given him a key.

I remember my mother crying, years and years ago, "Over nothing, Mary Margaret, don't tell your father."

"I won't, Mama," I'd said, "no, I won't," and I didn't, though he'd asked and kept asking and I was too young to know.

"Tell me," Reilly said, and where did it stop, this needing to know everything, where did it end? Charlie'd never cared, that I could remember, he'd let me alone and that's why I'd loved him.

*"You cannot fight the wind."*

My Latin philosopher, waxing so wise, and he might have been right that you can't fight the wind, but you know, you can *use* it—rig those sails, build those windmills for power. His eyes understanding me, amused and admiring, treating me like a woman, someone special, with respect.

"He wanted me to stay."

Reilly was very still in the seat there beside me. I curled my hands over the steering wheel, the fingers, and stared at the rings. My wedding ring, still on my hand.

When Reilly spoke, he was remote and controlled. "Did you want to?"

"I don't know." It came out as a whisper.

"Were you going to see him again?"

"No."

I wasn't.

I don't think I was.

"If he called you?"

"He wouldn't have called," I said. "He knew I was involved."

Because I'd said, "I can't." Because I *hadn't* said, "*I don't want to.*"

Reilly moved sharply, and then he had the car door open and was out. I had the steering wheel in a deathgrip, but he just spoke curtly through the passenger window. "Don't do anything until you hear from me."

"Reilly, I don't—"

"I'm *telling* you."

He was telling me.

"You know what it is?" I said. "It's this attitude you have that you own me," and I thrust the car into gear and spun away from him, leaving him there outside of his station.

# 9

Most people go someplace safe to cool down. They go to a gym, or they find a good friend, or they lock themselves into a room. Me, I drive freeways.

It's a drug for me, a narcotic. I go out and find an on-ramp and meld with the road. Zen-Freewayism, the New Meditation. Open yourself to the possibilities, go anywhere or go nowhere, go round in circles, great looping curves while you change up, shift down, stand on the brakes. Floor the metal again, swoop left, take on off.

Fly.

I don't have a Magic Kingdom card anymore, but I didn't see any CHiPpies. I wasn't watching, to tell you the truth, but none of them stopped me, so it must have been a busy day on the other side of Los Angeles. I came down past Agoura, climbing out of the valley, way out of range.

*"Don't do it anywhere near Sylvia de la Peña."*

You don't have to worry about *me*, Sergeant, sir. I always do what I'm told.

Usually, that is.

Not maybe today.

I geared down for the grade, the long sweeping hill. The thing was, you know, I was already moving, so I passed Thousand Oaks and kept climbing. I got to the top of the grade, and it was open before me, the broad stretch of highway curving down like a slide. It was easier to keep going, so I did. Camarillo valley. Oxnard and farms.

I got as far as Ventura, of all places, driving loosely by that time, driving numb before I finally looked around and started thinking. I pulled off on the other side of the city at an underpass, and made my way left towards the beach. There are stretches of pavement by the seawall along Rincon Highway there, the old Highway 1, which serve as sort of a parking lane, so I found a spot kind of lonesome and stopped the 'Ru in it. No one around me. I needed not to be sitting in the seat for a while, needed fresh air and a different perspective, so I climbed out and stretched, walked the few steps to the jetty rocks that were piled up by the roadside, staving off the ocean. I scrambled onto them and over, eased down half a foot, settled in with my spine to a crack in a boulder, and stared down the two yards at the water. Watched the surf massing. Ignored passing cars.

You can't run away from your life.

You can try, if you want to, but sooner or later it finds you and comes back to whisper. If De la Peña hadn't died, would I even have cared?

I don't think so. I hadn't had any plans to go see him. I hadn't thought much about him, to be honest, all weekend—I'd had my hands full with Reilly. *He's* what I want.

So you tell me why I was fighting with him, why I was spending this part of a bad day driving around.

Somebody close to me once told me, "God, Meg, you get those damned itches," and it's true, I suppose. I'm also not real good at scratching. I always seem to end up with my back on a post when a discreet little wiggle would have handled the trick. Take Reilly, for instance. Not ill-inclined. Willing to help—offering, for Christ's sake—and I couldn't take it. It was stupid of me, abysmally stupid, because he was my best road in there, direct to the case, and I've done my share of smiling for less. "Yessir, Sergeant, sir, you sure are a wise one," when the guy was truthfully thicker than stone. So what the hell did it matter with Reilly?

Well, he wasn't thicker, for one thing.

And it would have been too much like lying to him, for another.

Charlie would have had my head for me anyway, though, handed back in a basket. You don't blow off your sources. "Think smart," he'd be saying. "Get some facts. Play it easy." I just couldn't be easy with Reilly, was all. Couldn't play him so well.

And the other thing was that even if Reilly *could* tell me anything I might want to know about this case, I couldn't be sure that he would. I was pretty sure, actually, that he wouldn't.

His own little code of the West.

Police business wasn't *my* business—that's how he saw it. He'd investigate, all right, come back, ask me questions, maybe give me a couple of things. Little things that weren't privileged, weren't germane. Anything that didn't much matter. And while he was doing that, he'd be keeping the lid on, making sure that I didn't start any rabbits, didn't chase any hares. Didn't mix something that could blow up in his face.

It was fair. I could see it. It *was* his town. The man had his job there, his life, was expecting I knew it. Expected me to respect it.

A simple enough thing, loyalty.

*"Mary Margaret, don't tell your father."*

Okay, not so simple.

The water foamed at the base of the jetty, pulled back, launched again. Water wears away stone. It tears at it, tugs it away from its footings, even the big boulders like the one I was on. That's why they have to keep dumping in new rocks every few years or so, to hold back the ocean.

Build higher walls.

Fighting the wind *and* the sea.

A squirrel poked its head up from a nearby boulder and came flitting out, sitting there straight and looking around. I could have shooed it away, but it wasn't my place. It had as much right to the rock as I did, maybe more—it lived there, a hard life, existing on crumbs from the campers and whatever it could cull from the seaweed. I was just passing through, absorbing the warmth of the sun, moving on.

Hit and run.

Not even a cracker to throw him.

I stood up abruptly. The squirrel dove for cover and I felt kind of guilty, but I had that itchy, trapped feeling building again. I don't like the ocean much, don't know why I'd stopped there. There are too many things living under the surface. You wouldn't catch me going a yard in that surf, but there were sure enough people in wetsuits paddling out on their boards. Five or six cars were scattered along the half-mile of parking strip in front and behind me, mostly old junkers. A station wagon, some trucks, and there was something way off down the bridge part that looked like a van. They were the kinds of vehicles you'd take to the beach, to the salted-air fog. People were minding their fishing lines or sunning themselves in their chairs clear back down the strip as far as I could see, all the way down the curve to the beachhouses tucked in at the point. Nobody was looking at me, not even aimed in my direction.

I'm just paranoic as hell.

I shouldn't be standing there by myself, right out in the open.

I should be finding a phone.

I climbed back up the rocks to the Subaru, let myself in, and stayed that way for a moment with the engine turned on, watching myself in the rearview mirror while I put on some lip gloss. I capped the tube, put it casually back in my bag. Left the bag open on the seat there beside me. Eased my way along the parking lane, picking up speed as I signaled the pull-out and there was no one advancing behind me, no other car making time. I was a quarter-mile down the road to the 101 ramp before I finally saw movement, and by then I was turning the curve so I couldn't be sure. I kept on, melted in through the interchange where it joins 101. I lagged back a little there in the number 3 lane, and it was just the traffic sweeping past me, the selfsame cars that had been to my left. One white Mercedes crowded in, wanting me to go faster, and the driver gestured with his finger as he pulled around me, bullied by.

You'd think people with rich cars could afford better manners.

I drove idly back through the west side of Ventura, past the fairgrounds turnoff, the Seaward Drive exit. It was maybe three-thirty. There was a brown sedan way-back-when in the mirror that seemed to be going my speed. There'd been something brown at the end of the beach by the houses where something had glinted, but I hadn't been looking, hadn't really been seeing. Rule Number One and Rule Number One Hundred and One.

I pressed it a little.

The sedan didn't hurry.

I slacked off on the pedal.

The sedan didn't catch me.

I was heading back, you know, on the freeway for home. I was going the way you'd expect me to go.

I took the next exit, having signaled my moves like a good driver should, and way back behind me, an orange light started flashing. The exit was Victoria Avenue. Ventura courthouse is there, and the county offices. They're all built together into one sprawling complex. Also the main sheriff's jail. I rode the ramp up, took a left at the light. Two, three, four cars made the turn, and then so did the brown one.

It might just have business. Might be going shopping or something. Might want to pick up a sandwich from Restaurant Row there, off to the left. I got into the right lane in no particular hurry, flowing smoothly with the traffic, and, several cars behind me, the brown did the same.

The courthouse complex is three or four city blocks, all done up from the outside like a huge park with grounds. There are white sidewalks curving like snakes through the grass, and it's thoroughly landscaped, with neatly placed benches and trees. The main entrance is on Victoria, but there are other approaches from the surrounding streets, so I turned abruptly right at the light onto Telephone Road and wheeled the 'Ru over to the first left-turn bay. I might not have quite signaled.

The sedan overshot me three seconds later, speeding by in the farthest right lane. I got a look at the license tag, enough to remember. Scribbled it down on a receipt from my bag.

The green traffic arrow came on for my lane.

It should give the sedan pause, I would think, me going into the courthouse complex. Give him something interesting to write in his logbook. I wasn't about to make a U-turn right there, anyway, where he could see me in his rearview mirror, so I turned smartly left with the arrow and wasted no time driving in. The best bet was that he'd be making for the next corner, which, if memory served, was a ways up, was Hill Street or Hill Avenue, something like that. He might know there was an entrance there, too, might be looking to catch me inside by going in *that* one, or he might not know anything, probably didn't, in which case he'd be trying to swing back around, hang a U someplace soon there on Telephone Road, and come on in at the light where I'd turned.

It's a player's game.

There's a parking lot to the immediate left once you've entered the complex. It's screened off by trees—an employees' lot at the back of the courthouse, with a loading dock, that kind of thing. I've parked there before. The lot's not visible much from the street, and the sign says EMPLOYEES ONLY but, you know, there's no guard. I made the quick left, and at that time of day people are usually leaving so there were spaces aplenty around the perimeter. I jammed the 'Ru into park in the southeastern corner of the lot by the trees, the side facing Telephone Road. Grabbed my purse, slid out, got up the small hill in a matter of seconds and buried myself in the shrubs there, with a reasonable view of the entrance road and its stoplight.

The brown car and its driver came down Telephone Road. The driver hesitated at the intersection, sort of thinking of turning, and then he cruised straight on through the light very slowly, like a man who was trying to decide if I'd gone in, U-ed quickly around and scurried on out again, so I might yet be ahead of him going back to the freeway—or if I'd had business inside.

The best look I could get without drawing attention showed him short, very dark—tanned or ethnicity in southern California, hard to tell—but swarthy, at any rate. Bristle-boar mustache so he was probably not black. Looked fairly bulky. White shirt with short sleeves.

The arm muscle plain.

# 10

I called Mike from one of the courthouse pay phones.

I'd called Reilly first, actually, at the station, the STU office, his line.

"He's in a meeting," the terse guy who answered it said. "You want to tell me who's calling?"

I didn't, really. "It's Paula Williams," I said. "About an old case. I'll call back in a while."

Reilly was still there, then, still working. I'd thought that he would be, but it was better to hear it, I guess. To know for sure where he was.

I could have called his pager. I'd have gotten him more directly that way because it would have gone off in his meeting, beeping or vibrating, letting him know. It was a Ventura number that I'd have been leaving, though, 805 area code, the courthouse phone. Not a number he'd recognize, so he might not call back right away, and I didn't want to be hanging around.

I really should get a cellular phone.

I keep putting it off. It's bad enough that I have a pager, makes me feel sort of leashed, but we need it for the business when I'm out on a job. I usually leave it stuffed in my bag, though, forgetting to check it, so it isn't that useful—too easy for me to ignore. It had been vibrating like heck when I'd been climbing the hill, blinking furious numbers at me when I'd looked at it after the man in the brown car was gone. Office numbers. *My* office. Michael, I'd say.

Reilly hadn't paged me.

People have words all the time. They go away, work it off, they cool down. I figured he'd have gone into the station after I left him, majorly ticked but switching to cop mode, stuffing our fight to the side. Something to deal with when he got off at six-thirty, festering, maybe, definitely itching, but not what the man's getting paid for. Reilly has pride.

And he'd be thinking, too, that I'd be off feeling sorry, driving and cooling, rerunning a few things myself, so that by the time he called later, *if* he called later, I'd be more amenable—sullen, perhaps, a little bit touchy, but willing at that point to be reasonable and listen, even to admit I'd been wrong.

Reilly's so right.

I was feeling sorry.

I just didn't think I was wrong.

I would have talked to him from the courthouse, though, if I could have reached him then, because it wouldn't have been rehashing old news anymore, with somebody tailing me. It might not have anything to do with De la Peña at all, it could simply have been some guy at the beach thinking I looked too darned easy the way I'd been sitting right out there, but Reilly could run the car's license plate for me, which was mostly, I think, why I'd called.

Mike could run it, too, of course. He still has connections. I fingered the receipt with the scribbled-down license plate number and dropped another quarter into the phone. Pressed all the buttons for the office phone number and then my calling card code, and waited for AT&T to connect me.

Mike answered, second ring. "John Gill Security."

"It's me," I said.

"Meg—Jesus Christ, where the hell have you been?"

He sounded upset, kind of bristling. At me or because of me, I couldn't quite tell.

"I left you a note," I said.

"That was four hours ago. You've been at the station this whole goddamn time?"

"I had to see Reilly, after Jacoby."

He let out a breath, his fury collapsing. "Shit." Which pretty much summed it.

"We had lunch," I said. "Have you had any yet?"

"God, no, I've been sitting here waiting for you."

Waiting on edge, I guess—I should have thought of it. I'd been the same way fretting about him at the station this morning.

I ought to have called.

"I'm sorry," I said.

Mike's always impressed when I'm sorry. He made a really rude noise. It calms him down, though, to hear it. "So what's Reilly saying?"

"How's everything there, Mike? Any business things coming that you couldn't handle?"

He knows me. "How long?"

"Today and tomorrow. Probably not Wednesday."

There was one of those hard-to-interpret pauses. Then, "You going with Reilly?" He sounded carefully blank.

"No," I said. "I'm just getting away. I need you to cover for me."

"Cover with *Reilly*?"

"Yeah."

We've been here before, he and I—me for him, him for me, all situations. Last time it was a girl he'd been dodging. I let him think about it while I went through my bag, checked the cards and the cash.

"I'm not the hell telling him that I haven't heard from you."

Mike has a strong sense of self-preservation.

"You've heard from me," I said, "you don't know where I am, though. I went flying off in a huff."

"Did you?"

Essentially, really, that's what I'd done.

"He keeps bugging me, Mike." I was glancing around, making a quick inventory, trying to think what I'd need. I should have kept out the sweatsuit I'd brought back to the office this morning, all nice and clean, because it would have been something to wear, and then I remembered the dress in the storeroom. I still had the shirt there, too, and the heels.

I might not have to go shopping.

"Well, hell," Mike said. He was sounding more cheerful and I had a small pang of conscience.

"I'm just taking some time, Mike."

"Take all you want."

"Yeah." I hesitated. "Have you heard from Sylvia?"

His voice sobered quickly. "She called around noon. She's taking this hard, Meg—blaming herself. Kept saying that she shouldn't have done it, just over and over, but I guess the doctor has her on something. Linda finally got on and talked to me about it."

"Linda?"

"Her girlfriend—where she's been staying." He sounded that tad bit self-conscious suddenly, a tone in his voice, and I have an untidy mind.

I stared at the phone cord, silver and curling, and played the sound back in my mind.

The light dawns very slowly sometimes, with me.

"*Linda*?"

"Ah, Jesus," he said.

"You've been sleeping with *Linda*?"

"Christ, no, Meg, I haven't," but I was taking it apart, stringing it all back together. Not Sylvia. It hadn't been Sylvia at all.

"I'm not sleeping with her," Mike was saying defensively. "I know what you're thinking, but it's not that, okay? I'm just getting to know her right now."

Getting to know her. Somewhere I had another bomb starting to tick. "What was all this 'old girlfriend' stuff, Mike?"

"She *was*," he said. "I mean, *Sylvia* was, a couple of years ago, right? Not really a 'girlfriend' girlfriend. She was going to school here, and I brushed up against her, nothing important. We went out a few times, that's all. Then she left to go home and get married and I forgot her, okay?" He was honestly serious.

"You went out of the office fast enough Friday."

"Look, I ran into her—what was it, a month ago? Something like that. Over at Beverly Center, and we went out for a drink. Old times' sake, glad to see you, how you been keeping, like that. Nothing big. De la Peña was in a meeting, some muckamuck thing, and she had the evening to kill, that's all. Better than taking in a movie by herself. And she needed someone to talk to, you know? Somebody safe."

"To talk about what?"

"Being married," he said. "What she'd gotten herself into. She wasn't all that happy, Meg."

Really?

Surprise me.

"Didn't sound like *he* was, either," I said. "What'd she tell you?"

"Just general stuff. She was lonesome. Things were okay, I guess, the first year or so, and then they moved up here. She said she was glad to be back for a while, but it's different living in Beverly Hills—not like being at UCLA. Most of her friends had graduated and gone on, or they weren't such good friends anymore. You know how that goes. And De la Peña traveled a lot, wasn't around much."

Making those bucks.

Gilding the cage.

"So she wanted to get out?" I said. "Was she talking divorcing?"

"Naah," Mike said, "she was just talking. Glad to see someone she knew."

Yeah.

Maybe.

Mike's easy company.

"So a month ago, things were just lonesome," I said, "not much fun being married. He wasn't beating her up then?"

"No, I don't think so. Far as I know, Thursday night was the first. That's when she ran."

To a girlfriend's.

The one that Mike was just getting to know.

"Tell me about this girlfriend," I said, "this Linda. When'd you meet *her*?"

Another ambiguous pause. "Last Friday at lunch."

"I thought you were meeting an attorney."

"Well, yeah."

An attorney. Last Friday.

"*She's* the attorney? The one on the papers?"

"Yeah."

"Is *she* married?"

"No," Michael said.

This was great, what I wanted. Not what I thought I'd been doing at all. "You met this gal Friday?"

"We talked Friday night," Mike said. "Till kind of late. Sylvia was hurting, so she took some stuff, went to bed, and Linda and I just sat around talking. I had to wait, anyway, until after you'd called."

Like I'd held him up.

"I called you at nine-fifteen, Mike."

"I *had* to stay, babe," he said. "You know. I had to be there, in case."

In case De la Peña came calling, he meant, came stalking around. No good guy would leave ladies alone facing danger, and this way, Mike was a hero. A peacock. Spreading those feathers out, bright in the sun. I could see the whole thing. I just wished that I'd known it, wished that I'd known he was busy impressing this Linda while I was sitting there drinking last damned Friday night, worrying myself about the possibilities of Sylvia de la Peña.

It's not really Mike's fault, though. I'm the one who takes on.

"So you and Linda were just talking Friday night. Till when, do you think?"

"Till one, maybe two." He sounded slightly abashed but not sorry. No reason to be.

"You spent the night?"

"I slept on the couch," he said, "jeez," but I'm not his mother.

"The whole weekend?"

"Hey—"

"Oh, that's right, you were getting to know her," I said. "I forgot. Did you spend the whole weekend there guarding the bodies?"

"Yeah, I did, okay? I didn't have anything special going, and Linda kind of asked me to."

That explained the good mood then, this morning. "What's *Sylvia* think of all this?"

"Think of what?"

"You and Linda."

"She's not like that," he said, as if that were an answer. "She's a really nice girl. She, you know, went to school in a convent or something."

Some of the worst kids I've known were from Catholic schools. Biding their time.

"That doesn't make her a nun, Mike. She hasn't noticed you talking to Linda?"

"It isn't like that," Mike said for the umpteenth time, but this time I was trying to listen. "She just needed company. She wasn't looking for a fling, Meg, and I wouldn't have taken it, for Christ's sake, you know? I was just there to help."

Yeah, maybe. Okay.

"Why'd she call *you*?" I said. "Friday. What was the notion?"

"Well, she remembered me being a cop. I guess she thought I'd protect her, and once I saw the bruises, she didn't have to keep asking." He was sounding buffed again, rigid and tight, but I needed to learn things.

"Whose idea was the pictures?"

"I don't know," he said. "Linda's or mine, I don't really remember."

Linda, the attorney.

"You keep any copies of them? Have the negatives?"

"No," he said. "I gave them over to Linda. What's it matter?"

It didn't, not really. I just wanted a picture. I don't get to see many saints.

"What's Linda's last name?"

"Madrigala."

"She's Argentine, too?" With a last name like that.

"Yeah," he said.

"But she's with an American firm here? A law firm?" It had to be an American firm because they'd filed divorce papers. Gotten a restraining order kind of quick, from a judge.

"She's a partner," he said. "She's naturalized or something, I think, I don't know. She went to 'SC. Business law."

It was good, after all, that Mike had talked with her. "So her firm worked for De la Peña? His company? Is that how Sylvia knew her?"

"I don't think so," he said. "They met at some function, Free Argentina, or something. Sylvia was kind of alone there, didn't know many people and they hit it right off. That was a year ago, she said, maybe more."

"Free Argentina from what?" I said, but I could find it out later. No point in wasting the time. "Where does Linda live?"

"On Bellagio. In Bel Air."

Bel Air.

"Alone?"

"Well, yeah."

"She makes reasonable money if she's affording a house with a bungalow there."

"She might have old family," Mike said. "I don't know. She has a lot of antique stuff."

He hadn't asked much, not nearly enough, but then, he was getting to know her. Chatting, you know. Being suavely cool.

"What's the name of her law firm?"

"Why?" he said.

It would have been on the papers, but I hadn't read them. I'd just glanced to be sure De la Peña's name was on them, spelled out correctly, and Sylvia's, of course. Should have made myself a copy.

"I thought maybe you'd gotten a card."

"Well, I did," he said, "somewhere, but what does it matter?"

It'd be stuffed in his desk, maybe.

"I was just wondering," I said. "You know how I am. So you can cover things for me, the work orders and everything? There shouldn't be much. It was going to be a light week."

"Yeah, sure, I can." He was silent for a couple of seconds. "I think I won't stick around here today, though," he said.

Well, it was four at that point, four-fifteen. Most of the day was gone already, not many people likely to call—and the office is only a few blocks from Beverly station, where Reilly was working. Mike's got a pretty good sense of when to duck trouble. I can't seem to learn it myself.

"Yeah, no point in staying," I said. "I'll call you later, okay? You'll be home?"

"Probably, yeah. I think so."

Unless Linda called him, it sounded like. He'd gotten that little bit vagueish again.

Great. Wonderful.

"I'm going to get you a beeper," I said.

"Not for me," he said cheerfully. "I don't need one. No one expects to be able to find me."

I laughed and let him hang up.

I didn't ask him to check out the license plate number, the one from the brown car. I hadn't forgotten or anything, the paper was still there in my hand with its edges kind of crinkled where I'd mashed it around. The thing was I'd been listening this time, really trying to, anyway, trying to get a better fix on the problem.

If De la Peña *didn't* kill himself, someone else did, you know. Someone who'd planned it. Someone who might be keeping tabs, at least for a while, in case things unraveled.

I didn't want someone to know I was checking a tail out.

And I didn't want Mike sounding any different tonight when this Linda might call.

# 77

I left Ventura by way of its side streets, the local roads. Took rural 118, the back way, over to Thousand Oaks. There's a guy I used to know there—Andy Bates, an old friend from the department. He retired a few years ago on a disability pension. Had a gun repair shop in T.O. that was pretty much open when he wanted it to be—you don't like it, don't go there—which wasn't a philosophy change for Andy at all. It worked for him when he was in uniform, too. You don't want a real cop, don't call one.

It helps to be good, of course.

Andy always was.

I hadn't been there for forever, and he might have closed down or moved. People will do that when you're not paying attention. I might not remember the right street for the shop either, but I was pretty sure it was off the main drag, T.O. Boulevard. Since I was there and so close, it seemed like a plan to go look Andy up, see if he was still there, see how he was. Find out if he felt he could do me a favor.

I turned right with the ramp onto the 23 Freeway and went south for a ways past all kinds of construction, road graders and such in the center divider. Took the T.O. Boulevard exit, coasted through the several stoplights, and God was apparently riding right with me because the streets looked familiar. I located the side street and found Andy's shop. Parked in front at the curb.

Andy was open and was in with a customer, an unhappy-looking man. His place was a small industrial shop, about the size of a two-car garage. The Sheetrock interior was pasted together, strips visible, wires and ducts kind of added. Bars on the window. Stickers. He looked up from the counter and saw me. Nodded.

"McGee," he said.

"Andy."

As if it were yesterday. As if I hadn't been missing for nearly four years. I wasn't thinking he'd change much, but the fine bushy mustache was a pot-metal gray.

He turned back to the man on my side of the counter.

"Try me on Friday," he said. "Not too early."

It wasn't what the customer wanted to hear. He seemed high-strung, impatient. "Well, should I give you a call then or what?"

Andy thought some about it.

"Yeah," he said finally, "why don't you do that."

"About ten, say?"

"Ten's likely." It wasn't likely at all from the way he was standing, but the guy couldn't read him, was looking appeased.

"Well, good," the guy said. "I'm not, you know, trying to hurry you, but I need something to aim for, something concrete."

He'd have been better off shooting at sidewalks, but Andy was nodding, just watching him.

"So I guess that's it," the guy said. He glanced over his shoulder, tried to include me. "He does really great work."

"Yeah," I said. I moved out of the doorway, left him the path. He seemed ready to take it.

"Okay," the guy said. "Okay, then—so, Friday." We both watched him leave. He got into a Chevy outside, a Tahoe, nice and new, and revved it a little bit more than it needed before he moved out.

"You want to lock that door," Andy said behind me, so I stretched over and did it. Turned around and he was holding a gun, a Colt 1911, Government model. It wasn't aimed at me, exactly, it was sort of off

82

to the side, but it had a magazine in it and he was sighting the damn thing right there in the shop. "Been quite a while," he said.

I jerked my head at the door. "I thought you weren't going to deal with yahoos anymore."

"They keep coming around." He had a screwdriver out, had the Colt laid back down on the counter, was adjusting the over-travel trigger screw—something, probably, for the yahoo. They always want extras. He didn't look over at me. "I heard about Charlie."

I knew that he would have, knew that he'd say so, was halfway prepared. "I'm seeing someone else now."

"From the department?"

Our department. Charlie's.

"God, no," I said.

"Yeah?" Things didn't matter to Andy, which is what I've always liked about him. He'd known Charlie real well, but he wouldn't hold it against me, me going on. I didn't think he would, anyway. I crossed over to the counter.

"You still with Susan?"

"Still there," he said. Andy's girlfriend's a sheriff—or maybe his wife now, I didn't know. Things change in four years.

"How's life these days?"

"Boring as shit." He was sitting back, looking at me, the screwdriver loose in his hand. "You need something, girl?"

"I might," I said. "Might need to have someone checked into."

"Yeah?" He sucked at a tooth under the mustache, made a microscopic adjustment to the trigger screw. Looked back up at me without an expression. "You used to know how to do that."

"I've been somewhat proscribed," I said.

"Pro-scribed." He savored the word. Liked it. Found it darkly humorous. Aimed the gun again, a hairsbreadth to the left of my shoulder. "You still hanging with Mike?"

"Yeah," I said steadily. Could feel what was coming. The hammer snicked back and the barrel didn't waver.

"He pro-scribed, too?"

"In a manner of speaking," I said, "yeah, he is. You still taking your pills?"

Pin fell on an empty chamber. Click.

"Twice a day," he said.

Grinned.

And the thing about Andy is that he likes to see how far he can push it, how close to the edge he can take you. Took a captain too far once.

Why he's retired.

"Who's pro-scribing?" he said.

I scuffed my toe a little against the glass pane of the counter. Tried to find the right way to say it. "It's a Beverly Hills case, Andy. Suicide. Mike's a little mixed up with the guy's wife, nothing serious, but they don't want us poking around. I just wanted to know a little more about the guy and his background, but Beverly was getting kind of heavy about being the cops."

"So you came out to see *me*?" He was back to fiddling with the trigger screw, that bitty adjustment.

"Someone's following me," I said. "I dumped him out in Ventura, and I was taking the back roads towards the 101 when I remembered your shop. I thought I'd stop in and see what you were up to, how busy you were."

"I'm busy," he said. Sucked thoughtfully at the tooth again. "PD following you?"

I shook my head. "I'm pretty sure that it's private. It was one guy, not a pair, and there's no reason, really, for Beverly to do it. I got the license plate off him, but I haven't had a chance to have it run for me yet, find out who this guy is. I was kind of hoping, actually, that you still knew some people."

"I know people," he said. Looked at me for another indefinable moment. "I heard that you and Mike started a security outfit after everything went down with Charlie."

"Yeah," I said.

"Beverly Hills."

"Yeah."

He was waiting for something, but I didn't know what.

"You ever go back, Meg?"

To the department, he meant.

Our department.

"No," I said softly. "Do you?"

It was a strange, hungry moment, a look almost yearning.

"No."

"They keep sending me letters," I said. "The Association does. Retirement dinners and stuff like that. Mike's always saying I should go."

"Yeah. Sue tells me, too."

"You ever go to *her* stuff?"

"It's different," he said.

Yeah.

"This guy I'm seeing," I said, "he's with Beverly Hills."

"A cop?"

"A sergeant."

"Tough way to go," Andy said. He sounded suddenly sardonic again, darkly amused.

"What?"

"Sue passed her test. The sergeant's exam."

I was looking at him, feeling it.

"Sheriff's had all that affirmative action," he said, "after that lawsuit. Bumped up a whole bunch of females. She's a sergeant now. As of last year."

Mother-of-pearl.

"Well, that's good," I said carefully. "She ever learn how to shoot?"

He was grinning at me again, over the counter. "Hell, no," he said.

# 12

I went to earth in Brentwood. There's an old-style motel a few miles off the freeway, fairly easy access coming and going. I'd been there once with Charlie, which is why it occurred to me. You tend to go back to what's familiar. I don't frequent motels so I don't have a large pool of knowledge to draw on—other than where I used to work, of course, and there's no way I'd go to a motel in my city, even if Reilly weren't living there now. Brentwood was nowhere in particular, not near my home, the office, or Sylvia, so the odds of anyone figuring out I was there were pretty slim.

The key to finding somebody is their predictability—their lifestyle, their habits. So-and-so puts out the trash every Wednesday morning at six, so you can accost him then. X goes to the office Monday through Friday from nine to five-thirty, less an hour for lunch—that sort of thing. You can find him there. Meg has a home in Burbank and a business to run. We know where Meg's likely to be.

But Meg hasn't been scheduling a lot of work lately on Tuesdays and Wednesdays because those were her boyfriend's days off. And Meg has a partner who can manage the jobs for a day or two while she works some things out. The world doesn't have to know about it, she's just not where she should be. Check the house, use your key—she's not home, she's gone. No one knows where.

Not even Mike?

I smiled at the desk clerk, let him give me the room key. People don't pay much in cash anymore. More honest people in the world now, I guess, who don't mind their real name on a register.

"Thank you, Mrs. Abbott."

"Thank *you*," I said.

It was seven o'clock then, starting to get dark. I'd picked up a few things at the Thousand Oaks Mall, so I toted them across the small parking lot and into my room. I didn't really *arrange* them, I just kind of tossed the clothes into the one ancient chest of drawers, set out the toothbrush and stuff in the bathroom, and pulled the drapes shut. I used the room phone to call Andy, and left him my new name and the motel's phone number. I figured he'd know who it was.

Sue's voice was on the answering machine.

A sergeant now.

Sheesh.

Andy was checking on the brown sedan for me. I'd told him some more about what had happened with De la Peña, as well as the way things had gone down with Jacoby and Reilly that morning. Andy was thinking I was nuts, I guess, kind of looking at me that way, and I wasn't quite sure that he wasn't right. In the cold light of the afternoon, hearing myself saying it to him in the back room of his shop, surrounded by boxes of gun parts and magazines, real life as we know it, it did seem incredible. Unlikely. Harder to be sure that I wasn't just doing this because of hormones or an innate dislike of being told what to do. Bullied.

Rebellion.

But there had been the brown car at the beach, following me.

Andy believed *I* believed it, at least.

And the thing was that Andy and I, we went a ways back, had worked alongside each other. We hadn't worked really together, the way Mike and I had, because Andy was more Charlie's circle. The generation ahead. But we'd cycled around each other there at the department, knew how the other one did things. He'd give me that much of the benefit of the doubt, wouldn't automatically write me off as being female and wrong.

Unless, of course, it turned out that I was.

I'd given him the license plate number. I'd copied it over for him on a clean sheet of paper he'd pulled out of a drawer, adding the vehicle description and the little bit of physical I had on the driver. He was going to have a chat with a sheriff's deputy he knew there in T.O. and get back to me later. He'd offered to dig into De la Peña, too, if I wanted, but I'd turned him down.

I knew what *I* could contain, okay? And I wasn't so sure it would work if anyone else were doing it. I figured I could get in some low-key poking, a little bit of nosing around without harming anybody, without starting any fuss that I couldn't smooth over. I just needed to know something more about the whole situation, but I didn't know what the something was yet. I'd know it when I saw it, though, and as soon as I did, I'd pull back, get on out of it—again, without harm. Without making any messes that would blow up at the station, that would blow back on Reilly.

I owed him that much.

So I'd nicely said no. I'd told Andy that I needed to think about what I was doing, which really was true. I'd said I'd be staying somewhere else for the next day or two while I did all that thinking, probably hiding out, and I'd get back to him soon to let him know how to reach me.

I'd done that part now. I didn't know when he'd be calling, if it would even be tonight, but he could leave me a message to get back to him. It was seven-thirty, meanwhile, getting dark out. Time to set things in motion.

I went back across the parking lot and eased into my car, glancing very casually around. Another motel couple was out there, going to dinner, it looked like. Climbing into their car. I put the 'Ru into gear and swung out of the parking lot. Drove over the couple of miles on Sunset, turned onto the 405 for a little ways, and then took the Olympic exit, the south road in to our offices in Beverly Hills. I wasn't going to drive anywhere near Beverly PD. I believe very strongly in Fate, in not tempting it, because Fate has a way of looking out windows, strolling out for some air, spotting you at the moment you'd least want to be seen. It seemed best to avoid it and go the long way around. Reilly ought to have gotten off work an hour ago, but it wouldn't be the first time something kept him there late.

There were two cars still in the office parking lot. I had an impulse to dodge the corner, to park on a side street and slip casually back. I follow impulses like that. It saves me the emotional strain of second-guessing myself fifty thousand times. Impulses are instinct, the way I see it, and instinct's just experience that's well learned and working—if you can't trust your instinct, what the hell is the point?

You've got to be able to recognize whether it's instinct or plain old sniveling fear, of course.

So easy to do.

I parked on one of the side streets under an elm, shadowed my way back. It takes longer to park farther away and then skulk back and forth, and the time you spend exposed and more vulnerable while you're out on the street is also a factor, but I guess if I'd *really* been listening to those instincts, I wouldn't have gone to the office at all.

I just needed some things that were easiest there.

And I was thinking, anyway, that that part was fear.

There was a delivery van backed up by the stairs, but he's usually there towards the evening, picking up film stock or rushes, whatever, from the producers above us. That's where he parks as a rule, sort of out of the way, so he can take those extra few minutes chatting with the gal in the office upstairs if he wants to and not have people complaining that he's blocking them in.

Our office is street-level, under the balcony. I'd spent most of an afternoon applying window film after we'd taken over the lease—to help cut the sun, I'd told Ed, the manager, keep the carpet from fading, but as it happens, it also makes the windows reflective. Mirrorlike. You can see out well enough, but it's tough to see in.

I watched myself darkly walking up to the door, watched for any activity happening in the street scene behind me.

There was a Pontiac passing, a bluish Grand Am. It wasn't slowing or peering, it was moving right along, oblivious to me. The streetlights were starting to come on, though, yellow-orange spotlights glaring down through the darkening night. I unlocked the door, skinnied through, and relocked it behind me. Stood an extra moment by the door, letting my eyes adjust to the gloom.

I wasn't a burglar, I could certainly turn on the lights in my own office, but then all that mirrored protection would be worthless. The window film only reflects when there's more light outside than in—during the day, for example, with the sun shining brightly, which it wasn't anymore. I'd been at some pains to disguise my approach, had gone to some trouble to ensure that anybody getting off work late a few minutes away and driving by looking for me wouldn't know I was here, so a light shining out through the miniblinds with my shadow crisscrossing would be kind of specific. Counterproductive.

I have a little pencil flashlight at the end of my keyring. I also know my office pretty well. I put out my hands for bumping protection and felt my way through the dimness to the doorway that leads to the storeroom. Once I'd rounded that corner, it was safe enough to use the flash to light the stuff on the shelves. The black dress was still there, with the see-through shirt and the heels, piled where I'd left them, next to the envelope boxes. I didn't, unfortunately, have the leatherette purse—that was somewhere on the floor of my bedroom closet in Burbank, where Reilly had chucked it Friday night, taking charge—but I'd gotten a cheap-enough substitute one at the Thousand Oaks Mall.

It took me maybe a minute to peel out of my clothes. I folded them carefully and tucked them into the overnight bag I keep there on one of the lower shelves, putting them on top of the sweatsuit and the running shoes I'd brought back this morning. Only this morning? God, what a day.

I pulled the black dress on over my head, adjusted the fit, smoothed the fabric on down. It felt too revealing. Indecent. Exposed. I grabbed the cover-up shirt, sheer as it was, and wrapped it around me. It didn't feel any better. It was the same damn outfit I'd worn Friday night when I was feeling so good, and tonight it felt wrong.

It had to be Reilly.

Usually it's Charlie who's nattering over my shoulder, the little ghost carping, advising, whatever, but tonight the small voice was definitely Reilly.

Sapping me. Undermining my confidence.

*"I wouldn't have done it at all."*

Well, jeez, what do *you* know, you son-of-a-bitch? I think nobody asked you. I think nobody wanted you coming in with your attitudes and your damn self-assurance, making me small.

Something like that.

I tucked into the office bathroom, shutting the door. I went ahead and turned on the light there because there wouldn't be any visible spillover into the office with the bathroom door shut, and studied myself in the mirror. I just needed more makeup, that's all it was. Fortunately, Thousand Oaks Mall sells stuff like that, and equally fortunately, I'd thought ahead. I pulled the goodie sack out of my bag and scattered the contents onto the narrow strip of counter.

It's the story of my life, me standing over small bathroom sinks with glaringly ugly fluorescent lights. I should put up a pink shade or something.

Michael would like that.

I laughed at the thought in the mirror and felt better, grabbed up an eyeliner, and set to work. A dark blue line, very sophisticated. Mascara to match. Fringed eyelashes, blinking back at me, eyes slyly watching.

Pouting mouth. I drew Crimson Lustre over the lips there, gliding it on, outlining the curves. It was me, you know. Different.

I'd gotten perfume at the store, too—they were handing out small sample bottles so I'd taken one, I don't really know why. I dabbed some on my wrists and rubbed them together to warm up the scent, release it. It was jasmine, exotic. I ran a drop down between my breasts with a finger. Watched myself do it.

The dress was still maybe too low but I didn't feel tacky anymore. I felt good, I felt perfect. My mother always said that if you look good, you feel good, and maybe, after all, she was right. I resettled the shirt to be a little more open, tucked a stray bit of hair behind my ear. I smelled the jasmine again briefly as my wrist moved so close to my face. Dangly earrings? They were in the front tray of my top desk drawer, rescued from the In box this morning. I could slip out into the dimness and get them, except that I didn't want to be coming and going a lot through the office. I felt safe enough here in the bathroom, looking good, but confidence is a delicate thing.

*"Don't forget it again."*

"You're a jerk," I said to the man on my shoulder, "a bullying jerk," but it wasn't just him, it was me. Wanting too much, maybe. Caught up in something.

I looked at myself in the tacky black dress, and it *was* too tight, it *was* too revealing, but I was wearing it anyway, going to town. *"You won't stay for dinner?"* "I can't," I'd said, and I'd almost wished that I could.

What if I had?

What would I have known that I didn't know now?

Why he'd killed himself, maybe.

*If* he did.

Maybe that's what I wanted.

*"The truth will set you free."* That's one of those phrases people like to be quoting, but I've never found only one truth to anything. It's always perceptions, experiences, different interpretations. How *you* think something happened compared to the guy standing next to you—what you focused on, what you heard, what you thought you saw. It's why eyewitness descriptions are usually bogus.

And yet, we go get them. We try to interpret them for ourselves—*re*interpret them, really—compare them, correlate them, find the commonality, because we feel something's better than nothing.

Humans like to have answers.

Causes.

I had to know what had happened to De la Peña last Friday night.

I needed to know for my own sake what my part of it was, what difference, if any, I could have made.

It was worthless, I knew that. It wouldn't change a damn thing, wouldn't bring the man back, wouldn't guide me any better the next time I was facing someone over a table.

But you like to have answers.

This search had to mean *something*.

I couldn't just be doing this because I'd given Reilly a key.

# 13

It was a different crowd at Chaven's on Monday night. More work oriented, I'd say. Fewer moguls, and more moguls-in-the-making, there to dine with their clients instead of their little honeys. A number of female executives, too, it seemed. At least, there were several women in business suits, coats tailored and sleek, skirts properly long. I was more like a sore thumb than I'd hoped to be, so it was good that I'd brought a large jacket along. Good, too, that I'd left the earrings in the desk and had toned down the makeup.

Reilly's image was useful for something, I guess.

"Perrier," I said to the waitress, "with a twist of lemon."

She wasn't the one I'd had Friday night, but she seemed nice enough. Not like the twit who'd ignored me to swoop down on a table three feet away and assure the two gentlemen there that she'd be their waitress. They were gratified, I'm sure. Guys are like that. Mine was putting a small bowl of blue corn chips and something that looked like garlicky bean curd down on my table.

"Be right back," she said cheerfully and took off in the direction of the bartender. I was sitting in the same corner against the wall because it gave the best view of the room, and also because it was there and empty. You go to what's familiar, you know?

The bar wasn't very crowded at eight-thirty, nobody standing around looking for tables. I didn't know if people had already passed through on their way to the restaurant part, or if this was how they normally gathered, but there were fewer waitresses, too, than there'd been Friday night, so I'd guess this was a typical Monday at Chaven's. People saving their bucks for the weekend. Bigger bashes. More important people to be seen with.

I waited until the waitress returned with my drink, then paid her and put a fairly large tip on the table.

"It doesn't look busy," I said.

"Well, you know," she said, twinkling, "Monday night . . ."

Yeah, I knew.

"I was supposed to meet a friend," I said ruefully, "but I don't see him here. And me all dressed up."

"Oh, that's too bad." She was assessing my outfit, but relaxing a little. Strike the right chord. "Could he be inside?"

"Well, I was wondering about that. I mean, we didn't *say* dinner, I thought we were just meeting out here first, but—well, would you mind looking through the restaurant for me? Or I could do it, I guess. I just feel kind of awkward . . ." I let it trail off.

She was a very nice girl, and they weren't very busy. "No, sure. What's he look like?"

I described Rudolfo de la Peña.

"You just wait," she said. "I'll be back in a sec," and she went bee-lining off to the inner doorway, past the maître d' at his podium, flashing him a quick smile. He smiled stiffly back.

He was the same one from Friday.

He was glancing in my direction now as if I might look familiar, but the coat I was wearing hid most of the outfit, and I'm sure he saw a lot of people coming through there. In another week, or on a busier night, he wouldn't even have glanced. I drew the jacket a little more closely around me as if it were cold, which really it wasn't, and took a sip from my drink. Let my gaze wander past the two guys at the next table and looked lightly, quickly around the room. I was just another well-behaved female sitting there, waiting for her date. A little lost, perhaps, not quite certain, looking at her watch. Guy standing her up? What a heel.

Another fragile sip.

The glass very carefully put down.

Looking rather anxiously over at the dining room doorway. No sign of the waitress. The maître d', though, watching. The girl looking quickly away, embarrassed. Eyes drifting back in spite of herself. The man still watching. The girl's eyes sliding guiltily, stopping midpoint, with a poignant little shake of her head, half-humorous, telling herself to have sense, that she's not the first one in the world this ever happened to, and better to know it, face the facts, and then, oh, my God, the girl's rising, clutching the purse and her drink, ignoring the other patrons and walking towards the maître d', a little self-consciously but fairly determined, legs showing long and bare in the strappy high heels.

"The waitress was checking for me," I said sort of wistfully, but trying to keep a brave face. "I seem to have misplaced my date."

He'd noticed the legs, was being very professional. Stodgy. Looking briskly down at the reservations list on the podium. "The name, please?" A faint accent—French. "You had reservations?"

"I don't know," I said. "I think maybe so. We—well, we were here Friday and I couldn't stay then, something . . . came up, so he said let's do it Monday. Today. Tonight, I mean. At eight-thirty. I thought we'd just meet in the bar and talk about it, but he *might* have meant dinner." I realized then that the maître d' was still waiting expectantly, finger poised over the list, that he was politely still wanting the name, and I blushed like an idiot. "I'm sorry," I said. "It's De la Peña. Rudolph de la Peña."

The maître d' paused.

Maître d's in Beverly Hills know everything. It's their job, it's their power—they have to know who's in and who's not, all the little scandals, because that determines who gets the best table, who, regrettably, they just don't have room for tonight, "So sorry, sir." That way, too, they know who doesn't need a reservation—"Goodness, no, not for *you*, sir"—and who gets waved in past the line because the movie's a megadraw at the box office or they've just made a killing in Japan. Maître d's know the scent of old money, the staying power of new, and they can calculate to the nth degree the right level of condescension, familiarity, and/or obsequiousness that a patron might need to feel comfortably at home. They breathe out discretion. It's their stock-in-trade—like the old English version of a butler, you know? "The things I could tell you . . . but of course, I wouldn't. It wouldn't be proper. Never mind how many times I've seen Madame with the houseboy, or Monsieur dining out with a tidy little snack. Those goings-on aren't anyone's business but mine, of course, and theirs."

He knew Rudolph de la Peña was dead.

He had his eyes running over me again, recalculating, me in my too short, inappropriate finery, obviously from the really wrong side of the world, but not necessarily a girl on the make, perhaps just a romp who didn't know any better, how the rich people did things. I was doing my best to look like a frail, a wisp, a grateful little creature.

He'd know that De la Peña was divorcing, too. I doubted that he knew that *I'd* served the papers there at the bar last Friday night, but he looked a bit like he might be remembering me now, sitting at the table, talking.

With De la Peña.

We might have made future plans.

Wouldn't *that* be an interesting tidbit?

"She didn't even know he was dead?"

"No, my dears, she didn't, all broken up about it. And then I wondered if, perhaps, she'd try to go to the funeral. Just think of the scene." A delicate shudder. Everyone sort of ghoulishly delighted.

I blinked at him innocently. "*Did* he make a reservation?" I asked.

Another half a second's indecision, and then, "No, he didn't. You were here Friday night, you said? *Last* Friday night?"

"Yes," I said. "We met for a drink in the bar, and he wanted me to stay, you know, for dinner, but I . . . I just . . . really couldn't . . . that night . . ." I let my eyes drift rather sadly aside—the Mystery Other Woman, wishful, regretting. I shifted my bag and the glass of Perrier so that I was clutching them both in my right hand, leaving my left hand free to brush back a bit of stray hair from my face. He was noting my wedding ring, his eyes flicking over it. I always forget to remove it.

A *married* Mystery Other Woman.

Monsieur de la Peña's reputation was getting kind of a jolt there at Chaven's. I hoped it did some good, though, you know? Surely did hope so. Miss Sylvia might be ten times a virginal angel but De la Peña deserved better than being her joke.

"Did he call?" I asked anxiously, still worrying about Rudolph. "Did he leave any messages? It's not like him just not to show up."

Discretion was clearly struggling.

And it *was* a slow night.

"I think you should come and sit down," he said briskly. "In the back, perhaps? In the manager's office?" He was already motioning to someone from the dining room to come out and take over the podium, and he had one of those proprietary hands on my arm, ushering me into the interior.

"What is it?" I said, clutching frantically, guessing. "Has anything happened?"

"This way, please."

No scenes in the dining room. Not at Chaven's, no, no. One of the reasons their clientele likes them.

We were skirting the round, white-linened tables, aiming for a doorway at the back. There was a smattering of diners scattered around the room, most of them talking in animated but properly hushed groups of two or three. You could hear the indistinct hum of conversation, the clink of fine crystal as they sipped and repositioned their goblets. You could smell the warm aromas of French haute cuisine being sliced thin and tasted. The air was redolent with wealth and privilege, the carpeting thick underfoot.

I was being hurried along on the far side of the maître d' like a baggage, a bagatelle, an itinerant serving girl. Too many eyes that might see me, and wonder if Chaven's was losing its edge.

I was keeping up with the man—not much choice, actually, it was that or be dragged—but I was hanging back subtly, looking past him, trying to check out the room to see if my waitress was there, or the one I'd really come in for, the gal who'd been working in the bar last Friday night. She might only do weekends, but she'd seemed kind of connected, an employee who knew the customers by name, which generally means someone who's full-time, who's been there a while, who might have the pull to get choice of shifts. I'd bet that the good tip money during the week came from the dining room rather than the bar, so when she hadn't been outside, it had seemed worth the trouble to find my way in. It was just a notion, a plan that I'd had sort of hazily in the back of my mind when this whole Other Woman thing had started working out so well with the maître d'.

It's always good to have a backup, though, so I was still looking. If I spotted her, that would be one more card in my hand, something else I could play with or build strategy on.

We were almost to the end of the room when I saw her.

She and my perky waitress were standing together over one of the white-linened tables, quite obviously chatting, very cheerfully flirting with a lone male diner I didn't have any trouble identifying.

His eyes wandered over me, noted the dress, the maître d's grasp on my arm. Returned to me, deadpan and hooded, as I was whisked through the doorway.

It was, of course, Reilly.

# 14

There's a saying, so apropos, in the military. I don't know where it came from, probably Caligula. One of those ancient Roman-type guys.

"If your attack is going *really* well, it's an ambush."

It was good that the maître d' still had his grip on my arm, and even better that he wasn't paying attention to me just then because I might have looked for a second every bit as dangerous and bushwhacked as I felt. We were in an alcove off the kitchen with a server deftly avoiding us as he hoisted a trayful of food-laden dishes above us and back down again past us, almost balletic. Worth an extra buck on the tip if anyone besides us had seen it.

"In here," said the maître d'. He'd opened a door while I'd been turned half away from him, containing, watching the waiter.

I didn't know who this maître d' was now. His acceptance of my story was now much too easy. Suspect. People *will* believe things when they have a reason—greed or culpability—but this was looking a lot less like me being so smart and a lot more like me being outsmarted.

Reilly in place already.

On terms with the people here.

Even, perhaps, with the maître d'.

Except that I didn't know that for sure.

You get that adrenaline surge, you know, part of the aortic shock, the fight-or-flight reflex, and everything becomes heightened, very focused. The brain works intensely, on overload. The body readies. Time slows. I don't know if it's like that for everyone, but it's always been like that for me, for most of the cop guys I've known. When you work undercover, you have to be very careful with that. You have to hang on to your character, have to fight your own instincts and literally make yourself wait, be extra sure, because there are *always* shocks, there's always something that comes up unexpectedly and then it's a toss-up between precipitate action which might save your life or that subconscious move which will give you away, ruining everything.

I didn't know what Reilly was doing here.

He'd said he was going to talk with Detective Jacoby when he got back to the station, so maybe he had. Maybe he'd volunteered to look into the waitress and double-check the story, so maybe he was here officially, working. He didn't have to have identified himself as an officer, he could be posing as a diner, running the same sort of casual scam that I was. Pick up some info for whatever it was worth, no harm, no foul.

The waitress might already know him, of course, might be fully aware that he was a cop, because maybe he came in every Monday for dinner or maybe he used to hang out at the bar, stop in on the weekends looking for company. Hell, maybe he *still* did. I flat didn't know. We hadn't been discussing *his* drinking habits last Friday night—only mine.

Probably the maître d' would know who the cops were, too, so he might know Reilly. He might only know the Vice cops, though, having those dealings, or the high-profile ones—the captains and lieutenants, the upper ranks, the ones more important in the celebrity world. Or even if he *did* know Reilly, that didn't mean he knew why Reilly was there. It didn't mean that Reilly'd set this thing up to have the maître d' bring me back to the office, to catch me in private.

It comes down to the choices.

If the maître d' was his own man, I needed to maintain Other

Woman. Definitely needed not to alarm him by looking like anything else—Warrior Woman, for instance, or Trapped, Cornered Rat. I'd already controlled to that extent, already turned slightly away, disguising the gut-level response.

And now he was wanting me to go with him into a room.

"Yeah, sure," I said softly, pliably.

I needed his hand off my arm. It was okay that he was so close because I could take him that way, unsuspecting. If he suspected, though—or worse, if he *knew*—then his hand was a factor to deal with, a controller. I prefer not to clinch at close quarters with someone who knows that I've trained. There are still ways to get out of things, but they're more apparent, and any concealment at that point is gone.

I like concealment.

I walked into the small room, the office, with his hand still guiding but releasing me once we got past the door. It was a cubbyhole, not very grand—a working manager's office. The crammed-in desk, the computer, a phone, file cabinets with notes stickied everywhere. One extra chair.

He was closing the door.

Reilly might still be coming in, but I heard the faint little snick of a lock turning, the metal bolt going home.

Just the two of us then.

Tête-à-tête.

This part I could do.

I sank into the extra chair gratefully, Other Woman intact, clutching the purse sideways with the drink in the same hand, right hand, and my left out imploringly.

"Monsieur," I said, sounding that touch French myself, "won't you tell me?"

I have to be careful with accents, because I tend to pick them up too easily, respond with them, but sometimes it makes a subconscious rapport. He was unbending a little, a shade more gallant, although maybe it was just the bad news he was bringing.

"Madame," he said, "Monsieur de la Peña is dead. I'm very sorry to tell you."

I stared up at him, shocked.

Lost.

"What?"

"He's dead, madame. An unfortunate thing. Last Friday night."

"Oh," I said. "No." I was trying to put the drink on the desk, not to spill it, focusing that way on the glass clearly trembling there in my hand, and we needed some drama or else why was I here? The glass wobbled, overbalanced, and fell. "Oh, no," I said. "No." I dabbed ineffectually at my lap where the water had splashed me, rubbed helplessly at the spill on top of the desk. The maître d' had already found a box full of tissues from somewhere, had taken a handful and pressed them at me to mop myself up with while he attended to the few drops on the desktop, now dripping down the front of the cramped wooden desk. He was practically on top of me, of course, the short skirt of the black dress riding high while I swabbed at it. It was useless, you know, the skirt soaked very thoroughly, and anyway, my heart wasn't there. I covered my face with a hand and I cried.

"Madame," he said.

The tissues were sopping. I wiped anyway at my cheeks, at my eyes. "I'm sorry, monsieur." Wiped again. Tried very hard for control. "How could it be Friday night? I . . . I don't understand. Was there some sort of accident?"

"There, there," he said, patting.

He was pulling the rolling chair out from behind the desk.

Sitting next to me, handy.

We'd been in here already a couple of minutes, and with Reilly outside, fully aware I was in here, I probably didn't have a whole lot of time.

"He wanted me to stay," I said, letting the emotion part flow, and I buried again my face in my hands.

Well, I wasn't *entirely* buried, perhaps—my fingers were spread out, open like claws, and I have fairly good peripheral vision. I saw his left hand move, circle tentatively over my thigh. It touched the skin very lightly there and withdrew.

I shivered, sobbed, looked up at him blindly. Newborn kitten. So vulnerable. "What could have happened?" I cried.

His hand settled firmly onto my knee. Gripped.

"You need to be strong," he said. "Monsieur took his life."

"Took—?" I stared at him, caught. Noncomprehending. And then I understood it, and he had his other quick hand at my lips, leaning in lest I scream. Not at Chaven's, you know. Not in the back room.

"Sshh," he said. "Sshh, it's all right." His left hand had moved up in all the excitement, had my thigh muscle tight, thumb stroking over the skin. Predators everywhere when you're vulnerable. I flashed for a second on Reilly, making out with the waitresses, and I wasn't prepared for the sharp stab of jealousy. Yanked myself back to my role.

"I should have stayed," I said brokenly. "He wanted me to. Did *he* stay for dinner?"

"Yes."

I let the jealousy fuel it, let myself ask it. *"Alone?"*

He heard the note in my voice, the realish emotion, and paused for a second, his thumb almost touching the edge of my underpants. "But of course," he said. Was he preserving my image of Rudolfo as my true love, or telling the truth?

"I thought, maybe—oh, I don't know, I guess I thought maybe somebody else . . ."

"No, no," he said. "Monsieur de la Peña would never. He ate quite alone."

I realized abruptly then where the maître d's hand was, how close we were, almost intimate. Gasped. Moved back a little bit away from him, shaken.

"I'm sorry," I said, overcome, breathless, aware of him thoroughly now as a man and very confused. All my fault. It always *is*, for a woman, although in this case, I think you could truthfully say that it was. "I, just—was he drinking a lot after I went? Did he stay at the bar?"

He left the hand on my thigh as if he hadn't noticed it, was above such things, and patted my shoulder with the other. "No, no, madame," he said soothingly, as though to a child. "He talked for a little while with his friend, and then his table was ready."

"His friend?"

Again the jealous note. The maître d' saw that I was hurting, insecure about my own charms and needing reassurance. *His* reassurance. He chuckled at me comfortably while his shoulder hand drew me, very firmly, a little more towards him.

"A man," he said. "A friend of his from business. Truly there was nothing—although, perhaps"—he paused, struck, I think, by the notion—"perhaps the friend had bad news."

No one had asked him about De la Peña's last meal, then, to set him remembering. Nobody from BHPD had come checking. Well, really, why should they?

"Do you think so?" I said anxiously, as if hearing it was somebody else's fault would make it better. "Was he upset, do you think, by this friend?"

The maître d' was thinking his own thoughts, speculation, his left hand still absently massaging my shoulder. "Yes, perhaps. He was not quite so happy, coming in to the table. Polite, *tu sais*, as always he is, but more small."

More small.

The Lion, Rudolfo.

"I don't know all his business," I said, "only a little bit here and there. Was it his friend with the dark hair?"

"*Mais non*, quite blond. Tall, with the nose, you know, like a boxer." He said it "boxair"—our accents were both getting richer.

"A boxair?" I said, and I was seeing half an image from somewhere. "With the arms very thick?"

"Yes," he said with a disparaging shrug. "Not dressed very well, but a friend of Monsieur's."

Commoners. The hoi polloi. You just can't keep 'em out if the rich take them up.

Rich people's follies.

"Did he come in right away, then, after I left, this boxair?"

"He was here already," the maître d' said.

An agent in place.

I hadn't seen him, didn't think I had, anyway, although there was that tantalizing half-flash of an image. A blond boxer. Tall.

Someone at the bar.

"I never saw him here, Friday," I said rather petulantly, "if it's who I'm thinking. What could *he* want to talk to Rudolfo about?"

The maître d' shrugged. Not his concern, or more likely, he hadn't been able to hear. The bar had been crowded on Friday.

"Business," I said, sulkily, as if it were an ugly word. "Always business."

The maître d's hand started circling again. He had other business he wanted to get down to. Serious business. We'd already been here ten minutes.

"Oh, monsieur," I said, "no," but I was a fragile little delicate creature, fending him off. He knew what I needed.

"You're lovely," he said, pressing me into the chair. "How could a man think of business around you?" and his hands were all over me, palpating, squeezing.

"Oh," I said nervously, stopping him, "oh, what was that?"

He hadn't heard anything.

"At the door, monsieur. Someone trying to open—?"

The thought gave him pause, but not really for long. "It's quite all right," he said thickly. "No one will bother us here."

Well, wasn't that cozy? Not the first time, then, that the maître d'd used the room. And no one would bother him? Was *this* the house cut from the girls I'd seen Friday?

"I can't," I said, cowering, but he was wrestling my arms down. "Rudolfo—"

"He wouldn't want you to mourn."

"His friends would," I said.

That stopped him cold. I don't think he'd considered the notion of prey with connections—or prey that wouldn't count a quick nooky as part of the deal, the cost of doing business, you know.

He was breathing very hard, pushing back off me where he'd crowded me into the chair.

"It's all right," I said, speaking rapidly, meekly, "I know it was my fault. I, just—well, a man can't help himself sometimes, and I . . . I should have known."

"Yes, you should," he said severely. He was resettling his clothing, very Gallicly outraged. Took a few paces around the room, away from me. "You—you have put me in a very awkward position."

"I'm sorry," I said.

"So you should be. Yes. *Very* awkward."

"I didn't mean to," I said.

"I was just trying to comfort you."

"I know," I said. "I appreciate it, really. I *was* feeling kind of . . ." I let it trail wistfully into the realm of unspoken desires, longings. Possibilities. Shook myself back to reality. "But you can see that I can't. It just wouldn't be right, right now."

"No."

A little stiff, still.

Oh, well.

I was readjusting a few items of my own clothing, such as it was. "Is there a way out through the back?" I said. "I really don't want to go through the dining room again. All those people to see I've been crying."

"But of course, madame. When you are . . . quite composed." He wasn't wanting anyone to see I'd been crying, either, I guess. They might misunderstand.

"I think I'm all right now." I picked up the strap of the substitute purse, slung it over my shoulder, and rose, dabbing gently once more with the tissue at the corners of my eyes. "You've been, really, very kind."

He was unbending a little bit more. I was going to be reasonable, then, not throw any scenes, and he possibly even believed me. People will. In his mind, I'd guess, he was restructuring it anyway, himself as the saint swept away by my charms—nothing torrid about this encounter—and I hoped, truly did, that it was nothing he'd want to examine too closely or to discuss in anything but the vaguest of terms with any of his cronies—or with anyone, say, from the local PD.

Reilly, for instance, camped out like a spider.

"This way, madame."

He was unlocking the door, opening it grandly for me to disguise the metallic snick of the lock clicking back, and I was already moving the step or so sideways, out of the funnel, on the off chance that some-one was there.

Nobody was.

It was the same little curtained alcove outside, the same clatter of dishes from the kitchen area, and the same buzzing hum of conversa-tion from the dining room. The world going on. The maître d' was steering me again, hand on the back of my arm so discreetly. He led me through the kitchen archway and into the kitchen itself, waving aside a glance from a white-costumed chef and a guy who was chopping, onions it smelled like, on a huge wooden block. Big old sharp knife he was wielding. I wouldn't like to meet *him* in any kind of dark alley.

We were dodging cook islands and hanging pots, stepping around two waitresses hurrying to pick up their orders, aiming ourselves towards the back of the kitchen and a plain white door there. Double locks. It looked like a door to the outside to me, and that was sure enough what it was.

It opened out into the night, to a loading dock platform, not very deep. A couple of cement steps on the left-hand side led down to street level, to a grimy, shadowed corridor between buildings, with the bright lights and bustle of the main streets at either end of the alleyway. No one else seemed to be out there.

"You can find your way, yes?"

The maître d', I guess, wasn't planning to see me safe to my car. Maybe I should have asked that young guy with the knife.

"Yes," I said. "Thank you." I gave him one more tremulous smile and made my way down the steps. He was already shutting the door above me, cutting off the available light. I could hear him relocking. It's harder to go down steps in high heels than you might like to think, or possibly I haven't practiced enough. The left one caught on a rough patch of concrete and I almost tripped forwards, but I managed to catch myself, recover my balance.

Flat on my face in an alley. That would be good.

No one seemed to be watching.

I was parked on a side street somewhat north and to my left, so I turned right, heading south towards the open mouth of the alley there. I wanted to get some distance from Chaven's before I circled around west, and I've never minded walking a few extra blocks. There was only the thin striking sound of my high heels on the pavement.

Nobody else moving.

No little cat feet.

And then, behind me, very faintly, I heard a rustle. A brushing-by sound.

I had to readjust the strap on my shoe, the left one, which had caught on the step and apparently torn. Heels are just such a pain. I was limping already, very obviously twisted, so I hobbled a couple of steps to my right, leaned lightly against the brick side of the building there, and bent to repair the shoe, my hand reaching down and my head naturally turning. I saw the flicker of movement finally behind me, the blurry shape darting.

A rat by the restaurant Dumpsters.

How choice.

I straightened up and kept walking. Wobbled every third step or so just in case. Heard nothing else. I reached the end of the alley, turned right, and went west the half-block to Rodeo. Crossed left at the inter- section there and melted into the little chain of pedestrian strollers who were straggling south on the sidewalk. I have a tendency to like to walk quickly, but that would make me one of the few people moving, more of a noticeable target if anyone was caring, so I stared into the expensive display windows like everyone around me, wandered for- ward several steps, peered into another one, and so on down the row. It took me maybe five minutes to negotiate the block.

I sensed nothing suspicious, no one particularly watching. I had the coat buttoned firmly by now, of course, and my hair all atangle, so I might not have looked like I'd be worth any trouble. I was a block and a half down from Chaven's by that time, heading south. I went across the intersection there with several pedestrians who'd been clustered, waiting out the light. Everything still felt clear when we got to the opposite corner, so I turned west with two of them, sweethearts, a youngish couple who were holding hands, and we crossed with the light on the far side of the intersection—the cross-traffic and the bod- ies shielding my progress from anyone who might be hanging out at Chaven's corner. I took half a glance back and no one seemed to be there. The young couple peeled off to look in some windows. Jewelers' windows. Ring shopping. I kept going west by myself for a few more blocks before turning north and coming around. Headed east. Found my Subaru where I'd left it, still parked at the meter.

No one was in or nearby, so I opened it quickly, flicking the door locks back down as I slid into the driver's seat and slipped the key neatly into the ignition all in one move. Smooth. Had the 'Ru up and running and gliding out of the parking spot in less than five seconds. That's not good for the engine, but it's good for the soul. Makes you feel more secure. Capable.

The rearview mirrors were clear, reflecting nothing but streetlights and darkness behind me. Vague shapes of parked cars not moving at all as I pulled away.

I was feeling pretty good, you know? I'd gotten in, gotten out again, no muss or fuss. I still had my touch, and I'd done it all without wires or backup.

How's *that*, Sergeant, sir, for a has-been ex-cop?

Not too shabby, I think.

And I'd found out that De la Peña had talked to a boxer after I'd left Friday night—something I'd bet Beverly PD didn't know yet, if they ever would have known it at all.

He didn't have to be a boxer, of course.

A lot of club bouncers get broken noses, the same way that boxers do and for similar reasons. Most of them also have very thick forearms. And some gravitate naturally to bodyguarding in their spare time, that kind of work.

Some even hire out as PIs.

# 15

My beeper was going off. I'd forgotten about it again, actually. I'd left it on vibrate and chucked it under the seat earlier when I was leaving for Chaven's, and now that the 'Ru was moving, heading smoothly back for the freeway and away from Beverly Hills, I couldn't figure out what the heck was making that rattling noise underneath me. I fished around under the seat, in the metal of the springs, and finally found it. I was trying to keep one hand on the wheel and an eye on the mirrors while still watching traffic in front of me with a view to not ramming anyone, so it took a little longer than it might otherwise have done. I didn't want to pull over.

Mike had called twice, apparently, earlier in the evening.

Reilly'd just called.

He'd left me his cellular phone number, and it took me a moment to recognize it on the pager's digital readout because I don't call him a lot on his cellphone. It had to be him, though. The numbers were as near as I could remember, and nobody else had much of a reason to call me right then. Reilly pretty definitely did.

I wondered, a little guiltily, if he was still sitting there in the restaurant's dining room, waiting for me to come out.

I owed him a call.

In case he was worrying.

He might just be pissed off as hell, particularly with me in the black dress again, so he might just be wanting to lay back my ears for me, but it was also quite possible that he hadn't known what to make of me being hustled along by the maître d', looking kind of helpless and caught.

I mean, he knows I can do that, but he's also seen me like that for real once or twice. He was the one who'd caught me, so he'd gotten to see it up close.

I think if I were him, under the circumstances, no matter what either of us was officially or otherwise doing at Chaven's, I'd want to know, at least, that I was okay.

Or maybe I just wanted to hear from him. I don't know which it was.

If I'd had a cellphone myself, it would have made life so simple, but as things were, I didn't want to be pulling into a gas station somewhere to be using a pay phone. Not dressed in my get-up. I was already heading in the direction of the freeway, and the Brentwood motel was a short hop away. I could change there, which would be good. I could scrub off the makeup, and also I could ask the front desk for my messages, in case Andy'd had any luck yet with his Thousand Oaks sheriff. I could call Mike from there, too, and see what was up. Could check a few things in the motel's phone book. It sounded like a plan to me, so I merged with the on-ramp, heading north on the 405 Freeway. I didn't see anyone particularly tailing, and, yes, I was looking. It's a habit with me, hard to break. Hyper-awareness.

You get that way when you're always the rabbit.

Rabbit habits.

People tend to forget they have teeth.

It was dark, of course, and mostly what I could see were the headlights of the following cars. It's easier to figure out if someone's tailing you during the day because then you can see colors and types of vehicles, spot their driving patterns, whereas in the dark it's more of a blur of shapes and glaring lights. But if you spend some time practicing at night, you'll find that you're able to distinguish variations in headlight colors—one set of beams a little more blue, for example, sweeping along behind you, another quite white. You learn to keep track of who's where. There weren't any particular brightnesses that stayed in the distance or that seemed to be pacing me.

I went on past my exit, though, anyway. I could get off at Skirball and turn around, catch the 405 South there, come on back down.

I didn't think anyone could have followed me from Chaven's because I'd been pretty careful, but I sure didn't want to find out the bad way that I was wrong. A boxer with a broken nose who'd already had a chance to see me in the get-up I was wearing and who'd met with Rudolph de la Peña Friday night after I'd handed De la Peña his divorce papers didn't sound like someone I'd want to be meeting alone in the motel's little parking lot.

I didn't know what De la Peña's last instructions might have been, you know, while he was sitting there looking "more small."

I didn't even know if this boxer-person knew that De la Peña was dead. He might not. He might just have gotten his directions from De la Peña, his assignment, last Friday night, and he might not be checking back in for a week. Depends what the assignment was, right? *Somebody'd* followed me back from the beach, so they presumably also had followed me there.

It wasn't the blond guy who'd followed me, the maître d's "boxair" who'd been at Chaven's Friday night talking with De la Peña, because my beach guy was dark, unquestionably swarthy. The beach guy, though, had had noticeable forearms. The arm muscle plain. That's why I'd asked about the dark hair, thinking the maître d's "boxair" might be my beach guy, trying to make any kind of connection.

And the maître d' had come back with "*Mais non*, quite blond."

The arms, though, might be the connection.

Not one but *two* boxers.

Ex-boxers, maybe. Maybe working together.

Bodyguards that De la Peña was using, perhaps, to do him a couple of favors, some jobs on the side, like checking into Mike and Mike's business. Mike's partner. Following both of us around, trading off.

The Torino in the parking lot, for instance, that was outside my office late Friday night.

I'd thought of it then, damned if I hadn't—from me to Mike and then on to Sylvia, but Reilly'd been looking at me like I was just out there, over the line, a drunken ex-cop who'd gone into the nighttime waving her gun. Flourishing. Brandishing. Chock-full of paranoid theories.

Well, of course, I *hadn't* known much then.

It *was* all just theories.

I hadn't known at the time that De la Peña was dead.

I was making the right-hand turn onto Skirball, heading the half-block down to catch the 405 on-ramp going back south, when the wording of that suddenly hit me, replayed itself for me.

*Was* he dead then?

What time were they saying he did it? Before I'd spotted the Torino—or after?

Jacoby had simply said Friday night and I hadn't asked him, it hadn't occurred to me. I'd thought vaguely, a quick flash of a picture, of De la Peña drinking heavily there at the bar, Chaven's bar, and then going home crocked, disillusioned, somewhere around nine-thirtyish, ten.

He hadn't, though.

He'd had his one drink with me and then talked to the boxer. Gone in to dinner. Eaten alone.

He could have had more to drink during dinner, lots more, but the maître d' hadn't mentioned it, hadn't even implied it, had said—what was the phrase that he'd used?—"Polite, *tu sais*, as always he is, but more small."

Didn't sound like a drunk.

Not a habitual drunk, anyway, or even that night.

I turned onto the 405 South, still thinking. Blended into the traffic coming down the big hill.

He could have started sloshing the drinks back when he got home, I suppose, driven into despair the way Jacoby was thinking, but again, it was the feeling of things not being right. Actions not adding up.

I needed to know what the time of death was, what the time frame had been.

Reilly had gotten to the office after eleven, that much I was sure of, so the Torino could be placed there then.

I didn't know when it had gotten there, though. It hadn't been in the parking lot when I'd driven in, just after eight, so the Torino had shown up sometime in that three-hour slot. Kind of a gap there. And the thing is, you know, I'd been sitting at my desk in the darkness with the miniblinds partly open, with the radio playing and the bottle in front of me, watching the headlights sweep by.

I'd have noticed car lights coming into the parking lot. They'd have had to come by me.

I hadn't been so down in deep river that that wouldn't have sparked me. I always have the extra eye open. I may not put together all the things I take in, each one doesn't come to the forefront of conscious-ness, but some part of me always registers the fact that they're there.

Even drunk?

I think so. I don't drink very much, and then only in what I consider safe places, so that's harder for me to tell.

It's a security thing with me, though, and I'm pretty darn sure that my security bump would have gone into overdrive, flashing its warn-ings even if the rest of me couldn't respond right—maybe even more so if I couldn't respond. I'm quite sure I'd have seen the car's headlights coming in.

Which meant they'd been off when the Torino entered the lot.

I took the exit ramp at Sunset, turned left at the ramp, and then right at the light to go over the several miles to the motel. I searched the brainpan again, the wellspring of memories, saw myself driving into the office parking lot last Friday night. There'd been no Ford Torino parked in the corner. I'd had nothing to drink at that point to confuse me, and my security bump would have warned me, would have wondered, at least, who was there that late when I was already edgy and the job hadn't gone right.

So the car hadn't entered the lot in the daytime when headlights would naturally be off, hadn't been left innocently sitting there, parked.

It had entered at night, *after* I'd gotten there, and had come in deliberately darkened, had maneuvered way back to the corner, under the overhang there.

I'd noticed that, too, Friday night.

I hadn't pursued it then, hadn't followed the thought. I'd been busy persuading Reilly I wasn't in danger, that his notions were wrong, his restrictions uncalled for. "The world doesn't turn around *me*," I'd said, which is generally true, but in this instance wasn't.

Seemed like it, anyway.

Now.

And my security bump was activating, was screaming its warnings, was flashing all over the place because it had noticed that, quite a ways to the rear, a set of pinkish-tinged headlights had gotten off the freeway behind me, had turned, several times, the same way I'd turned, and was following me now down the road.

# 16

You can run, but you can't hide.

Wanna bet?

That's another one of those phrases I love. People like to pronounce it as if it were gospel, but the reality is that you can do both. You can't, obviously, if you startle off like a jackrabbit, great leaps and bounds. That just tells the predators that you've noticed so they'll come leaping after you, and yeah, then you'd *better* have a prime set of legs. Or wheels, as the case may be.

Subarus aren't noted for their power.

They will, however, turn on a dime.

Okay, maybe more like a quarter.

The point is, if I made a bootlegger turn and went squealing straight back at this guy, he might get the notion I'd caught on to him, hey? And I didn't know what sort of wheels *he* had. I couldn't tell in the mirror—he was hanging just far enough back to be darn near invisible except for the lightbeams. It might be the Torino. It might very well not be.

No percentage in risking it.

I turned sedately left at the next street, signaling like the very best kind of good person, like someone who cared about laws and nice neighborhoods. I drove carefully down the residential block next to all the cars parked along the curb. Turned left again. I might have been going a little bit slowly, eyeing the homes like somebody looking for— a number? A vehicle? A particular driveway?

No one was turning the last corner behind me, but there was a glow back there on the street now, not moving. Someone sitting, perhaps, thinking. Studying. Those *Thomas Guide* street maps. They come in so handy. I'd already pulled mine up out of the door pocket. I use it all the time when I'm going to a new job, setting up a security system or picking up parts. I know a lot of the L.A. area, but some of those bitty cross-streets start and then stop again three or four times. Very confusing. Annoying. City planners at work.

And I know, I know, some of these streets were laid out before there *were* city planners, but that's where that eminent domain thing comes in. It isn't *my* property. They're welcome to condemn it and drive the roads through. It might upset the people who live there, of course. Might lose their votes. I haven't noticed that bothering city councils much.

I pulled hesitantly over to the curb in front of a house with its outside lights on. It looked kind of welcoming, all lit up, like it might be expecting a visitor or an old friend like me. I left the engine on, idling, while I used the light from the gauges to illuminate the *Thomas Guide* page. I could have turned on the overhead map light—that's one of the Subaru's features—but besides lighting me up for the whole world to see, it would effectively destroy what remained of my night vision. Peering at house lights had already done quite a number on that. Through the halo, I was keeping an eye on my left-side mirror, which was still reflecting that slightly warm glow from around the corner at the end of the block.

This guy had one hell of a long patience cycle. Most people would have been jiggling in, craning to see, checking to find out if I was going on into the house. *His* lights weren't moving.

And then they were off.

I was blinking through black and bright spots, trying to scan down the page to figure out where I was, and the glow in the side mirror vanished.

Which meant what? That he'd just cut the lights?

Turned the car off?

Was out now and coming?

A guy on foot in the dark is harder to see.

More maneuverable.

Better choice of terrain.

On the other hand, I had the speed now unless he was lulling me.

Damn modern cars, though. They have all these safety features. You can't shift out of park without pressing the brake, which activates the taillights, sends out a red flash of color, bright red like a strobe light, highlighting the night. It washed the street scene in crimson behind me. There was a human figure ducking back at the corner—a guy for sure, hard to say about size.

I had maybe two seconds on him. He'd make for his car again so I needed to hurry—but it's that running thing, you know, that startling off, that flip of the fluffy white tail. You have to fight your precipitate impulse, be smarter than that. I eased off the brake very gently, let the 'Ru glide forward, no hurry, not me, just someone who'd pulled over for a minute to check on an address, maybe, or even a map. Lost her way in the dark maze of streets. Not looking over her shoulder, not suspecting any evil. Minding her own little business, whatever it was.

You can follow me easily.

Anytime.

I signaled the next right at the corner, paused there, light blinking, to check for any oncoming traffic both ways. A really solid citizen. There was no traffic coming, so I proceeded with caution into the turn.

There were no lights behind me.

It was dark out, really, so I couldn't go very quickly, wouldn't want to be speeding on one of Brentwood's residential streets. It wouldn't be safe. You never know who might pull out of a driveway without looking. I slowed just that little bit more to be certain. Let's not meet by accident, hey?

Insurance companies love me.

I had the street to myself.

Nobody in front or behind me, apparently.

It's dangerous to drive without lights on, you know? Not a really good notion. I had mine on, of course. Saw the bitty shape of what might be a cat in the headlights, jammed on my brakes. It maybe wasn't a cat. It disappeared very quickly, and the red wash of my taillights showed nothing behind me. I should get brighter bulbs for the taillights, I guess. Have that better visibility.

I pulled over towards the curb again, not quite all the way. I slowed. Stopped. This time, I put it in neutral rather than park, put on the handbrake, let the thing idle. Looked at my *Thomas Guide* map page again. There was still no one appearing behind me. I had the window rolled down for the cooling effect of the night air and I couldn't hear anything but my own motor humming and the distant reverberative whoosh of the traffic on some other street, quite possibly the freeway.

I wasn't very far from the motel, was the problem. A couple of blocks at best. It was idiotic of me to have come so directly, to have been so effing sure I hadn't been followed. The car wasn't appearing in the mirror behind me, but I didn't think for a second I'd lost him. Not with a simple maneuver like this one. Not for a guy who'd followed me apparently, unseen, from Chaven's. He was waiting somewhere where I couldn't see him but where he could see *me*. I didn't have all that high-tech look-through-the-dark infrared kind of scope stuff with me because, well—I just wasn't prepared, okay? Out of the loop. I'd pack it from here on in. Part of the emergency first-aid kit. Me and the Scouts.

I could go south and west a few blocks, the way it looked from the map page, head for San Vicente Boulevard and lead this guy around Santa Monica's streets for a while, or even head farther south, for that matter, through Torrance and Long Beach. Or I could turn right around and run past him again to make sure he was following, dodge up to Sunset and jump back on the freeway, go north into the Valley and try to lose him up there.

Or I could just drive straight to my motel room, park the Subaru directly out front, and let him sit there keeping tabs on me all night long, earn his keep. I don't like the notion of people watching my door, though, you know? It's bothersome to me.

There was nothing in the mirror to spark a decision, no lightbeams reflecting, no vague darkish shapes.

And the thing is, I might just be paranoid as hell.

Maybe nobody was following me because nobody cared. Coincidental driving paths. That happens.

The human figure might have been ducking back because he'd been startled while taking the trash out or something from the house on the corner. My unexpected flare of red light. Him in his pajamas, perhaps, a loose robe and slippers, not wanting to be seen. That happens, too.

The world doesn't turn around *me*.

I wheeled the Subaru abruptly, not quite on the quarter, and went back the same way I'd come. I met nobody else out driving the streets. Nobody was apparently lurking in any of the front yards or side yards, shying away. There were lots of parked cars, but none that I recognized—not a black Ford Torino, not the brown beach sedan.

I really had to get to a phone.

I drove for another couple of blocks, aimlessly switching directions. Crisscrossed around. Passed a few other vehicles, out driving like I was. Backtracked a little, didn't see them again. How many spooks can you fit in a taillight?

The answer: you only need one.

# 17

I called Reilly from the Brentwood motel room. I'd left the Subaru parked around the corner as a good-faith sort of gesture, an offering to the gods, and I'd skulked in through the shadows. I'd taken off the high heels first. I love those dang things, I always feel so illicit strutting around in them, and the stiletto heel's good for raking down a shin or for stomping the spike through somebody's foot, but they're absolutely useless for any kind of running.

I didn't know that I'd have to run, it just seemed like a notion.

Also, I sneak better, Indian-style, in bare feet. And out there in Brentwood, there's no broken glass on the sidewalks to worry about. It's a city ordinance or something.

No one appeared to be watching. I'd taken my night bag out of the Subaru's trunk—that's the bag I keep at the office with the sweatsuit, running shoes, and other clothes—and I could have switched into my Nikes, but why waste the time? I had the motel room key in my hand, the *Thomas Guide* clutched, and I just kept on moving. I snaked around the edges of the parking lot without incident, which happened to take me past all the parked cars. No one seemed to be hiding in any of them.

You don't relax, exactly, but the alarm kind of wanes. It becomes part of the background, ready to swell up again if it needs to, but no longer jangling.

I checked the motel room out thoroughly anyway.

Nobody there but us chickens.

I took the extra two minutes to peel off the black dress, and yes, I hung it up carefully on a hanger. Pulled on an old shirt of Charlie's from the assortment of clothes in the bag.

Then I called Reilly.

The cellphone number rang and rang, and I was thinking that probably he'd already gone home, that I should have just called him there. It was close to an hour since I'd gotten his page. I hadn't meant it to be so long, but I'd wasted a lot of time dodging. He might have gone back to the station, but I didn't know that and I didn't really want to be talking to anyone there. There was no point at all in my calling his pager, because you can only leave a number on those, and I wasn't going to leave the motel number for him to call back to. He has access to those backwards directories—the ones where you look up the phone number and it tells you the address and city.

I didn't need to be dealing with *that* one tonight.

But I didn't want him worrying, really.

I just didn't know where he was.

I was about to give up and call the answering machine at his apartment, leave him a message, when the cellphone stopped ringing.

"Yeah."

"It's me," I said.

There was an ungodly long pause.

"Reilly?"

"Yeah."

Flat.

Uncompromising.

"Where *are* you?" he said.

I shouldn't have called him.

"I'm just out," I said. "I didn't want you to worry."

"I'm not worrying."

Oh.

Okay.

He wasn't saying anything else and I didn't know where we were in this thing. I sort of wished I could see him, get a look at his face. Sort of was glad that I couldn't.

"What were you doing at the restaurant?" I said.

Another lengthy pause.

"Waiting for you."

God.

"Reilly—"

"How long are you going to do this?" he said.

"I don't know. A day or two."

"Wednesday?"

What did it matter?

"Yeah, maybe," I said.

"And I'm just supposed to hold off? That's how this works?"

I didn't know—was it?

"Look," I said. "All I'm doing is trying to understand it, okay? To see what it is."

"It's a suicide."

He bit the word at me. Harsh. Absolute. The term we all live with. I could see myself on the bed in the mirror.

"You talked to Jacoby?"

"Yeah, I did."

"But it doesn't add up right," I said, and the figure in the mirror was wavering and tired, looking smaller somehow in Charlie's big shirt. "De la Peña didn't care that much about his wife leaving—"

"Then he did it for ego. What the hell does it matter?" Reilly's voice sounded tired, too.

"Because someone's been following me," I said.

We had another thin moment of silence. I hadn't meant to say that exactly—in fact, I meant not to, so I still to this day don't know why I did.

His voice was very controlled, almost a drawl. "*Following* you?"

Oh, God. The nuances.

The echoes.

Somebody lurking.

"I think it's a PI," I said steadily. "I don't know for sure. De la Peña had somebody following around after Sylvia and Mike, I think, that's how he knew who I was, and maybe the guy never got the word to lay off. It's just odd, Reilly. With me checking things."

"Yeah," he said.

*Very* odd.

Strange, you know, really.

Because he wasn't asking me anything else.

"I have a friend of mine running the license plate," I said. "I got all the numbers."

"Did you?"

It was definitely a drawl this time, and I don't have anything like the long patience cycle Reilly has.

"That was you, then?" I said. "Following me tonight?"

"Tonight?"

You can humbug your way past any situation if you just act like you maybe didn't quite get the question.

"Yeah, *tonight*," I said emphatically. "After Chaven's."

He was considering ways to answer me. Playing those damn STU games of his, getting ready to jive me. It was good, after all, that he wasn't there in the room.

"You know," I said, "I *really* don't like being followed around."

"Well, you know," he said softly, imitative as hell, "I *really* don't like my lady friends going out on their own."

"Reilly—"

"As long as we're being so clear on this," he said.

Dammit.

Goddammit.

You could look at this following-me issue a number of ways, and the problem was that I could see it the cop way. It's just how things are.

When relationships start going to hell, you fall back on your training because what else is there? It's ingrained in you to be skeptical—to doubt, be suspicious. Nobody's reasons quite what they say. It's why cops have a hard time being married. Everybody wants to believe in their nearest and dearest, but when your nearest and dearest starts acting out on you . . . well.

Then there's a stronger need for control.

This wasn't the same as stalking me, was it?

Or was it?

*"Over nothing, Mary Margaret, don't tell your father."*

"Where are you?" I said.

"Outside your door."

Here? He couldn't be.

"You didn't follow me *here*," I said.

"No."

"What then?"

"Not a lot of motels in Brentwood, Meg."

There weren't.

There was only one, in fact.

This one.

"I could've been going to Santa Monica."

"Yeah, you could've," he said.

There are a lot of motels in Santa Monica. But I'd gotten on the freeway south of Beverly Hills, gone north, U-ed, and gotten off again at Sunset. That's a long way around to be going to Santa Monica, when I could have just cut west on the surface streets to begin with, if that's where I was heading.

"You pull the notion of a motel out of a hat?"

"No," he said. "Not until you did your taillight trick on the street back there."

Taillight trick.

The red wash of light.

"That was you on the lawn, then?"

"Yeah."

"You didn't come after me."

"I figured when you started being easy to follow, that there was a reason."

So he'd hunkered back and considered the matter, I guess. Decided I was leading him deliberately away. Cast his mind around for what was in the vicinity and found a motel.

"I'm not registered here."

"'Susan Abbott' is," he said. "With a Subaru."

There was that drawl back in his voice, and I really need to be more creative when I'm making up names. At least not use his lieutenant's last name, right? I think he was taking it as kind of an insult.

A little bit of a gauntlet thrown down.

I don't know why I'd picked it, exactly, but yeah, I might have had more than one reason. That subconscious, bubbling, you know?

"It was just a thing," I said.

"Yeah."

I was facing the mirror, holding the phone. Me in the shirt on a bed in a motel room. "Are you going to come in then?"

Another one of his pauses.

"No."

Okay.

Fine.

"You going on home?"

He didn't bother to answer.

"Reilly—"

"You're doing what *you* have to do," he said, "right? That's what I'm hearing?"

"Yeah."

"So I'm doing what *I* have to do."

Christ, he was watching my door.

He was pissed off as hell at me, really, he was, and with cause, you know—I couldn't deny it. I'd been leading him around half the night—

well, I hadn't known it was him, but he didn't know that—I was doing what most would be making him crazy, but he wasn't stomping in and he wasn't throwing orders, he wasn't trying to drag me out by the hair. He was respecting it, dammit.

Respecting *me*.

"I don't want you to sit out all night, Reilly."

"We'll see."

It was an odd half a moment, tentative, wistful. Me in the motel room and him on the phone, but outside, just a few feet away.

"Don't come in, though," I said, "without calling me first. I'm on kind of alert here, okay?"

He was absolutely silent.

"Reilly?"

"Right," he said shortly.

# 78

I called the front-desk guy for my messages. I didn't let myself think about what Reilly might have told him, if he'd sold him a story or if he'd just badged him to look at the register. I simply identified myself as Ms. Abbott in Room 41 and asked if anyone had called. The desk guy didn't sound particularly interested, so maybe cops came by all the time asking questions, or else Reilly had kept it discreet. Another damn point for the sergeant because he could have done me. ·

Andy had called about a half hour before. He'd left his first name and no phone number. He'd figured I'd know what to do after that, I guess, and that way the world wouldn't have all his info. Cops and ex-cops are careful like that.

I called him at home, punching the number in and using one of my credit cards to charge it so the world wouldn't have all of *my* info, either—or at least so that the front-desk guy wouldn't have a computer printout of my outgoing calls in case anyone happened to come by him, asking. Andy picked it right up. It sounded like a TV or something, kind of loud, there behind him.

"Sue's out working?" I said.

"Yeah—goddamn Graves."

"Well, she's still a new sergeant," I said. They almost always get Graveyard shift for the first year or so, shunted back to working Patrol. Breaks 'em in, keeps 'em humble.

"Plays hell with my sleeping," Andy said. "You got a pencil?"

I had a pen.

Had some paper.

He gave me a name and an address.

"The vehicle comes back to this guy," he said. "Problem is that it's not a real address."

"Yeah? You looked it up?"

"Had some time," he said. "Thought I would."

The address was a street in Van Nuys. I had the *Thomas Guide* open on the bed, was already checking the index myself.

"No such hundred block," Andy was saying. "Could be a typo. Happens. Vehicle's a '94 Oldsmobile, though, so you'd think he'd have had problems registering it the last couple of years. Renewal going back to DMV nondeliverable."

Yeah, you'd think so.

Unless he was friends with the mailman or something. Had worked it all out.

Fairly premeditated.

Or unless he'd lived there a while and the block number was close, so the mailman would know him and deliver it anyway.

Like 1199 instead of 1099.

"Gosh, darn, Mr. Smith, DMV hasn't fixed this yet?"

Or whatever.

"Thanks," I said.

"Not a problem." There was a second, and then he laughed rather grimly. "Sue wanted to know who Susan Abbott was. At the Brentwood Motel."

Oh.

Oh, my.

She'd heard the message I'd left him before. She must have called the number and gotten the front desk, though, to have found out it was the Brentwood Motel. I hadn't said.

"You can tell her."

"No, I don't think so," Andy said. "I'm kind of liking her calling home every hour to see if I'm here."

"Andy—"

"You give me a call," he said, "when you've worked out your deal there. We'll go shooting or something."

It isn't my business what everyone does.

I know that already.

And God, I'm not someone to preach—I was doing so well with my own stuff, you know?

"Andy," I said, "you're one idiot man. You tell her it was me, that you were doing a favor, and then we'll all go out shooting, okay?"

He laughed again, derisively.

"You bringing your sergeant?"

Now *there* was a question.

"Yeah, sure," I said lightly. "Why not?"

I called Michael next. He'd paged me twice, which would make it seem urgent, but he wasn't home. Urgent things tend to take on a life of their own, so he might have been out handling whatever it was. I didn't know. I mean, it was a while ago that he'd paged last, and it was really quite likely he'd just gotten tired of waiting. I would have paged him then so he'd at least know I was trying, but, of course, he doesn't have a pager. We're a fine high-tech pair: Mike with his phobia about pagers and answering machines, and me knotted up by the cost of a cellphone. It isn't the buying of the thing that stops me each time, or even the monthly fee. It's those goldang roamer charges and long-distance add-ons that don't show up on your bill for a couple of months. It's also the notion of someone snagging your number as you're driving around. I hate having to call up and change things all the time.

It would have been handy to have a phone earlier, though. I might have to rethink it. Maybe keep one turned off in the car. They can't snag the number if it isn't turned on. Reilly keeps saying I should do that, have one for emergencies, and I just haven't wanted to deal with it. I haven't needed to, before now, but maybe I should.

Drag me kicking and screaming into tomorrow.

Drag Michael, too.

I didn't want to keep dialing Mike's number until he got home. Didn't want to be sitting here, either, my lone self, waiting around.

Kind of had a block on the door.

*"You bringing your sergeant?"*

I could, you know.

Maybe.

I picked up the room phone again and dialed Reilly's pager because I didn't know if he had his cellphone turned on. Left him the room number, 41.

I figured he could figure it out.

Then I slipped out of Charlie's shirt and into my sweatsuit. I was tying the last knot on the Nikes when the room phone rang.

"Yeah, what?"

He always affects me. It's his tone, or the unexpected richness of his voice curling into my ear. It fogs me or something so it's harder to think.

"You want to go for a ride?" I said.

"Where?"

"Van Nuys," I said. "I just want to drive by a couple of places, see if there's anything."

"Tonight?"

"Yeah, the guy might be home," I said. "He might not be, but it's something to do. I thought maybe you'd like to go with me."

"Why?"

"Well, it's easier than you following me and making me paranoid."

We had kind of a silence.

"I meant, why'd you want to go there?" he said very dryly.

Oh.

As in "What were you planning to do?" A fair enough question, all things considered.

"I just want to locate the address," I said, "I'm not going to go trooping around his house or anything. The DMV comes back to the wrong block number, so I wanted to cast back and forth, check out a couple of the likelier typos, see if I can spot the car anywhere." It might be locked away very tidily for the night, invisible in its two-car garage, but sometimes you get lucky. And it beat sitting here. Got me out. Got me moving.

Being with Reilly.

Although . . .

"Meg," he said, sounding that little bit bent out of shape, "who is this 'guy' you're talking about? Why are we going to look at his address?"

Ah.

Well, I *had* told him, but he'd been sort of focused, I guess, on his own role.

"I wasn't just blowing smoke at you earlier," I said, "trying to trap you. There was a guy this afternoon who was following me back from the beach."

"Beach?"

"I went to look at the water," I said. "After lunch."

He was processing that, adding it up. Filing it away under "Places Meg Goes When We Fight."

"What beach?"

"Ventura."

There are a lot of beaches in Ventura.

"Anyway," I said before he could ask more specifically, "I got the license plate number like I told you and had somebody run it. The address comes back wrong, but I want to check out the possibilities. Do you want to go?"

He wasn't going to let me go by myself, we both really knew that, but he also knew that he couldn't quite stop me and I'd already put the kibosh on him following me around. He didn't like the notion on the one hand that I was pulling his strings, but on the other hand, I was letting him in. It was kind of a moment for him, working it. He can get very stubborn.

"All right," he said finally.

Okay, then.

Well.

The next major question.

"Did you want to drive?"

There were all the echoes of the past weekend between us, reverberating down the phone line.

"Oh, yeah," he said flatly. "I'll drive."

# 19

It was dark in the cab of the El Camino, and a whole lot too close. Reilly had pulled into the parking lot in front of my motel room and sat there idling while he waited for me to come out, like the kind of date that your parents wouldn't have approved of. He didn't even come around to open the truck's door for me, just reached over and unlocked it so that I could get in.

"Where're we going?" he said.

I had the address and the *Thomas Guide* with me, and I was busying myself looking at pages. His overhead light doesn't work—it might be the bulb or the fuse, but it's mostly the intent—so it was good that I had my keyring flashlight to see by. Those things are so handy.

"Up the 405 to Victory," I said. "And then over east about eight or nine blocks."

"All right." He headed the El Camino smoothly out of the parking lot, aimed it down Sunset towards the freeway. I wasn't asking him where he'd been parking to watch me and he wasn't mentioning the black dress. Yet. We were having sort of edgy best behavior. His eyes had flicked over me, climbing in, and he'd noted the sweatsuit with a half-nod, a closed, meditative look, but he hadn't said anything. I didn't doubt that it would come up at some point. He has a harboring nature.

*I* don't, of course.

It's a long sweep up the 405 through the Sepulveda Pass. Dark. Not much to look at. He had the radio firmly switched off, and I guess I could have reached over and turned it on, but then we'd have to be polite about "Do you mind?" and "Which station would you like?" and you can't always be sure with Reilly how the manners will hold. He has a very direct way of responding sometimes. I figured he'd turned the radio off on purpose not to have the distraction. Not to let *me* have the distraction.

The silence was slightly oppressive, you know?

Heavy.

"So how are you?" I said.

"Great." He had that little set to his mouth.

I looked out the window. We surged up the big hill for a while, climbing, and then sailed down the other side. There were other cars running beside us. Trucks. We made it past the divide where the 170 Freeway branches off and we were coming up on the Victory exit before he spoke.

"You have Mike run the license plate?"

He said it very coolly, like he knew that I had and it didn't really bother him, he was just confirming, but there's something about the way he says Mike's name, getting it out without moving his jaw much. I don't think he means to.

"No," I said. "I haven't told him yet."

He considered that for the length of the exit ramp, the pause at the signal light. Turned right onto Victory.

"Why not?"

I didn't know how to say it. He was sitting beside me the same way we'd been, in this same goddamn vehicle, last Friday night. Me even in the same sweatsuit. Him fairly ticked off and not talking much, cool but aggressively thrusting. We were both very consciously this time not touching.

Guarded.

Withholding.

It was a hell of a thing, no good way to be, so I told him what maybe he needed to hear. "You were in a meeting," I said. "And then it just didn't seem right to tell Mike."

He looked at me sharply.

"You called the station?"

"Yeah."

"Who'd you talk to?"

"I don't know," I said. "One of the guys in your office."

"What time?"

I didn't know. "Three-thirty, four. I don't remember. Why?"

He was coming alive at me, looking better but ticked. Fulminating. "Did you leave your name?"

I had—I—oh. "Paula Williams," I said.

"God*damm*it," he said. Exasperated as hell but still feeling better. "Why can't you just leave your name like a real person?"

I don't know. Too many cops taking notes? Nobody's business me calling?

"Why?" I said. "You know a Paula Williams?"

He just looked at me sideways. "You start practicing," he said crisply. "'This is Meg Gillis, tell Joe I called.'"

"Well, it wouldn't have mattered," I said. It did kind of matter, but I didn't know why.

Other than him knowing that I'd tried, that is.

Which was maybe most of the point.

I shrugged at him, looked away. We were into the retail part of Victory Boulevard between Van Nuys and North Hollywood, more storefronts and streetlights. Stoplights. There was a lot more traffic, with the street names harder to see.

I touched his arm and nodded across him. "I think that was where we wanted to turn." It would have gotten us up to the first of the start-

and-stop blocks of Milford, the Oldsmobile's possible street. I didn't think it was likely to be the right one because the block number was wildly off, but it's best to do things methodically. Start at the beginning and eliminate up, or down, as the case may be.

"We'll come back," Reilly said.

He was driving. That made it his choice. Me, I would have U-ed and gone back right away, but before I could open my mouth to say so, he had his left hand coming off the steering wheel, reaching over and covering my hand where it was still on his arm, sort of capturing it there, his fingers rubbing the skin.

A way to say "Sorry" without having to say it, maybe.

"Sorry we're fighting."

"Sorry for doubting you."

Or it might just have been to soothe me, you know, pacify me, get me to go along without fussing. You can interpret silence however you want to. My fingers were already stroking back, though, in rhythm, responsive. The body takes over, sends its own messages: "Yeah, okay—so maybe I'm sorry, too."

"Tell me about this guy following you," Reilly said.

I could do that. I needed to, probably.

We turned at the next left, Colina, went up that street and then right onto Milford, and drove down the two blocks of that bit of the road, scanning in and out while I told him about the beach guy and dodging through Ventura. We looked more particularly at the house matching one of the numbers on the list that I'd written of possible typos, but it seemed pretty much like all of the houses around it. Single-story. Anonymous. There were several cars parked at the curb and in the driveway, but there was no brown Olds sitting out.

Check that one off.

We went back out to Victory and east to the cross-street. Up again and over. This bit of Milford was three blocks long, and except for some people standing around on the sidewalk who took exception to us driving through and stared at us hard, it was a lot like the other bit. Small stucco houses. A mostly Latino population from what I could see. A couple of vans. No brown Olds.

Check, with a question.

East a few more blocks on Victory. North on the cross-street. We looked at that bit of Milford, came back down. We did this routine another four or five times. The general tone of the area was the same, block to block—some houses were more kept up than others, obviously tended, some had the scraggly grass and the free-blowing weeds. Neighbors, you know. What can you do? I saw no sign of an Olds, although there were brown cars aplenty, four-doored and ancient. Cars tend to have a longer use-life in California, not so much because the weather is nicer or because Californians just naturally take better care, but purely and simply because we don't put salt on the roads. Salt mixed with snow tends to rust through the metal, although they *are* making cars out of plastic these days.

East again. North. It would have been easier if the dang road went through. I'd gotten up to mentioning Andy in a roundabout way, an old friend from the department, because I knew Reilly would be wanting to know who I'd gone to, whether he was willing to come out and ask me directly or not.

We were cruising the 11100 block of Milford when I reached out lightly and touched him.

"When we come around again," I said, "go by here very slowly."

He dropped our already sluggish speed down. We came to the cul-de-sac end of that part of the street, circled it, came back around. He hesitated momentarily there in the radius as if we were lost or confused, then pulled the El Camino over towards the curb, shifted to neutral, and very obviously bent to consult the *Thomas Guide* on my lap.

"What's up?" he said quietly.

There were no brown cars parked out on this block of Milford, Oldsmobile or otherwise. There was, however, a black 1994 T-Bird, a two-door coupe, large, sitting in the driveway of the house across the street from us. The house number matched one of my possibles—was 13 734 instead of 13 134.

"You speak any Spanish, Reilly?"

Because the T-Bird had a sticker glued to its back bumper and the bumper sticker, as best I could tell through the dark, said: ASOCIACIÓN DEL REPÚBLICA ARGENTINA POR LA LIBERTAD.

Which, to me, looked a whole lot like "Free Argentina."

# 20

"What's Free Argentina?" Reilly said.

He was still in Lost Tourist mode, using the *Thomas Guide* as a cover, holding it open on the steering wheel and carefully writing the T-Bird's license plate number down in one of the three-by-five notebooks he always has on him, as if he were jotting directions. I was facing the T-Bird across him, so I'd been reading the number off to him, Reilly never even looking that way.

"Hell if *I* know. Mike just said that's where Sylvia and her divorce lawyer met, at some sort of party. A charity thing or whatever. It sounded like one of those Hollywood causes."

Reilly'd worked his share of those. Protection. Can't have the pretty people taken off by real radicals. We'd had quite a few where I'd worked, too—they tend to happen wherever the money converges and people have time for philanthropical notions.

"What name did the Olds come back to?"

"Ernesto Ayala."

The name could be Argentine.

It could be Mexican, too, or Colombian, for that matter—from any country, really, of Spanish descent, and certainly L.A. has a diverse population.

It could even be Cuban.

It's just that given the glaring similarity of the street address, and the T-Bird there with a bumper sticker about Free Argentina, the name seemed most likely to be Argentine.

Ernesto Ayala.

I could go in and ask.

Reilly was sitting between me and the house like a barrier, though—an off-duty sergeant. I think I'd told him that I wouldn't go skulking around.

"So," I said, "this is good that we found it."

"Yeah."

He was releasing the brake, shifting back into first, gliding us away from the curb, down the street.

"We'll come back here tomorrow," he said, "if we need to."

We?

"You're not working?"

"I'm off Tuesdays," he said. He looked quizzically sideways at me, and it's not for a second that he thought I'd forgotten, it's that he likes to maneuver me into a corner. "What did you *think* I was going to be doing?"

Laundry or sheepdogging me. Flip a coin.

He'd asked it ever so innocently, though—mildly surprised, all natural good manners, just a really nice man who was trying to help. Devoting his weekend to me: "I simply wanted to drive you around, sweetie-honey. Help you work this thing out." No hint whatsoever that this way he'd be there in position to keep me constrained, contained, under wraps. Keep me from climbing out to visit people like Ernesto Ayala, for instance.

Well, okay, there was sort of a hint—he had that devil glint in his eyes, deliberately there so I'd see it and spark. He isn't really, you know, a nice man.

"You're such a lowlife," I said.

"Yeah?" He laughed at me openly then, shifting gears, in a surging good humor. Flew us along Victory, still heading east. "I want to go by my place, get some things. Since we're this far out, I might as well be comfortable if I have to spend the rest of the night in the truck."

I guess. My house in Burbank was closer. He had some clothes there, too, in my closet, but neither of us wanted to say it, I think. *I* didn't, anyway. Memories still raw of last Friday night. His apartment was better.

We caught the on-ramp for the 5 Freeway where Victory runs into Burbank Boulevard, the five-corner light there, just a short skip from my house. Reilly wasn't looking at me, he was focused on traffic, on shifting, on getting us around the other vehicles and through the intersection before the signal turned red because it's a really long light when you're having to wait—and so the issue of houses and proximity didn't even have a chance to come up.

He wanted me in Glendale, at *his* place.

Was pretty well making it happen.

Okay.

We got off the 5 at Colorado Boulevard and then turned north onto Brand past the Glendale Galleria. Reilly doesn't live very far from Glendale PD. There was a time when I wouldn't even drive into Glendale, but I've had six months to get used to the notion. I still don't go very often. He knows it. I know it. That's why he has to come and visit *me*, generally speaking. I've only been to his apartment a handful of times.

I have a key now, of course.

Reilly was looking at me sideways, not being obvious about it or anything, just the now-and-then glance. Watchful.

I was a cop once in Glendale, okay? Charlie and I used to work there, used to drive these same streets. Even the damn stores haven't changed in four years. They've added some buildings. Taller ones. Skyscrapers, or what passes for skyscrapers in a bedroom community.

A unit pulled up behind us at the red light on Wilson, blinking to turn right there—probably transporting to the jail, because it looked like someone was in the back behind the grill, but I couldn't see who the driver was from my sideview mirror. I probably didn't really want to know.

"We'll be there in a minute," Reilly said.

I hate being an open wound. I'm not so obvious that *other* people ever see it or comment, so I don't know exactly why Reilly's got the channel. He had a hand on my kneecap, was resting it there. The signal light changed. He needed the hand back to shift, and he wasn't moving it, hadn't maybe noticed the light.

"Reilly—"

"Yeah."

He'd noticed. Had his eyes narrowed thoughtfully, and then he'd taken his hand away and was nudging the stick into first, prompting the El Camino forward again, moving us out of the intersection.

Another couple of blocks.

We went east on California, north on Louise. He pushed the automatic opener and drove through the security gate and down the little ramp to the underground parking under his building. It was all lit up down there, of course, that late at night, but even so, you scan the other cars for occupants. Reilly was out of his seat fairly quickly and had come around the back of the El Camino before I'd gotten my door all the way open, was standing there in the vee of it to help me get out.

"I'm not broken," I said.

He just nodded without listening, was looking around. Handed me off, sort of ushering, right hand to left, while he shut the ElCo's door behind me. Locked it. Walked me out between the cars. He was tense now, a little bit tight and masking it, so something was up.

"You making dating points, Reilly?"

"Yeah, I'm impressing you," he said. "Trying to lure you up to my apartment." There wasn't any levity lurking this time. He was solemn as sin and just as forbidding, but I hadn't seen anything around there to worry about.

"What—?"

"I need to get a few things," he said very quietly. "I'm not leaving you down here."

By myself in an underground parking garage.

Was that what he was chafing about? Whether I'd go upstairs willingly or he'd have to drag me?

"Nobody asked you to leave me," I said. "It's creepy down here at night—you think I *wanted* to stay?"

"Hard to know," he said, and maybe it was. He reached past me to the concrete wall and pressed the elevator's call button. Stood back from it, watching me.

He lives on the second floor, which is really the top floor since it's only a two-story building, not counting the parking garage. I don't know why we weren't taking the stairs. The elevator dinged to announce itself, though, right away, and the door slid open beside me. He wasn't hurrying any to move, of course, just sort of standing there the way he does, and I never have five million years to wait on him.

"Are you going to get in?"

He contemplated me. "Yeah," he said slowly, "yeah, I think I am," and he's a rat, a darkly sexual rat, because he meant something else, and he'd set me up to say it, and he was laughing at me openly now, me turning red.

"I swear to God, Reilly—"

"No, no, Meg, don't swear," he said. "He might be listening," and then he swept me into the elevator car. Kissed me very thoroughly all the way up as if there'd never been anything but loving between us. Disarranged a few things besides my senses and my mind. I don't know why he has that effect on me because I can be so blisteringly angry at him one minute that I could take all his skin off, and the next minute *I'm* the one melting. They say it's hormonal—the exact same chemical changes produced by the fight-or-flight reflex, the same adrenaline flush that sets your nerves jangling, only in this case, it isn't fear, it's what they call love, or, at least, what they call physical attraction. It's disconcerting as hell, is what it is—except, of course, when it leads somewhere good.

He had his arm loosely around me all the way down the hall, warm somehow and comfortable like a jacket that fits. I'm not quite sure how we'd gotten here from two people who wouldn't even touch in the car, but I wasn't going to make too much of it just then. I don't like to fuss and it was massively better than being at odds.

He kept the one arm around me while he unlocked the door with his other hand, the security bolt—harder to do than you'd think. Opened the door and scooted us through. Locked it again.

"You want something to drink?"

I was okay. I didn't know anyway, if he meant "alcoholic," if he was referring to anything, because he had half a look in his eye. God. One minute fine, the next minute not, and if this was dizzying hormonal love, you could *have* it. I like settled and staid, myself. Secure.

"No, thanks."

"You sure?"

I was sure.

"Didn't you have to get your things, Reilly?"

He was looking sort of guiltily caught. "Well," he said, slowly, a man feeling his way, "I probably should tell you that I had a motive for luring you up here."

I braced myself for whatever it was. "Yeah?"

"I have a computer."

A computer? I knew that.

"I have Internet access, Meg."

I was half-comprehending. And then he was smiling very brilliantly at me, oh-so-pleased with himself for surprising me. "It occurred to me," he said, drawling, "that you might like to see what we can find out about Free Argentina tonight."

Oh my God. What a thing.

He was actually helping.

I found myself grinning delightedly back at him.

"You mean this *wasn't* to ravish me?"

"Well, I like you grateful," he said.

# 27

I was grateful. I was *very* grateful, as a matter of fact, because there was an amazing wealth of data up on the Web about all kinds of facets of Argentine life. I'd had no idea. It would never have occurred to me to look for it this way. I'm more of a dinosaur than I'd thought.

Reilly'd settled me in at his desk in the corner of the living room and he showed me how to call up and use the search engines, the programs that scan the Internet after you type in your subject, looking for references to whatever you wanted to know. I don't have a clue how it works other than electrons and magic, but the results are just awesome.

"I was going to get Josh one of these," I said, "but Caroline bought him one for Christmas."

"You should get one anyway," Reilly said.

Yeah, maybe. I thought you just played computer games on 'em, to tell you the truth. Bigger toys for the boys. Blow up more things. Reilly was sitting back on the couch, kind of sipping a soda and watching me. He had papers of his own laid out on the armrest—he always has paperwork—and he'd gone off into the kitchen earlier with his cellphone to make a few calls.

One was to the Beverly station, I'd gathered, to one of his guys there working the night shift. That was taking Reilly into the Danger Zone, because these days with the privacy restrictions, cops are limited as to the checking they can do into people. You've got to document everything and you have to have a good reason. It can't be personal, right?

It used to be that you could just punch in the names, search the files, whatever you wanted, but there were abuses with that, I'm not saying there weren't. A cop having a property dispute with his neighbor, for instance, so suddenly the neighbor's being run, and his or her personal information being divulged. I had a cop from LAPD once who wanted me to check on his sister, he said, see if we still had a local record on her or if it had been cleared off our files. Her last name was different than his on his name tag. It didn't strike me quite right. If I'd known the guy, maybe I would have done it, but as it stands, I told him to go get it okayed by the Watch Commander. If the *girl* had come asking, with ID and everything, that would have been different, too, but I didn't figure it was my business to give this guy information about her. He was a jerk, aggressive about it when I first told him no, and I don't mind disobliging jerks with the letter of the law. He never went in to the Watch Commander, either, at least on my shift. You have to follow your instincts.

So the thing here was, and it worried me more than a little, that Reilly having his guy at the station checking any of this was pushing it some. Cops have been fired for that. Sergeants, lieutenants, and even a captain or two, going down for abuse of authority. On the other hand—barely—I *was* connected to the De la Peña case, such as it was, and this Ernesto Ayala or somebody using his car today had been following me. I guess you could make the point, if you had to, that it was a legitimate inquiry rather than anything personal, such as, say, Sergeant Reilly wanting to know who'd been following his girlfriend around so that he could go have a little chat with him. It was still borderline, kind of dicey, so we'd better hope that we never actually had to explain it. It was more than I'd wanted Reilly to be doing, a lot more, which I think is why he'd settled me in with the computer and then taken himself off to the kitchen. He hadn't said anything about it when he came out with his soda, but I have pretty good ears.

I couldn't figure out how to bring it up, though, how to say something like "Don't get too deep here, Reilly." He knew that already—he's been a cop a long time. It's just, you know, that cops are human. They have their emotional moments, too, forget about consequences.

I was staring at him, I guess. He raised an inquisitive eyebrow.

"Find anything?"

Not the right moment to verbalize fear.

"Yeah, I did," I said, "lots. Argentina just started exporting beef to the U.S. again, did you know that? Seventy years of restrictions, and now they're sending us steaks. Only to specialty restaurants, though. It's a trade agreement or something. There's a press release about it on their embassy page."

He was laughing at me.

"That's Free Argentina?"

"Oh," I said, "no, I didn't find that yet. There's an 'indigenous native population,' though, that looks very promising—the Mapuche. Sort of like our American Indians. They've been forced off their lands any number of times in the past four hundred years, and right now they're fighting back with some legal actions there and in Chile." I was scrolling down through the Web pages to find it. "Here it is, see? The Mapuche's official government-in-exile is over in France because they elected some French guy king in the eighteen hundreds and then he had to flee Argentina. His descendants have a Web page, pictures of the current king standing in front of an old French mill, but I couldn't find anything specific there about Free Argentina, so I've just been noodling around, getting an overview and trying out different things. It's amazing, all these links. You can see a live picture from any of the provinces just by clicking on 'em, check out the weather, get maps or their radio and TV stations, and one of the business Web sites even has a bunch of stuff about their cultural heritage and what makes up the

Argentine character. They're wanting people to invest, did you know that? Americans and American businesses."

"I didn't know that," he said tranquilly. Humoring me, but I didn't mind. It was kind of comfortable.

"Yeah, since 1989," I said. "They've been really working on that since Carlos Menem took office. Well, actually, it probably started in 1982, when they lost the war for the Malvinas Islands to the British. You remember the Falkland Islands thing? Prince Andrew in a helicopter?"

"Not really," he said.

I laughed over at *him*. "You've got to pay more attention to world events, Reilly. The cute guys."

"I guess so."

"Absolutely," I said. "No other reason. Anyway, after losing the islands and the war, the Argentines gave their military juntas the boot. The military guys had been eating up the economy with their internal power struggles since the 1940s—that was Juan Perón's little stint in power, remember Evita?—so the Argentines voted to restore democracy and free enterprise and they elected Carlos Menem as Presidente in 1989. I didn't know it was this bad, but they had something like five coups and three countercoups just between 1976 and 1983. Bloody. All kinds of human rights violations, apparently. There's a Web site up here dedicated to the Desaparecidos—the Disappeared Ones. There were over three thousand people, they're saying, men, women, and children, who were arrested and then vanished during those seven years under the guise of wiping out left-wing terrorism. There's supposed to be widespread evidence of detention centers. Torture and murder. The military records of it were all destroyed during the war, though, according to Menem. He's been trying for the last few years to put out a blanket amnesty for that time and move the country on, but the families aren't letting it rest."

"I'd think not."

Me, either. Not if it were a member of *my* family.

"It's a lot," I said, looking at the screen. "Any part of it could be Free

Argentina. *And* Argentina's got a bigger presence in L.A. than I would have thought. I was checking out their embassy pages, and besides all the press releases about trade agreements, that steak thing I told you, they list places to contact in the U.S. There's a consulate general's office right over on Wilshire Boulevard, about a mile from Beverly Hills, and then there's a directory of what they call Resident Centers. The L.A. area has *ten* of them, Reilly—a couple downtown, one in Sherman Oaks, one in Canoga Park, one in Burbank, and one in Beverly. Next closest is Florida with five, and a handful of other cities who only have one apiece."

"You definitely need to get a computer," he said.

Maybe. I'd probably spend too much time on it, though. Turn into a computer junkie or something, always on-line.

Of course, then he wouldn't have to worry about me going to bars. I wondered if he'd thought of that, and looking at him sitting back over there, so cozy on the sofa, I figured he had.

"Yeah, I could check out the chat rooms," I said agreeably. "I've heard about those."

He gave me one of his very dry looks. "I'll put on the parental lock for you."

What a guy.

It's good that we know each other.

We were smiling back and forth, just really easy, and you forget about the things that will tear you apart.

"You ready to go to bed, Meg?"

I was, I guess.

"It's pretty late."

It was, actually, almost two in the morning. I hadn't realized.

He stretched a little bit, there on the sofa. Looked fairly sleepy. "Kind of a long drive to Brentwood," he said. "But I will if you want to."

I'd paid for the room already. It was housing my stuff.

"You just don't want to sit out in your truck."

"I'm not going to sit out," he said lazily, "you already told me that I

153

could come in. On the other hand, I've got a very comfortable bed down the hall. Probably bigger than the one you've got there."

Well, yeah, it was.

Firmer, too.

"Bigger isn't always better, Reilly."

He snorted at me scornfully.

"Girl, someone's been telling you lies."

Maybe so.

He looked sleepily complacent, placid as a fed cat lolling back on the couch. No kind of pressure, and I *was* pretty tired.

"You know how to turn this thing off?" I said.

He did.

We snuggled our way down the hall. Shucked off our clothes, climbed in under the covers, and his bed *was* big and comfortable, his pillows just right, and we slipped off to sleep holding on to each other. Somewhere around four or five in the morning, he woke up to find me, leisurely, easily, no particular hurry, and it isn't the size of the bed, you know, really—it's all how you use it. I was floating hazily, happy and warm, when for some reason I thought about Mike. Mike and his two calls on my pager. Reilly stirred, and it was probably nothing. I kissed his shoulder, his chest, shifted my hair out from under. It couldn't be that important. I'd get hold of Mike later. It was just the notion as I drifted again that nobody except Reilly really knew where to find me.

## 22

I woke up kind of early. Reilly was still sleeping. Guys are like that, or at least the cops that I've known that well are. They can sleep pretty much anytime, anywhere, conservation of energy, and I can't understand it, much less do it, so it must be one of those genetic-differences things.

Of course, Reilly was in his own bed, so that might have been part of it.

I slid off the side of his bed very carefully so as not to disturb him, borrowed one of his tee shirts, and padded down the hall to the living room. The computer was waiting for me.

I'm not totally computer illiterate—I know how to turn the things on. Reilly'd had me type in his password, so I knew how to do that now and how to get on to the Internet. The only other thing I needed was orange juice or coffee, and Reilly had both in his kitchen. He wouldn't begrudge me.

I flipped the switch on the computer and let it warm up, let it count through its numbers and check out its ROM or its RAM or whatever, while I took care of my own basic needs. I showered and lotioned in the guest bathroom, next to Reilly's two kids' rooms. He has a boy, sixteen, and a girl, fourteen, who come over some weekends. It's tough with his schedule. I haven't really quite met them. I've seen the pictures and everything—he's got some on the wall—and they don't live that far away, forty minutes or so. I just haven't wanted to take the next step yet.

I brushed my teeth thoroughly with the toothbrush I'd left there. Moseyed down to the kitchen, set the coffee to brew.

I went back in to check on the machine, and its screen had gone to a conservative black, so I knew that it was ready. Tapped the mouse, and the screen lit back up. I clicked AOL, typed the password, got up and connected, and clicked on the Internet grid there in front of me. Search engines on Go, Captain. Aye, aye, then, Scotty, let's find Argentina.

From "Argentina," I got to "Government Of" and "Political Parties." Also, the "Dissidents" page. It floors me, you know? All spelled out there, with street addresses and everything. Many of the dissident groups had Web links, where you'd just click on the highlighted names to get to their home pages. I wonder if all the underground American militia groups have the same thing now. No need to keep those expensive government files on 'em—just click on the Web.

I scrolled through the several pages of information and clicked on all the links, looking for anything on Asociación del República Argentina por la Libertad, but apparently they hadn't registered. They probably needed a fund-raiser to buy them a home page—and, well, you know, if memory served, they'd been *having* a fund-raiser in the L.A. area about a year or so ago. That's where Little Miss Sylvia had met her attorney.

Linda Madrigala.

Search engines are great. Magic. You type in "Madrigala" and click the Go button, and voilà—faster than several speeding trains, each leaving a coast and meeting in the middle at an unknown time—your server produces a dot-com.

"Madrigala.com" to be precise. Http://www and all of the rest of that. And about five seconds later, while your mouth is still hanging open, up pops a home page.

Madrigala Internacional.

With offices, believe it or not, in Buenos Aires, Tokyo, and beautiful downtown Century City. Century City, USA. About a stone's throw from Beverly Hills.

Reilly was right.

I *did* need a computer.

The coffee machine was beeping in the kitchen so I went and fetched myself a cup. Dumped in the several handfuls of sugar and creamer that makes the stuff drinkable, stirred it around. Brought it back to the living room to sip while I stared at the Web page some more.

Mike had mentioned old money, lots of antiques. Well, yeah, I would guess she might have that—if she was related, of course, but Madrigala isn't the most common name. I copied the Century City address and the phone number onto a scrap piece of paper. She might not work there, actually, because Mike had thought she was a partner in a law firm, and this was pretty definitely an investment operation, or at least that's what it looked like. Maybe imports.

I typed in "De la Peña."

Search engines aren't *reliably* magic, however: "Requested gateway not found."

I went back to Madrigala.com. It was still there. I looked for highlighted words, or anything else to click on to, quick, easy links. It didn't have any.

Cheesy kind of outfit.

I tried "Madrigala, Linda," which just took me back to Madrigala.com. I tried "De la Peña, Rudolfo," I tried "Free Argentina," I even tried typing in "Argentine Flame." That got me to "Asociación del Fútbol Argentino," because soccer is *fútbol* to most of the rest of the world. There was a list up there of *jugadores*, the current players, apparently, and their jersey numbers, and there were also several buttons on the left side of the Web page that were labeled in Spanish.

It stood to reason that the buttons would be labeled in Spanish since I was back in the Argentine homeland again, but my Spanish abilities are unfortunately limited. I speak mostly a street slang kind of Spanish, and it's Mexican street slang at that. Other than being able to recognize gang names and to rattle the Miranda card off *en español*, I haven't had to *read* a whole lot of Spanish. I can puzzle it out, but I'm slow. So I just went to the left side of the Web page and clicked on each button in turn.

"*Mensaje de bienvenida*," I pretty much figured to be a welcome message, and that's about what it looked like. "*Selecciones Nacionales*" appeared to be the *jugadores* selected for the current national team—World Cup time, you know? I went through "*Datos Institucionales*" and "*Entidades Afiliades*" before I finally came to something that looked like a history page. I don't know why I was looking, exactly—it just seemed like something to do. I clicked on the button, and there it was, a picture of the national team that had astonished the assembled countries and won the World Cup back in '78.

The Argentine Flames.

He was younger, Rudolfo, than when I'd met him, obviously. It was a grainy photo, black and white, and it didn't do him justice, but he was clearly the third from the left.

He was triumphant, they all were, grinning and macho and somehow so vulnerable in their newfound celebrity, the fans in the arena behind them going wild. Young celebrity lions. Easy women and wine. I'd seen clips on the Web last night about Diego Maradona, a troubled Argentine *fútbol* star, and his recurring problems with the high life, with drugs. Where had the Flames gone from that moment in time?

"*I should have stayed with my first wife.*"

The things people say.

"*When someone comes, so interested and alive, and they remind you, too well, of what you were, what you could be . . .*"

Was it the lost glory you were reminded of, *miejo*?

Or was it lost love?

And did you *lose* it, Rudolfo, or was it perhaps that you threw it away?

That fighting-the-wind stuff that made you so wise.

Wise men don't put bullets through the roof of their mouth. They don't eat their guns. Despair happens to all of us, to anyone who can feel, anyone with a heart and a functioning soul, but you fight *that* wind with every ounce you have in you, you look for the good. You build higher walls if you have to, to keep out the wind, but you make sure to frame windows, places for the sun to come through.

You look for the love, *miejo*.

And when you can't do that anymore, then you go to the desert and you burn the pain out of you—you take a bottle to it, or fists, or you drown it in tears. You lock it away a thousand feet deep, way down inside of you, so it can't get out to hurt the people you care for.

Did you forget that part, my flame Argentino? Is everybody right and I'm wrong?

I turned my head and Reilly was watching me from the archway. I'd heard him, vaguely, getting up and moving around in the bedroom, the shower, but I hadn't heard him come down the hall. I didn't know how long he'd been standing there.

"I was just looking," I said.

"Yeah." He was closed, noncommittal. Carefully blank. Silence between us. It might only be early morning, the way people are when they haven't had breakfast.

"Did you want some coffee?"

"Yeah." He turned and went into the kitchen, monosyllabic. I backed out of the Internet, signed off AOL, switched off the screen. Followed in with my cup.

"I found some other things on the Web," I said.

"Yeah?"

We just keep going sideways.

He was pouring himself a cautious cup of coffee, sipping gingerly at it as if it would burn. Concentrating on the handling of it, the feel, and I could have stayed in there, I guess—"What's wrong? What's the problem?"—and maybe I should have, but it seemed pretty clear that the problem was De la Peña, or, perhaps, even more than that, me.

Doing the things Reilly didn't approve of.

Didn't matter how well.

"I'm going to get dressed," I said. Put my cup on the counter and fled down the hall.

I had hardly anything there in his closet—an overnight bag with some underwear in it, a shirt or two hanging. A pair of jeans. At least it was clean stuff. I was three-quarters dressed when he opened the door.

He blinked when he saw me, so I don't think he was expecting me to be changing yet, hadn't come in on purpose to catch me off guard. I'm pretty quick when I'm moving, and this time I was flying, as much from lack of clothing choices as a need to be gone.

"I forgot about the cat," I said before he could say anything. "I've got to go by and feed her. And pick up the mail."

He was impassive. Stolid.

Leaning against the doorjamb, looking at me.

He had the vehicle. Mine was in Brentwood. It kind of depended on him.

I hadn't thought all of this through last night, had gone with the moment, the chemistry-thing.

*"You bringing your sergeant?"*

I couldn't.

I shouldn't have tried.

"Or I'll just get a cab," I said lightly, as if it weren't an issue. "It's a long way over there for you."

"You picking a fight, Meg?"

Me?

"Seems like," he said, and he does know me well.

"No."

I wasn't, exactly.

Picking it, I mean—the fight we were about to be having.

He was very quiet a moment, thinking.

"We have to talk about some things," he said finally, and I'd always thought that was supposed to be *my* line.

"It's the same thing it was," I said. "You don't want me doing this."

"No, I don't."

That was honest.

"But I've been helping you anyway, Meg."

"Not really," I said.

"Yeah?"

Yeah.

"Took you around last night," he said, rubbing his hand at his jaw. "Got you here. Accessed the Internet."

"Because you didn't think I'd find anything, Reilly."

He was just silent, looking.

"Because last night, it was all theoretical," I said. "Last night, we drove around Van Nuys looking for haystack numbers, what were the odds? And I was going to go anyway. Might as well go along, huh? Only we found it—found *something*. In not such a good part of town. So you got me away from the house on Milford, got me safely here in your living room playing armchair detective. *Where in the World Is Carmen Sandiego?* 'How Many Ways Can You Spell Argentina?' Like that. While *you* called the station and had one of your guys really working, tracking things down. Did you call in again this morning?"

He had. I could see it. On his cellphone from the bedroom. I looked at him steadily.

"And the T-Bird comes back to the same guy, doesn't it? Ernesto Ayala. Probably at that same typoed address on Milford."

His eyes lidding over.

"Right," I said. "But they couldn't find anything on Free Argentina, so nobody knows what it means. It's not all wrapped up yet, a package for you to hand over. And today's a new day."

"They've got some leads they're following," he said. "I was going to go in."

"You should do that."

He took in a breath. "I'm going to," he said tightly. "After we've talked."

We were talking.

"I want you to hold off, Meg. Leave it alone for twenty-four hours, let me see what I can find out."

Twenty-four hours.

Those magic round numbers.

He wasn't asking too much. I loved him, didn't I? Wanted to please him?

"And in twenty-four hours?" I said. "What then?"

"We'll have a better idea what it is."

"Well, twenty-four hours *ago*," I said, "everyone knew it was suicide. Twelve hours ago, even. Ten."

"Meg—"

"It's not," I said rawly, "that I think that your guys aren't good. It's not that I think you're mistaken. You're probably right and I'm probably wrong, almost certainly am, and I know it. So if I'm wandering around on some stupid quest for the dead, what's the harm in me going? Why is this such a threat?"

"It's political," he said.

Political—what the hell was political?

"De la Peña was an Argentine national, Meg."

Ah, Christ, yes. A *prominent* Argentine national, with a gunshot death and a half-beaten wife. The Argentine consul would be taking an interest.

"Jacoby's already had two of the attachés up with the Chief," Reilly said.

Okay, very touchy. The diplomatic involvements and all the repercussions for Beverly Hills. For Reilly's department.

So much for dropping in at the Argentine consulate to ask about soccer and travel brochures. Reilly was reading it, reading me, looking brusquely sympathetic.

"So I can't go *anywhere*?"

"Not much."

Son-of-a-bitch.

"You knew this," I said. "Last night."

"Yeah."

When he'd driven me away from Free Argentina. If he hadn't been with me, I could have walked in.

"What was all this, then?" I said. "This 'Come on up to my place, baby, and let's see what we can find on the Net'?"

He grimaced with distaste, not liking my tone. "I thought it would be something to do," he said roughly. "Give you something."

Keep me sweet. I almost said it out loud.

But then he'd thought they'd have an answer this morning, which would have rendered the whole problem moot. Big Daddy handling things.

"I'm not going to sit here all day, Reilly."

"You could use the computer. Dig a little deeper."

Into what?

"I don't have to go in for the whole day, anyway," he said. "A couple of hours this morning, and then I'll be back. We could go look at things then."

He was honestly serious.

"You never got me that embroidery hoop," I said.

"Meg—"

"At some point," I said, "you have to accept that I know what I'm doing." He was starting to respond but I just rode right through him. "I won't go near the consulate, Reilly. I won't visit the residences. I won't touch the precious hair on an Argentine head in any way that would make your lieutenant uneasy, but I am *not* going to sit here in Glendale while you go to work. I don't know what I'm going to do yet, but I'll think of something as I go along that satisfies your require- ments, okay?"

"No."

"Reilly—"

"Ayala is out there," he said tersely. "We don't know where he is. Van Nuys drove by this morning and his car's not at the house."

163

"So I'll have to be careful."

"You *aren't* careful." He was almost agonized, trying to reach me. "You take goddamn chances because you think you're so good. *I* followed you last night."

"And I spotted you," I said. Truth is truth, but sometimes you can say it better, make people easier. "This guy doesn't even know where I am right now, Reilly."

"He will if you go flinging around."

I don't fling. Well, not much.

"I'm going to go looking," I said flatly. "I'm not an idiot, Reilly. I'm not going to find some guerrilla group and take it on by myself, guns a-blazin'. Free Argentina is probably an orphanage fund, and who knows—maybe Ernesto's the chauffeur, right? Was just taking the kids to the beach. If it's anything more than that, no problemo—I'm outta there and I'm calling you up. Okay? This does not have to be a big deal."

He's had too many people saying "Yes, sir" to him, have I mentioned that part? Makes a guy feel entitled. In charge. He was looking at me then like spanking was an option and the harder, the better. He gets, I don't know, kind of set.

"You are not going back to his house, Meg."

Sergeant Reilly, "pro-scribing" again. I had a quick flash of Andy, darkly sardonic.

"Fine," I said.

"I mean it."

Like he'd meant I couldn't think near Sylvia de la Peña. I still owed him a postcard.

"Sure," I said, "right. Can I go to the library? It's okay with you if I ask questions there?"

"What kind of questions?"

"*History* questions," I said. "Jesus Christ, Reilly—world history, okay?"

"Which library?"

He was riding me, driving me down the way he does. I just looked at him. He looked ruthlessly back at me, sort of tapping his hand against his thigh, and what was he going to do—sit on top of me all day long? He wanted to get in to his guys, and he knew goddamn well now that I wasn't going to stay here meekly, surrounded by Glendale.

"This is how it works," he said curtly. "You're taking my truck. We'll trade off at the motel."

So Ayala wouldn't notice me, maybe, if he was out scouting for Subarus. I guess I could do that.

"And you're taking my cellphone."

I could do that, too.

"You're going to call me," he said, "and let me know where you're going—every place that you're going—*before* you go there."

I just looked at him.

"You'll be out working."

"That's why you have my pager number," he said.

# 23

We fed the cat. Well, more accurately, I put fresh food and water out for her in the enclosed porch by the back cat door—I don't know where she was. Out chasing her own breakfast, I'd guess, in the neighbors' ivy. That cat could survive without me for weeks, which is a fortunate thing, actually.

I'm not a good mother.

Bills and junk mail were the only things piled up in the mailbox, but I brought them in anyway and tossed them on the dining room table to deal with later. My bill-paying room. I had a message on the answering machine from Josh, giving me the time for his baseball game Saturday, the Little League Astros, and he kind of halfheartedly told me that I could bring Reilly. He likes Reilly, but it's the notion, okay?

Of somebody else in my life.

Reilly was listening, heard the lukewarmness.

Noncommittal. "You want me to go?"

I'm trying to be careful walking that path. I don't usually do much with Reilly on Josh's weekends because I've been trying to give us some time, trying to ease us all into it. Be surer of things. Not make us pretend right away to be one happy family.

"Did you want to?"

He shrugged at me. "Sure."

Little League hot dogs.

"Okay, then," I said. "If you're not working."

"I can probably go in late. I'll check."

It felt very odd.

This would have been enough of a step by itself, but here we were, matter-of-factly making a date for next Saturday, a few days away—a future together on the other side of this Argentine problem, this small disagreement.

Reilly employs things. He's very strategic. It's a useful trait for an STU sergeant, but maybe just that little bit off-putting at home.

See, this way I had a bigger stake in not crossing him, not getting him bent out of shape or getting bent out myself and ripping us open.

Apart.

"I'll call Josh back later," I said. "After he gets home from school. I don't really want to talk to his mom."

Reilly nodded, unconcerned. Maybe he hadn't thought of it that way. Maybe it's just me.

"You ready to go?"

I was ready.

He whisked us out, took Olive Avenue south through Burbank to where Olive turns into Barham Boulevard there by Riverside Drive and the television studios, and we caught the 101 South. We'd missed the worst of the morning rush hour, but it was still fairly ugly. It always seems to be, these days. Crowded. We got off at Cahuenga, went west into the stop-and-go on Sunset. That road runs straight through into Beverly Hills.

"You want to stop at your office?"

Mike would be there. I needed to talk to him, but I didn't especially want Reilly to.

"No, that's okay," I said, "you have to get into work."

"I don't mind."

He has these really nice manners he uses sometimes. That makes it harder to say, "Oh, yeah? Well, I *do*." Fortunately, I was raised to have nice manners, too.

"I don't want to hold you up," I said. "And anyway, Mike's supposed to be handling things, so I wasn't even going to go in today."

"All right," he said equably, not one whit perturbed. He had his attention on the traffic, you know. Maneuvering through it.

We drove carefully into Beverly Hills on Sunset, passing the Beverly Hills Hotel on the right, just after Rexford Drive. Rexford's the street where, a few blocks farther south, the city hall and the police department coincide. *I* didn't look over that way when we went by it—I don't know if he did or not. We got to the part where Sunset wraps around UCLA, and followed the curves past the 405 Freeway into Brentwood and my Brentwood motel.

Reilly pulled up and parked in the spot directly across from my room.

"You checking out now?" he said.

It was nine-thirtyish. I didn't have to check out till eleven. I needed to get hold of Mike, though, and there was a phone I could use undisturbed in the room.

"I'm not sure," I said. "Probably."

He nodded. Was kind of engaged there working the truck key off his keyring, concentrating on it.

"I was thinking," he said idly, "that you might want to go down by the beach with me for dinner."

Now that he knew I liked beaches. And since we were so close to Santa Monica with its waterfront dining.

And since we were making these dates.

I didn't know where I was likely to be at dinnertime, but I'd have his cellphone if I had to be late. It would make the man easier.

"Sure."

"You might want to keep the room, then," he said very casually, watching something behind us in the rearview mirror. "I'll pay for it."

It's hard to quit being a cop.

See, that way we didn't quite have to decide whose idea it might have been to stay out another night, and that way he'd know where I'd end up this evening. Another way of keeping control.

Or maybe he was honestly trying, you know?

If it was just that I was wanting variety. If he'd been working too hard lately and hadn't been around enough, taking me places. Reilly has *his* baggage, too.

"Okay," I said. "I'll keep the room. We'll argue about who owes who later."

He looked at me sideways. "Service fees?"

"Use fees," I said and plucked the key out of his fingers, handed him mine. I kissed him intensely so he'd know that I loved him, and then climbed myself out of the ElCo. He was getting out on his own side, ready to go to my 'Ru. I locked the passenger door and shut it, smiled cheerfully at him over the top. "It's good that you're getting some overtime, Reilly. I think I'll order the lobster and steak."

He was already back to looking grim. Reluctant. "It's nine thirty-five, Meg. You call me by twelve."

Yassuh, Boz.

"I will," I said.


If it were Mike, I wouldn't have had to think twice. "I will" means "I'll try to," means "If I remember." "If nothing else gets in the way." With Charlie, too, really. With Reilly, it means "Yes, I'll set my watch to go off at five minutes till, so I don't miss the moment and I don't keep you waiting." A little too much like a pain.

On the other hand . . .

Mike wasn't at the office. I got myself on the answering machine, so I said a few things to my voice like "Okay, it's me—are you there, Mike? Pick up," but nothing like "Jiminy Christmas, Mike, where the hell are you?" Jumping Jehoshaphat, and all of that stuff.

I dug around then and finally found my pager on the floor by the side of the motel's bed. It had slipped off, I guess, yesterday evening while I was tugging my sweats on to go out with Reilly, and I'm a fine one to throw stones about being unreachable, you know? Mike had paged two more times—once last night, kind of late, from his apartment, and once this morning, kind of early, from the office.

He might just be avoiding Reilly. Hit the office quickly and get out for the day. It wasn't unlikely.

It was four pages, though, in a row.

The front-desk person, this morning a girl, didn't have any messages for me. There was no reason she would have. The only one with the motel's number, really, was Andy. And I guess, technically, Andy's wife, Susan.

And, of course, Reilly.

The girl had no problem with my keeping the room one more night.

It was 9:55.

I tried the office again. Tried Mike's apartment.

I hadn't kept the damn number of Linda's bungalow that I'd called Friday night. It might still be in my trash basket at the office along with the stripped-off press-on nails. I might even find Linda's business card somewhere there on Mike's desk. He'd said that he'd gotten one. She might know where he was.

I didn't know that I wanted to be asking her.

Or I might find a big note from Mike.

I had nothing much else I could do, so I locked everything up and drove straight to the office.

There were a number of cars in the office parking lot I didn't recognize, but nothing black or brown, nothing with a Latino bumper sticker. At that point, I'd have looked twice at YO ♥ MAZATLÁN, and yes, I have a notion where Mazatlán is. I haven't ever been there myself but it would have been close enough to the South American continent to have gotten my interest. As it was, I made a passing gesture to the Great God of Caution and parked the El Camino across the street. It cost me seventy-five cents in change for the meter, but I wasn't going to be there for more than two hours, and that way I didn't have to worry about someone blocking me in or my having to waste any time getting out of the parking lot if I wanted to leave in a hurry. It was farther to cross unprotected, but nothing's protection, really—it's all just degrees of concealment.

Mike wasn't there.

He hadn't left me a note.

My trash can was there, though, with the nails still rattling around. We have someone come in every other Monday to vacuum and wipe down, and they *will* dump the trash, but I usually do that myself. It's easy enough, just a step to the Dumpster out back in the alley, and since I hate looking for papers and wondering if somebody accidentally knocked them off into the garbage, we've worked out an agreement. The point was that the nails were still there, but the Friday note wasn't.

No bungalow phone number.

I didn't *know* that I'd crumpled it up and thrown it into the trash can. It seemed like I had but maybe I'd stuffed it into my purse instead, that leatherette bag, last Friday night, in which case it was somewhere in the bedroom closet in Burbank. I flat couldn't remember. It hadn't mattered at the time.

I poked quickly through Mike's trash and also through the trash in the bathroom, because I'd been bothered and pacing around Friday night, so maybe one of those fit the memory of chucking the thing, but there was no crumpled piece of paper with a phone number on it in either basket.

Okay, no phone number.

Linda's card.

No card. I went pretty thoroughly through the junk on Mike's desktop, but, you know, I'm an idiot. Mike doesn't remember numbers. He'd have the card in his wallet so it would be handy when he wanted to call her—Linda wasn't a business account.

I have phone books at the office.

Linda wasn't listed, but Madrigala Internacional was.

So was Rudolfo de la Peña.

I didn't *know* that Sylvia de la Peña was still at the bungalow. She might very well have gone back to her own house. The man who'd allegedly beaten her up was gone now, dead, leaving her, I would think, in possession.

Her house wasn't the Argentine consulate.

It wasn't me going anywhere near her, it was simply me looking for Mike, so I picked up the phone and pressed in the numbers.

"*Hola?*"

The voice was accented.

Latino.

Male.

I had no particular cover story worked up, nothing that I'd intended to play, but I wasn't expecting a foreign man to answer the phone. I was expecting Linda or Sylvia, Mike, maybe, a maid. I was still looking at the phone book page, my finger marking the listing to keep me from losing the number, and so I said the first thing that came into my head.

"Rudolfo?"

There was a pause and then,

"*Sí?*"

Whoa.

No.

I had to be sure, have him give me the name. "Rudolfo de la *Peña?*"

"*Sí*, De la Peña," he said.

# 24

What do you say to a dead man?

I'm qualified for this, as it happens—I talk to dead guys all the time. Not usually in Spanish.

*"Inglés?"*

"Yes," the dead man said. "Who is calling?"

Dead men aren't always dead. Sometimes it's insurance fraud, that kind of thing, headless bodies left lying around.

They don't generally answer their phones after that, though, announcing themselves.

A wrong number?

He'd said De la Peña. I glanced down again and it was the only one listed. De la Peña, Rudolfo, no street address given.

The man was repeating something, rather forcefully now, *"Quién habla?"* alternating it with "Who is this? Who's talking?" and he was clearly, impatiently, wanting an answer.

He wanted to know who?

Well, why not—what the hell—you can't let the dead people push you around.

"Sylvia."

I said it the way *my* Rudolfo had said it on Friday, rolling the *l*: "Sill-vee-ah."

*"Sylvia?"*

He sounded kind of shocked, actually, but hey.

"Where you are?"

Ah.

Not "Sylvia who?" but "Where you are?" This guy somehow knew her.

Knew her well?

Sylvia was under a doctor's care these days, drugged to the gills by what Mike had been saying.

"I'm . . . at a friend's," I said softly, slurring.

"Where?"

Jeez.

"I don't know."

There was a rush of furious Spanish from the guy's end of the phone line, harsh orders and overtones, but it was wasted on me. I need to learn the damn language or carry a recorder.

"No . . ." I said, " . . . no."

He spat more Spanish, bullying. I tried to grasp phrases, but he was speaking too fast and it was truly beyond me. He would pause periodically, expecting answers from Sylvia that he just wasn't getting because hell if *I* knew what to say, but he interpreted silence as resistance, I guess—resistance that his anger had no effect on—and he finally gave in with a very ill grace.

"You tell me where you are, Sylvia."

He was there in her house. Answering her phone. Yelling at her in Spanish, giving her orders, but I didn't have to satisfy him, I could ask my own questions.

"What do you want?"

"You know what I want," he said, "*puta*."

*Puta* means whore.

I know that word in a whole lot of languages. Catcalls, jeers, guys clustered and looking. Cars slowing down as they're passing by. I wore a wire in those days. I wanted one now. God, did I want one.

Or some little bitty pocket recorder. Legalities be damned.

And I don't have any tape recorders in the office, exactly, but I do have an answering machine, which was sitting right there on the filing cabinet behind me. It won't tape a phone call simply by your turning it on while you're talking because answering machines don't work like that. They only activate to record if someone's called in and you didn't pick up the receiver before the designated number of rings. By then the machine's started the tape-cassette winding and the record function working, so at that point, it will tape both sides of your conversation for a minute or two. It won't otherwise do that.

It will, however, record an *outgoing* message on that same cassette tape whenever you'd like it to. The "Sorry, I'm not here right now" message that you can change anytime just by pressing a button and voicing it over, speaking with your mouth fairly close to the grille on the machine's built-in microphone.

Fifteen seconds' worth of tape, maybe? Twenty?

Not much, but more than I had.

The only thing I wasn't sure about was the beep at the end. How loud it would be, if he'd hear it.

Oh, well.

I swung lightly around and stood up, taking the phone cord with me. It stretched. "I *don't* know what you want," I said. "Tell me, Rudolfo." I had the machine door flipped open and my finger on the Announcement button. Pressed it. Leaned in towards the grille.

He laughed incredulously. "You call me Rudolfo? Rudolfo is dead."

Well, I knew that part, right? I just hadn't been quite sure that *he* did. The dead take forever to learn things. He was reveling in it, apparently, gloating: "You have no one now, Sylvia. The hombre won't help you, no one will help you. You see what you have done? You see what your ways have brought you?"

I saw something else.

"You hurt me," I said.

"You deserved it—*puta*."

"No," I said, and his voice deepened, got impossibly gentle.

175

"Where you are, Sylvia? Where is it you hide now? You think I don't find you, bring you back home?"

"You hit me." My voice might have trembled a little.

"You make me to do it—you don't behave. What was that man, then, huh? The 'old friend' where you stay? I know who he is—" and the damn beep went off then, right next to my mouth and the receiver end of the phone. His voice changed up an octave. "What is that, you record me?! You, you bitch—" and then he abruptly was gone.

I hit the Playback Announcement button. Listened to the whole fifteen seconds' worth. *"You call me Rudolfo? . . ."* right up through *"I know who he is—"*

There was nothing legal about taping him. No admission in a court of law. I didn't precisely need "legal" at the moment, though—I needed to know the name of this guy. I needed Mike to know who he was, so that he could be watching, and so that he—or I—could have more of an informed chat with Sylvia.

"She have another boyfriend, Mike?" and he'd just said "Hey!" like I was throwing dirt on an icon. Sullying, you know?

I'm so like that.

I popped the tape out of the machine. It meant I had to fetch another one, record a new outgoing message, but as it happens I already had a box of extra cassettes in the storeroom. Serendipity. I'd had to replace one a couple of months ago, and they're cheaper if you buy them in bulk. Maybe that's why I'd even thought of it. I'd been spending a lot of time in the storeroom lately, changing clothes right next to the stuff on the shelves. One way to keep track of the inventory.

I was halfway to the back when the phone started ringing. There was no machine working to answer it, or I would have left it. I picked it up at Mike's desk.

"John Gill Corporation."

"I know who you are," the dead man said.

# 25

I really don't like this new phone company feature, this "Press a button and call back your last caller" deal. It's nothing but trouble as far as I'm concerned, for all that they tout it as a technological marvel. If I want someone calling me back, I figure I should have to leave 'em the number.

"Who am I?" I said.

"Margaret Gillis."

The same damn "Mar-ga-re-ta."

"Yeah? Well, I know who you are, too," I said. "So do the cops."

He laughed.

"You know nothing."

And you don't have to answer a psychopath, it's not really wise, but sometimes I'm willing, especially when he's calling into my goddamn office.

"Free Argentina," I said.

And then for good measure, I added, "Asociación del República Argentina por la Libertad."

Dead absolute silence.

I had time to remember that I hadn't called Reilly yet, that Reilly didn't know I was here. That while I had this guy on my phone line I couldn't call out, couldn't get people hotfooting their way to Rudolfo's, surrounding the house with the psychopath in it—and that Reilly's

177

cellphone, which I could have been otherwise using to dial for help while I kept this guy talking, was safely locked away in his damn El Camino on the other side of the street. Why would I need Reilly's cellphone while I was there at my office, you know?

That's the beauty of having two phone lines, though—I can put people on hold. They don't have to stay there, but they can't tie up my only available line. I had my hand stretched out with the thought, ready to push down the Hold button and then the private line button, so I could Touch-Tone like hell for Reilly at the station.

On the other hand . . .

I had extra cassettes.

"You still there?" I said snidely. "*Rudolfo?*"

"I going to cut you," he was starting to say as I eased the phone down onto Mike's In-box tray and raced for the storeroom. Somewhere, goddammit—I knew they were there, I'd just seen them. I was shoving stuff aside, the boxes of envelopes, scanning the shelves. I spotted them at the back next to two stacks of message pads, so very organized, God, I was good, and I snatched three or four of them out of the box. They were individually plastic-wrapped, with cellophane rip tabs, except that of course, when you're hurrying, they don't rip at all. I was back in by the phone, over Mike's desk, discarding the torn pull tabs, gnawing the plastic wrap loose with my teeth. I got one free fairly quickly, all things considered, but there wasn't a sound from the phone.

"*Hola?*" I said.

Someone was breathing.

Breathing is nice.

Ranting is better.

"How exactly are you planning to cut me?" I said. I needed to move over and pick it up on my own phone. Mike's wouldn't reach to the answering machine.

"You find out," he said. "Soon."

And then he hung up.

Dial tone.

One of the several things that occurred to me then was that I didn't know where Rudolfo's house was, how far away. And that I didn't know for sure that this guy had been calling from Rudolfo's home phone. He might just have checked what my number was and jumped into a car—Reilly's not the only one with a cellphone.

Or this guy might not even have *had* to hit the call back button to find out who I was. This guy knew my name, so he obviously knew more than the phone number, might very well know where the office was.

This guy might have friends.

*Asociación* usually means more than one person.

Hello.

I probably didn't want to be standing here then, making my phone calls to Reilly. Listening to the "Sorry, he's not in, can I take a message?" routine, or even "Yeah, he's here, just a minute" while Reilly got waved to and finished his unhurried chat, not moving very quickly to pick up the phone because he was ticked, maybe, that I was only just now checking in.

I was already stuffing the original cassette tape into the top flap of my bag. Had the bag up and slung over my shoulder, ready to go. Reilly would need the machine, though, to play it—it wasn't too big to detach and take with me—because there was no point in handing over an urgent tape of something if he had no way to hear it. I didn't know if Beverly PD even had a microcassette player—they've got all kinds of state-of-the-art stuff, more than *we* ever had, but that didn't mean they were spending their money stocking different-size machines on the off chance they'd need one someday to play my cassette through. I unhooked the phone lines up top. Had to shove the filing cabinet a little bit sideways so that I could pull out the electrical plug, got my hand on the cord and just yanked.

A minute, all told?

I had the keys ready, my knife in my front pants pocket. I looked through the miniblinds, saw nothing moving, so I opened the door and slipped out. I relocked it behind me with my eyes on the world.

The dangerous part was crossing the open space to the ElCo, but I have some practice with gliding, with hiding, with drawing my aura in like the folds of a cloak. Withholding attention. It sounds sort of bogus, but you become nondescript. Blank. I don't know a better way to describe it. It makes you invisible, almost—with the emphasis very strongly on "almost"—keeping in mind that if a predator's marked you, the best it might do is confuse him or her for a second.

You might only *need* a second, though.

It's better to have it than not.

I got my key into the doorlock of the El Camino, opened the driver's door and slid in. Locked it with the movement as I started the engine and eased away from the curb. I could have fished out the cellphone then and called Reilly, but the station's just a few blocks away, and I was kind of busy with mirrors and checking the traffic, leaving my nerve ends strung out there like tendrils, trolling the area.

No one seemed to be following.

I made it the couple of blocks north and over to Rexford. Pulled into the city parking garage. No one turned in behind me while I was taking my ticket, while the wooden barrier arm pulled back and rose. I drove slowly forward to clear it. It lowered. There was still no one there.

I turned right and went quickly up the ramp to the second level. I wanted to be close to the PD's entrance bridge there, and I was able to find a parking space halfway up the slope on the opposite side of the structure, the non-Rexford side. You're not so visible from the street inside the parking garage anyway, but each little extra thing helps.

Degrees of concealment.

I climbed out of the truck and kept my head tucked down over the answering machine in my arms, my bag clutched close as I hurried the rest of the way up the concrete slope towards the pedestrian walkway that bridges over to Beverly PD. There were two loiterers in the area, one locking up his car, one transferring what looked to be library books from his front car seat into a satchel. I passed them in modest confusion, obviously intent on gaining higher ground unmolested, my *objet d'errand* held like a barrier against my chest.

I reached the second level's corner, scooted through the opening there, and turned onto the bridge. It's really more of a ramp than a bridge, running alongside the outer wall of the PD like a balcony once it's crossed the little distance between the parking structure and the station. I stayed as close to the building as possible as I trucked up the ramp. Got to the PD's entrance and went in.

They've built a little booth for the front-desk officer recently, a tiny office space set back against the left wall in the lobby. Now you get to talk to the officer through a formal hole in the bulletproof window, while he talks to you by way of a microphone system. It isn't as citizen-friendly as the previous open-air podium the PD'd been using, but it is, I think, much more officer-safe. *I* feel safer for the officer, anyway. I feel safer for both of us, actually, because I figure he's got to come out of the glass cage to grab me.

I left my secretary persona at the door.

"Hi," I said like myself, "is Sergeant Reilly around?"

This guy didn't know me.

He smiled at me nicely and used his telephone to check. Thanked somebody there.

"I'm sorry, ma'am," he said through the glass, "he's away from his desk."

I had the damn answering machine in my arms. Shifted the weight.

"Somewhere in the building?" I said.

"No, ma'am, I don't think so."

Reilly could be gone for hours, then, the whole day, even—I didn't know what he was doing. I'd tucked his cellphone into my bag as I'd climbed out of the El Camino, so I had it with me. I could take one of the benchseats over there by the staircase and page him. I'd have to wait then, of course, for him to respond.

"Is Jacoby in? Detective Jacoby?"

The officer was taking a little more interest—first Sergeant Reilly and now Detective Jacoby. He picked up the phone link again to dial upstairs, and I had that flash of Jacoby looking at me, not unkindly, in the interview room. Those tar-pool black eyes. The sergeant's girl-friend enmeshed.

"I'm sorry," I said. "Just a minute, okay? I need to make a phone call first. I'll be right back." I didn't give him any kind of time to think about it, I was already moving for the outside door. I couldn't just sit on the bench in the lobby using the cellphone now because that wouldn't stop him from calling upstairs, that would only look like I was intending to wait, simply doing a little necessary business while he went ahead and found Jacoby for me anyway.

"Hey," he said over the microphoned speaker, but I'd made it safely by then through the door. He wouldn't come after me, which is another reason why I love that glass booth. A barrier both ways.

I took the bridge to the right that leads over to the library, consistent with my going-somewhere-to-make-a-phone-call story. The officer could watch me that far on the overhead cameras if he wanted to, and he had no way of knowing I was carrying a cellphone. I made the slight jog to the left and went down the first set of stairs. Curled low then and sat myself in the far corner of the bottom step there, up against the column, out of the way. Not out in the open, but not really hiding—just casually enjoying the sunshine, the lunch break, for any fellow travelers over the bridge. I smiled at a hurrying executive-type coming at me. She smiled briefly, a reflex, and took the stairs beside me two at a time.

I ought to give the tape to Jacoby. I just flat didn't want to. I wanted Reilly to be there, to hear it. I wouldn't mind, then, if Jacoby heard it, too, in company, but we already had a history, he already thought I was a twit, and I just couldn't hand it over to him without any backup. It was the only copy I had.

Who else then? Abbott—Reilly's lieutenant?

The one whose surname I was wearing at the Brentwood motel. The one with the qualms about my rightness for Reilly. I trusted him, I guess, as much as anyone there, but—"Hi, Lieutenant, could you keep this tape for me? It's of me sort of butting into a police case, and probably dragging your favorite boy down the tubes with me when the whole thing blows up, but, hey, can you do me this favor?"

And the thing was that Reilly might very well have been covering the tracks at the department, keeping me quietly out of the picture as far as anyone higher up was concerned. Abbott might have no idea.

Until I came squealing in, of course.

Precipitate impulse.

I stared down at the sun-bright courtyard below me and thought it all through again.

I couldn't keep the cassette with me.

If this dead guy, this "Rudolfo," *was* following me with his hand on a knife, then the cassette would be most of what he was wanting—his voice on the tape I had, legal or not. Cutting me would be extra, a bonus.

And Reilly wouldn't know, then, where to start looking, if something happened. If I didn't make it.

I pulled out his cellphone and called his pager, got the recording. Keyed in his cellphone number as the one to call back. He should get that wherever he was, whatever it was he was doing.

I hate sitting around waiting, but it gave me more time to think. Smile at a couple more climbers. Enjoy the damn sunshine. Work out what I needed to say.

The cellphone rang.

"Yeah?" I said.

"Meg?"

Just the sound of his voice was unnerving. I'm such a coward. There was noise behind him, traffic sounds.

"Hi," I said.

"What's up?"

I guess *I* was. My turn on the stage.

"I just wanted to tell you that I left a cassette for you at the station. It's on the outgoing-message part of my answering machine from the office because that's all I had to tape with. I brought the whole thing in for you—the machine, I mean—so just hit the Announce button, okay? When you get back."

"Where are you?"

He never asks what you'd expect, like "What's on the tape?"

"I'm outside," I said hastily. "Listen, it's a guy who thought I was Sylvia. I was trying to track Mike and I thought he might be with her, thought she might have moved back home by now, so I looked the number up in the Beverly phone book and called it. This guy answered. He said he was De la Peña, Reilly."

"De la Peña?"

"Yeah. He identified himself as Rudolfo. I asked him twice."

"On the *tape*?"

"No," I said. "I didn't expect it, so I didn't start taping till later. He was busy asking who I was, so I just, you know, told him Sylvia. He didn't say 'Sylvia who?'—he started right in yelling at me, mostly in Spanish, so I'd say he knows her, and he knows her pretty well."

He was silent a second. "He was at Sylvia's house?"

"About fifteen minutes ago," I said. "He's the guy who beat her up, Reilly. I got *that* part on tape."

Reilly thinks sometimes without breathing. At least, I couldn't hear him breathing and I was listening. I only heard car noises, sort of muffled. The phone against a jacket or hand, covered over.

"All right," he said abruptly, coming back on. "The tape's at the station?"

Well, technically it was.

"Yeah."

"You there, too?"

There was something about his tone, very casual suddenly, like he wasn't maybe that far away. Moving in. Or like he had somebody on another line closer to me than he was, able to reach out and touch me. Everyone has cellphones these days. In any group of people, you can probably find three or four. You could borrow one or even two of them if you had to, just by asking your guys, because I had Reilly's cellphone right there in my hand and it didn't sound at all like he was calling me back from a pay phone.

"What's going on, Reilly?"

"Going on?"

'Scuse me, ma'am, didn't quite get the question.

"I have to go," I said. "Bye."

"Meg—" *That* tone was real and rising, a warning, but I was already pressing the End button on his cellphone, cutting him off.

I pressed off the Power button, too. Wouldn't want anyone stealing his numbers.

I ran back up the steps to the bridge ramp, stuffing the cellphone into my bag. Hit the PD's door flying. Fortunately, there was nobody in the lobby except for the cop in the booth, the same cop I'd left. He wasn't on the phone.

"You have an envelope?" I said breathlessly. "A big one, interoffice type? I've got to leave this machine for Sergeant Reilly, and I'm in kind of a hurry."

He was looking at me oddly.

"I just wanted to throw it into something," I said. "I told him he could borrow my spare one, because I guess his own isn't working, but it looks sort of dorky, leaving it off here like this. I couldn't find the box anywhere."

The cop was having a little trouble following me.

"You know Sergeant Reilly?"

"Joe?" I said. "Oh, yeah—yeah, I do. Pretty well, actually." I gave him a very big cheese-eating smile because I figured it wasn't any of his business who Reilly was seeing, and then I shifted into Harmless Little

Woman mode. I didn't want him thinking I was leaving a bomb. "I went out just now and called him, and he was wanting me to hang around for a while until he gets back, but I can't do that—I told him I couldn't—I've got this hellacious big meeting with some independent producers about my new film. I just feel sort of *stupid* handing this over like this—I thought he would be here so I didn't wrap it or anything, put it into a bag . . ." I eyed the answering machine dubiously where I'd laid it down on the little shelf ledge on my side of the bulletproof glass, so that the officer could see that I was in a quandary, that I was having second thoughts now about whether I should leave it at all. "Still," I said, torn, "he *did* say he needed it today if I could get it here. Oh, I don't know, I'm such an idiot." I smiled ruefully at him. "*Do* you have a big envelope?"

He did.

It was right there in a drawer beside him, a large manila envelope of the city-interoffice variety. I printed Reilly's name very quickly in the next unmarked space, with the pen that the officer slid through the little tray to me. I had pens in my bag, but why quibble? He was being gallant and nice. I like cops like that. Maybe Reilly wouldn't feel that he had to disillusion him any when he got back. I signed the register clearly as myself, leaving a package for Reilly. Thanked him again. The package wouldn't fit through the little tray, though, so he had to come out of the door on the side to take it from me.

"I've got to run," I said. "Oh my God, I'm so late. You'll make sure he gets it?"

"Yes, ma'am."

He really was a nice guy. Probably hadn't worked there very long.

I skated out the front door, going right again towards the library, then heading left to the parking structure by way of the bridge fork that crosses the open area over the courtyard between the three buildings. You're more exposed to the world that way, people better able to see you up top there, but there isn't the blind corner back into the parking structure that the PD's ramp has. I hate blind corners. You pie 'em the best way you can, scope 'em out without seeming to do so, but there's still that moment of glory when you have to step into the unseen unknown, hoping to God the whole time that there's nobody lurking.

Me, I'd rather go around.

I kept to the middle of the bridge, away from the edges, the railings. That made me a little less visible from below. I went fairly quickly. I'd already told the front-desk cop I was late, so it wouldn't be remarkable if he happened to look out and see that I was hurrying. People will do that, and I wasn't racing in a manner to draw any attention, I was just moving very smoothly very fast.

Cutting right along.

There's a half-step there by the parking structure, coming out of the sunlight into the relative shadow, and I swept a quick glance left to right as I passed it, aiming first at the back view of the other ramp's blind corner. I registered nobody there as I scanned through the arc, the 180-degree turn. There was a vehicle coming up from the lower level, I could hear the gears grinding down for the climb, but there was no pedestrian waiting on my level, nothing hostile in sight. I melted back into the wall beside me as the car came up and rounded the curve. Mom driving, and a daughter, preschool age, in a car seat behind her. Doing the library thing. I left them jockeying into a space on the other side of the wall and hied myself down the driving ramp.

Eight more feet to the El Camino, halfway down the concrete expanse, both sides full of parked cars. I scanned them while I was moving. Another vehicle was coming around the far corner, maybe thirty feet from me, turning onto my level. Coming kind of fast, a black car.

*Yo ♥ Argentina?*

I had time, barely, to step to my right, between a Dodge and an Astrovan, to turn my head, look for keys.

The car hurtled by.

I didn't think he'd make the next turn, flying as fast as he was, but he did, jammed hard on the brakes, hauled it around. He revved up again climbing through the bend, so I guess he was still in a hurry. I heard a car door slam on the level above. I was really hoping the mom had her hand on her daughter, walking her carefully out between the cars, but I was already the eight feet farther down the level, had the ElCo's door opened and slamming. Firing the ignition. Backing right out, not waiting the thirty seconds for the engine to warm up, the oil to circulate. I could hear my dad saying how bad that was, takes years off the life of the engine, but right then I was thinking of *my* years, you know? Took the exit ramp down.

I ignored the main exit to Rexford Drive on my right, went on down and around the one level to the back gate. It's too visible sitting out at the booth in the middle of the three structures' courtyard, blocked in by the barrier arm while the guy clocks your ticket and counts out your change. The back exit lets you out on Civic Center Drive, and you're decently *inside* the structure while you're handing the man there your ticket and money. More of a private transaction.

"You have a good day," the guy said while the barrier arm rose.

I was sure going to try.

My pager was rattling at me from the floor on the passenger's side, but I pretty much expected it to be Reilly, ready to lay back my ears. I didn't recognize the call back number. Numbers. There were two of them.

Mike?

I Touch-Toned the first one, the earliest number. Connected.

"*Hola,*" the dead man said.

# 26

It isn't a puzzle how a dead guy gets my pager number. Until I'd ripped it out of the wall a half hour or so ago, my office answering machine gave it out routinely to anyone who called in—sort of as an after-thought, an in-an-emergency kind of deal. Nobody'd taken me up on it in the six months since I'd gotten the pager, but that didn't mean nobody had never written it down. Apparently, *this* nobody had.

I hung up on him.

Okay, more precisely, I pushed the End button, and then I jammed off the power. I should have stayed on the line with him, I know—should have tried to play him, get more information, but hell if I felt like it. I was tired of reaching out and touching damned trouble. I eyed the second number on the digital pager display. There ought to be Caller ID for pager numbers, you know?

Michael or Reilly?

I was heading west on Santa Monica Boulevard at that point, having taken the south way around. If it was Reilly and I hung up on him a second time, I could pretty much kiss that goose good-bye. It wouldn't be sitting at all well with him that I'd done it the first time, but we could maybe—maybe, maybe, maybe—get by it. If everything turned out okay, that is, fairly soon, and I managed not to twist his feathers any more in the meantime.

It might just be Mike, it probably was—but I couldn't bring myself to key in that damned second number.

I *could* push the End button, of course, as soon as I heard who it was, but I don't know much about cellular phones, and I wasn't willing to bet they don't have Caller ID or that nice call-back-your-caller feature like everything else does these days. Hit that pound sign, or something. Read back the number on the digital display. What were the odds Reilly wouldn't know his own cellphone number and therefore wouldn't know it was me, hanging up on him again?

I was already on the road towards Santa Monica, running up on the left-hand turn for Century City in a matter of seconds.

Century City.

The business hub of the world.

And, well, now that I thought of it, I had an address in my bag for Madrigala Internacional there, the possible employer of the attorney Linda, who could possibly tell me where Michael might be.

*That* was a legitimate reason for stopping in.

You couldn't really quarrel with that.

And office buildings generally have phones in their lobbies, some sort of pay phone, a land line from which I could call any old number I wanted, could hang up if I had to, without leaving confirmed evidence of deliberate wrongdoing. "Who, me? Call from a pay phone? What?"

Two diplomatic birds with one stone.

Immunity.

And an office building couldn't qualify as an Argentine embassy. Consulate. Whatever.

I signaled the turn with the thought, got into the left-hand lane. Took Avenue of the Stars, backtracked on Olympic, and ended up on Century Park East. Turned into the building's parking garage. Found a space, parked in it.

Sat.

I'm not psychic—I'm paranoid. I wouldn't normally have gone anywhere near Madrigala Internacional without checking the layout, getting a sense of what they were all about first, so the fact that my warning bump was agitated and fretful was a result of the circumstances. I knew that. I've learned not to ignore the warning bump, though. I sat in the El Camino in the parking garage and used Reilly's cellphone to call Mike's apartment one more time.

He didn't answer.

I called the office. It just rang and rang.

And then I called Susan Abbott at the Brentwood motel. She wasn't answering her room phone, naturally, so after an interval, the courteous guy at the front desk who'd tried to connect me got back on the line. Could he take a message? Why, yes, thanks, he could.

"Please tell Susan," I said very clearly, "that this is Meg Gillis. It's, what—eleven forty-five now? Tell her I'm going into Madrigala Internacional's office here in Century City, looking for Linda Madrigala"— I spelled it all out for him and gave him the address, and then—"so if I don't call back in an hour or so, tell her that's where she can find me."

"At Madrigala Internacional?"

"Yes," I said. "Thanks. And, ah"— oh, hell—"would you just add at the bottom there that I'm sorry?"

"You're sorry?"

I'm an egg-sucking idiot, really. "Yeah," I said. "Just put 'Sorry,' okay? I don't want her to worry, but I couldn't wait."

It was all I could think of to do.

It gave Reilly a place to start looking if this whole thing went south. He'd end up at the Brentwood motel at some point today, and I was pretty sure he'd be interested in any calls Susan Abbott had gotten. I could have just phoned his machine at the apartment and left a similar message, but he can call home to pick messages up. I don't know how often a day he actually does that, but this way I could safely figure I had a few hours. He wasn't likely to go back to the motel till tonight. Dinnertime.

He'd understand it then.

I hoped.

Or, really, what I hoped was that he wouldn't have to.

I slipped the pager and the cellphone into my bag and went up through the stairwell into the building. It had a wide-open lobby, spacious, with floor-to-ceiling glass windows that fronted on Century Park East. The windows were tinted, naturally, against the heat of the sun, and tempered so that they wouldn't easily break, but the world's visibility through them added to the overall feeling of lightness and grace. I approached the nice guard at the desk, who pointed me down a side hall to the alcove where the telephones were.

I used my credit card again to finance the call, touching in the second number from my pager. Kept my finger on the pay phone's silver hook, ready to disconnect at the first hint of Reilly.

"Hello?"

I didn't know who it was. Some guy. It didn't sound like a cellular phone.

"Somebody called my pager and left this number," I said.

"Ah, yes—Ms. Gillis. Hold on just a minute."

I don't like people I don't know knowing my name. Particularly snooty-sounding people. I held on, though, for what seemed like a lot longer than a minute.

"Hello?"

It was Mike.

Distinctly, unequivocally him. Such a rush of relief.

"Hey, Michael," I said.

"Meg? God*damn*, Meg—where've you been?"

Happy to hear from me, too.

"We've got to get cellular phones," I said. "I've been rethinking that, big-time, chasing after your pages. Where are you right now?"

"At Tovarsen's, doing the motion-detector."

He sounded very frazzled. Tovarsen's? Oh, yeah, in the Valley. I'd thought that was set up for next week, though. I guess it was good that one of us was working.

"What's up?"

"We can't find Sylvia," he said.

# 27

There are some things I don't like to hear. One of those things in particular is that a woman who was recently battered is missing from shelter at about the same time that the psychopath who hurt her is loose on the town.

Loose with a knife.

"Since when, Mike? Last night?"

The first of his pages.

"Yesterday afternoon," he said tiredly. "Between five and five-thirty. We've been looking everywhere, Meg—hospitals, clinics, old friends. I don't know what else to do."

"Give me the circumstances, Bo."

"Yeah," he said. "Right. Linda called me last night. She'd gotten home about five-thirty and went out to the bungalow to see how everything was. There was a nurse who was supposed to be sitting with Sylvia because she'd been pretty hysterical after she talked to the cops, and Linda was afraid, you know, that she might hurt herself. She had to go to work, though, Meg—she couldn't stay there the whole day."

No, she couldn't.

"Where was the nurse?"

"She was still there. She thought Sylvia was sleeping, so she'd gone in to fix some dinner, but when she checked back after Linda got there, Sylvia was gone."

"Gone how?"

"It looks like she wandered out the front door," Mike said, but I know him.

"Suspicious circumstances?"

"No sign of it." He sounded really beat.

"The door wasn't locked?"

"The nurse can't remember. She thinks she locked it when Linda left the first time, but . . . It's just a dead bolt, babe. Sylvia would've only had to turn the knob—you don't need a key on the inside."

And with the nurse busy clattering pans in the kitchen, she hadn't heard any click of the bolt drawing back.

"I thought Sylvia was under sedation," I said.

"Well, that's the thing. The doctor had her on Xanax."

Xanax. Whoa. That'll warp you some. It makes you drowsy and clumsy and really, really out of it, so maybe that's what was bothering Mike. It doesn't mean that you *couldn't* get it together to sneak out the door, I guess, but most of the people I've seen who were on it weren't capable of that much coherency.

"Why would she go?"

"Linda thought maybe she'd come to see me."

"You?"

"She said Sylvia kept talking about me yesterday, all mixed up with other stuff, rambling. Probably because I helped her last weekend. But how would she get to me, Meg? She didn't have any money for taxis or anything. God, she wasn't even dressed!" He was upset again, I could hear it. Anxious.

"Nightgown?" I said.

"Yeah, something of Linda's. Pajamas or something."

Because they'd put her to bed.

"Did Linda call you right away?"

"Pretty much. She got me right around six. I was just back from the gym."

"So you went over and searched the area? You and Linda?"

"We drove up and down the damn blocks, babe. Poked everywhere, and asked all the neighbors, the ones who were in. Nobody'd seen her. Not a clue."

But she could have been passed out under somebody's bushes or in the back of a car speeding elsewhere. He didn't need to hear me say it.

"You said you checked all the hospitals?"

"Yeah."

Twelve hours ago. More or less. I hate damn round numbers. Hated to ask it.

"And the morgue?"

"L.A.'s," he said.

It really is hell knowing where to start looking.

"Well, the Xanax would have worn off," I said, "don't you think so, by now?"

"Yeah."

And she hadn't, obviously, called in, so I didn't ask that.

"Did you tell Beverly PD?" It was technically LAPD's jurisdiction, over there at Linda's. LAPD wouldn't take a Missing Person's report, not yet, it hadn't been twenty-four hours, but under the circumstances, I would think BHPD would be willing to have Patrol keep an eye out for Sylvia, in case she was trying to get home.

"Yeah, I went by and talked to Jacoby this morning after I stopped at the office."

Ah.

This morning.

Mike's page for me from the office.

And then he'd gone over to the station to see Jacoby.

"Kind of early?"

"Eight-thirty or nine."

Reilly'd called his guys from his bedroom about seven-thirty this morning, so he wouldn't have heard it from anyone then, but Sylvia's disappearance might have been a hot topic when he got to the station around ten after dropping me off at the motel in Brentwood. So Reilly most likely knew that Sylvia was missing when he answered my page.

Which would pretty well explain his reaction when I was telling him about taping the guy on the phone, about me telling the guy I was Sylvia.

The guy being the one who'd beaten her up.

"Did you go by her house, Mike?"

"A couple of times."

It was a natural place to look, if she was slightly drugged and hazy and had somehow found her way.

"Anybody there?"

"Just some guy, a repairman or something. He hadn't seen her."

A repairman or something.

Not a repairman at night—

"This *morning*?"

"What?"

"You went there this morning, Mike?"

"Yeah."

Holy Mama and Mother of Pearl. My fingers were tight on the phone.

"What time?"

"Hell, I don't know—after I talked to Jacoby. Why?"

Mike would have been there nine-thirtyish? I'd called the house at eleven.

"Was this guy Argentine?" But Mike wouldn't know that. "Latino?" I said.

"Yeah, I think so."

"He had an accent? Spanish?"

"Yeah."

Okay.

"What'd he look like, Mike?"

He was following my tone, picking up on it. "Short—five-eight or five-nine. Medium build. A hundred and seventy pounds, kind of muscular, no obvious marks. Black hair, and a mustache. What's the deal, Meggie?"

"Big mustache?" I said. "Coarse hair?"

"Yeah."

It sure sounded like my friend from the beach.

"There was a guy at Sylvia's house this morning around eleven," I said. "I called over there looking for you."

"So?"

"So he's the guy who beat her up, Mike. I've got him on tape."

There was a noncomprehending silence for a second, and then— "De la Peña beat her up."

"No," I said, "I don't think so. He denied it, I told you that."

"Meg—"

"Mike, there weren't any marks on his hands." I was staring at the phone cord, the twisted, silvery coil. His ring had been the same color last Friday night, glinting in the barlight—platinum, maybe, but carats for sure. Manicured nails on those resolute fingers, the clear polish shining as he lifted his liqueur glass and sipped. It's not easy to hit someone repeatedly, hard enough to leave bruises, without getting any marks of your own, particularly if you're hitting the facial area with all of its angles and its unpadded bone. You'd have scrapes, at least, some abrasions. Would a manicure fix that? "Goshdarn, Mr. D, you go on and soak 'em—whatever have you done to your hands?"

"Listen to me," I said urgently. "I told this guy on the phone that I was Sylvia, I acted drugged up, you know? Dazed. I asked him what he wanted, and he said I knew what he wanted and then he started calling me names. He was calling *Sylvia* names, Mike. *Puta*, like that. Whore. I told him he'd hurt me, and he just laughed and said I deserved it."

"Goddammit, Meg—"

"No, *listen* to me—I don't know what it is, Mike, okay? I don't know that she was screwing around, I'm not saying that. Maybe this guy's off his rocker imagining things. Maybe he just flat out attacked her and that's why she ran."

Mike wasn't having any little bit of it. "She said it was De la Peña."

He gets an idea lodged, you know?

Still—

"'De la Peña'?" I said. "Or 'my husband'?"

"Look," he started angrily, firing up, and then he stopped cold. "Oh, hell."

"'*Mi esposo*,' Mike?"

"Yeah."

I hate that term. It's irrational and I know it. Circumstantial. A long time ago, when I was new, they transferred a call back to me. I was working the desk, working dispatch that night, and nobody else much spoke Spanish. I had some, my street slang. She kept moaning, "*Mi esposo . . . mi vida*," and I'd sent out the units but I was trying to get more. "He hurt you?" I said. "*Su esposo*?" And she wouldn't tell me he did her, she just bled to death on the phone.

That might have been driving me, I don't know. We are what we are.

"So maybe she had a first husband," I said. "Whatever. Even Catholics divorce. The main thing is to find her and get her in. We can sort it out once she's safe."

"This guy's out there looking for her, Meg."

I could hear all his fear, his frustration. It's the awareness of things that go wrong in the world, and your own limitations.

And Sylvia in a nightgown somewhere, lost and confused.

"She'll be okay, Mike," I said. "Because I'm pretty sure that, right now, this guy's looking for me."

I had to go through the whole thing then for Mike—the phone call, the taping, my flight from the station.

"Reilly doesn't know about the 'cutting me' part, babe, okay? You don't need to tell him."

"I'm not telling him anything."

Well—

"You've got to give him the description," I said. "Him or Jacoby. I think they'll have played the tape by now. It's not an absolute—it might not be the same guy. I mean, there isn't a positive link because there's the ninety-minute gap between when you were there and when I called the house, but I really want Beverly PD to know about him anyway."

Especially if it was the guy from the beach, the man with thick arms.

"Did he say what he was doing there, Mike?"

"Fixing stuff, I thought. I don't remember if he actually said it or not. He was carrying a hammer and some screwdrivers when he answered the door."

He hadn't attacked Mike with them, though. I was feeling a little cold there in the alcove, facing the hall.

"Did you tell him who you were?"

"No, I don't think so, not really. I just said I was looking for Sylvia, and I thought maybe she would've come home."

"Did you mention Linda?"

Kind of a pause.

"God, yeah, I did. I gave him the number in case Sylvia showed up."

Spilt milk.

"You'd better call her, too, then."

"I will," Mike said.

"She at work?"

"Yeah, I think so."

Thirteen floors above me.

"Tell her not to go home by herself, right? And maybe have the cops check out the place."

"Yeah, I'm going to call her now. You think Reilly's at the station?"

He probably was.

"I would just call Jacoby," I said. "There's no need to go by. Keep it short and sweet. You almost done there?"

"Just about. There's a couple more things, but I can catch them tomorrow. Tovarsen wasn't really expecting me."

You know, I'd *thought* it was set up for next week. A prime example of why I handle the schedules.

"You be careful," I said.

"Yeah, you, too, 'Gie. When am I talking to you again? This pager stuff just isn't cutting it."

"I know," I said. "I keep forgetting to wear it. You want me to call you at five?"

"I don't want you out there that long."

He was getting that take-charge attitude going, too. Is it a guy thing, a cop thing, a friend thing? I guess I'm as bad—I kept hearing the psychopath's voice: "the 'old friend' where you stay . . . I know who he is—" I didn't really want to go all afternoon without hearing from Michael, either. We were going to have to do something about cellular phones. Get walkie-talkies. Tin cans with string.

"I don't know what all you'll be doing, Mike."

"Not a whole lot else." His voice roughened. "I'm going to call and give Jacoby the description and then I'm going out again looking for Sylvia."

Driving the streets. Calling her friends one more time. UCLA.

"So you don't know, really, where you'll be when," I said.

"I'll end up back at Linda's," he said. "At the bungalow."

"Mike—"

"The guy's welcome to come, 'Gie—I don't mind it at all. And I just don't know where else she'd go back to."

Sylvia.

"Okay," I said. "Then let's make it five o'clock. That gives us both enough time. I don't have the number there, though, or the address."

He gave them to me. I wrote them down on my scrap of paper, the same one I'd taken from Reilly's desk when I'd copied the Madrigala information off his computer screen. Which reminded me—

"There's one other thing," I said. "If there's a change of plans or whatever, leave a message about it for Susan Abbott, Room Forty-one, at the Brentwood Motel. Or if you don't hear from me, let's say by five-thirty, then get hold of Reilly and tell him, okay? About the motel."

"I don't like this," he said.

Well, see, that was two of us.

"Not to worry," I said lightly, as in Famous Last Words. "This guy doesn't know where I am."

# 29

The dead guy might not know where I was, but *I* surely did. I was in an alcove off a building lobby in Century City, hanging up the receiver on a pay phone on the wall. I hadn't quite managed to convey that to Mike. "Me? Oh, I'm just here in the lobby of your new girlfriend's building. . . ." I couldn't somehow see saying that. "Call and warn her? No, hon, I'm right here, I'll just run up and tell her. . . ."

Life's full of guilt and betrayals. You learn how to live with it.

I wasn't really there spying on anyone. I was just looking around, getting a little background, a little *necessary* background. This girlfriend came attached to a death, okay? Under disturbing circumstances.

I had some time to spend before five, and I had no particular other direction to go. I was already here. And she might not even work here—I didn't know for sure that her law office was part of Madrigala Internacional—so what would be the point of discussing it with Mike? Better to find out I was wrong by my own stupid self.

So I finished hanging up the phone on the wall in that alcove off the building lobby in Century City. Building lobbies have directories, and they sometimes also have guards, but this guard hadn't minded me much. I went back down the corridor.

He looked up and saw me.

I smiled nicely.

He smiled back.

Two polite people. Nobody else in the echoing, cavernous hall. We looked away from each other again quickly so as not to intrude or to seem to invite, and I moved on to study the building directory.

I absorb things.

I'm the kind of person who stands right in front, reading every last entry there on the wall while you're trying to crane past me to find out your particular office and floor. It's a character flaw, but it's useful to me. I look at the wall coverings, the decorating schemes. I notice little details like the matching seams in the carpeting, the juxtaposition of marble tile and brass inlay, the water stains that indicate building repair. Reconstruction. Gives me more of a feel for the place.

This building had fifteen floors.

Madrigala Internacional was on the fourteenth. I looked all over that dang directory, but I couldn't spot a nonsuperstitious thirteenth-floor suite of offices listed at all.

I could have taken an elevator, I guess—there were three of them, shiny and brass-faced in a row at the back of the lobby. Nobody was using them. I'm just a stair kind of person—an exercise fiend. What's fourteen floors?

And this way, I could open the stairwell door very quietly, no dinging bell to announce my arrival, no big double doors whooshing open onto a reception lobby or something, with people looking up to note my arrival.

I'm a *stealth* exercise fiend, see? I like to keep my exertions to myself.

The stairwell was back by the telephone alcove. I double-checked something, very obviously, in my purse—my appointment book—and then looked at my watch. Dang. Looked at the directory again, fairly quickly, the listings, looked at the watch one more time, and then made up my mind. Better go make that one other call. I retraced my steps past the guard again, smiled briefly, apologetically, and hurried back towards the telephone corridor. He'd sort of looked up from the magazine he was reading, and then back down again when he saw where I was heading. Been there. Done that. I skated past the alcove and through the stairwell door on one breath.

It was an office building stairwell, nothing fancy. Beige paint, concrete steps, iron railings. Pipes and some shut-off valves. Signs. Sometimes, in hotels, they'll dress up the bottom floor or two of the stairwells with paneling and carpet—it looks better, I guess, when the door swings open from the lobby floor. They hadn't bothered here. It was purely utilitarian.

I made my way up the stairs and stopped at the second-floor door. Some buildings lock their stairwell doors, setting them up to open only from the inside so that you can't reenter on a different level. They don't mind you going all the way down to the lobby, but they don't want you prowling the floors in between. Some buildings even rig up their doors with alarms. I hadn't seen any sign of a roaming guard, but that didn't mean that there wasn't one. I hadn't noticed any security cameras in the stairwell, either, but we sell some that are tricked up to look like fire sprinklers in the ceiling, so again—better to find out the bad news, if there was any, on the second floor, rather than all the way up on the fourteenth.

I tried the door.

It opened.

No audible alarms went off. No guards or Rottweilers came running.

I tried the handle on the other side of the opened door. It turned very easily both ways.

I closed the door again quietly and went on up to the third floor—same-same.

Fourth floor—ditto.

Fifth floor was locked.

That was kind of interesting.

I couldn't remember, off hand, what the directory'd said about the fifth floor, who it was who occupied those suites. Secretive people.

# Hook

The sixth-floor door was unlocked on both sides, with the hall beyond it looking innocently beige all the way to the bend. I went out into it, keeping an eye on the several closed white doors with their discreet golden suite numbers tacked into the wood. I pied a cautious arc around the corner and saw another straight corridor with more of the same, closed white doors and numbers. The three elevator portals opened onto a slightly wider lobby area, facing a floor-to-ceiling tempered-glass window with some sort of frondy potted trees placed so they'd frame it. They might have been giant ferns. I'm not good with plants. There were two ladies, fashionable heels and skirts, admiring the view through the fronds while they waited for one of the elevators to arrive. At least, that's what it looked like. They were chatting with each other calmly and the call button was lit. The corridor continued on past them, closed white doors on both sides of the hall, but down this particular stretch of the hallway there were gold placards screwed onto the doors below the suite numbers, announcing company names and occupancy.

I went back to my empty stairwell.

Seventh floor was open.

Eighth.

Nine through eleven.

Twelve was locked.

I went back to eleven.

It looked like the same type of innocent corridor as on floor number six, in subtle shades of gray this time, the same bend, the same view of the hallway with the elevator portals. No frondy plants framing the window, no ladies-in-waiting. It was a very quiet floor, so I slipped very quietly myself down the hallway and stopped beside the elevators. They have to post a floor plan of the building on every floor, with the exits clearly marked and so on. It's a building code. Fire safety stuff. They usually put them right next to the elevators to direct everyone to the stairs in case of an emergency. People aren't supposed to take the elevators then. That's because they could inadvertently go right to a floor that's on fire, say, where the car would automatically open its doors and draw in the flames. Whoosh. Not a good thing.

Of course, technology came up with a method to fix that little problem, too. In the event of a fire emergency, with the alarms going off and so on, the elevators are supposed to recall themselves instantly and automatically to the ground floor, where they lock themselves down and *won't* respond to call buttons being pressed up above. That's another good reason to know where the stairwells are in any high-rise, and not to waste a lot of time standing around waiting for elevators that won't come, when the building's on fire.

I studied the floor plan. It had the same general outline as the floor I'd scanned earlier. Two stairwells noted. The stairwell I'd come up was to my left, around the bend, and the second stairwell was at the far end of the hall, to the right. I padded on down the hall, still quietly and with an eye on the closed office doors, and tested. The stairwell door there wasn't locked. I went on in and up the flight of stairs to floor twelve. That door *was* locked. So much for that clever notion. I slinked—slunk?—on up the stairs and around.

There wasn't officially a thirteenth floor, since it could bring you bad luck, I guess, so the stairwell door here was marked "14."

Madrigala Internacional's floor.

Just for the heck of it, I put my hand on the stairwell's doorknob.

The door was locked.

We all value our privacy—certainly *I* do. And I also think people should have to come to my front door and ring the bell if they want to see me, rather than slinking around to the back door and trying the knob. I'm not saying I don't understand locked doors. I absolutely do.

The explanation could be as simple as "It's a company and they rent the whole floor." They don't have those individual tack-numbered suites with doors they can lock when they're going to lunch, so they've found it simpler to lock off the entire floor. That would stop casual visitors like me who go hiking stairwells just to see what's around.

Some visitors who hike stairwells like to lift purses, for instance, from unwary people with untended desks.

Or maybe they did top-secret research there, do you think? With security clearances required and so on. *I'd* pick a Century City office building for that.

I considered the doorknob.

It required a key.

I've picked a few locks in my time—purely for practice and the knowledge, of course—and it doesn't need much in the way of tools of the trade. Things have gotten more electronic these days, but technology keeps pace, even for bad guys.

It would be a pain if the dang thing was alarmed, though.

I contemplated the door.

One of the lesser-known features of the building code in L.A. is that besides the elevator recall, all locked doors must automatically *unlock* in the event of a fire alarm. You can't have people trapped in a multistory building, unable to get down the stairwells to safety for lack of a key. Rescue workers unable to reach them, that sort of thing.

I went up to the fifteenth floor, the top one. The stairs above went up and around to the roof, but signs on the wall were very clearly meant to discourage anyone from continuing up there. Signs don't discourage me. *People* do, but signs don't. However, when I got to the very tip-top, the large words on the door there in English and Spanish and some type of Arabic said, EXIT ONLY TO ROOF—DOOR IS ALARMED, and that was sufficient for me. When a door is alarmed, so am I.

I returned to floor fifteen, and it was an important floor, I'd think—the penthouse suites—but its door wasn't even a little bit sticky, not locked at all. I opened it slightly and peered down the hall. There were people there chatting briskly near a door halfway down, papers in hand and attaché cases, a slung purse or two. They appeared to be moving towards the elevator well. Lunchtime dispersement. I pressed the door almost shut, barely open, and waited for the *ding* of an elevator arriving. It came. The chatting swelled higher. The doors *ding*ed again and closed. I couldn't hear any sound of people talking or moving, but I gave it another twenty seconds, counting them off to myself to be sure. One one thousand, two one thousand, three one thousand, four.

I opened the stairwell door more fully and looked through the gap. No one was left in the hall, so I went out fairly quickly, looking around. There was a pull-station right beside me on the wall—a pull-station being that six-inch red square with the lever inside that you're supposed to yank down in the event of a fire. It sets off the alarms and lets everyone know there's a problem.

The problem is that, once yanked, it's clear evidence of tampering. You can't put the lever back up and walk away whistling. It also very specifically reports the emergency location back to the guards. It identifies itself electronically to them as, say, Pull-Station, Stairwell Two, Floor Fifteen.

I absolutely didn't want to pinpoint any trouble that precisely, or to have it look like anything the least bit deliberate.

On the other hand, there were smoke detectors built into the ceiling every thirty feet. I was standing right below one. Smoke detectors are wired to share a common electrical loop, so they can only report an emergency in a general area—East Corridor, Floor Fifteen, for example—meaning that there would be several places that people would have to go to, to check. It would take those people a little more time to test all the detectors and return things to normal.

And one of the better-known, more-annoying aspects of smoke detectors is that they'll go off for dust or a puff of wind or cigarette smoke, at which point they get the door locks unlocking just like the pull-stations, but there aren't any of those broken connections to find. They also don't alarm the whole building and bring out the fire department in force, because everyone knows they can go off for nothing. It would set off the audibles and the strobes on this floor, and certainly the building engineers or the guard would come hurrying to discover which detector it was and to shut it back down, but it wouldn't occasion any remark or a search. They'd just want to be sure that there wasn't a fire, and then everyone would go right back to work. No reason not to.

As long, that is, as nobody came out of an office right now and spotted me standing under this particular smoke detector right next to the stairwell, waving my several wadded-up burning pages of appointment book at the thing. I don't smoke, but I always carry at least one book of matches—I like to have flame when all other light fails—and I can act fairly quickly when everything's a go.

The smoke wafted, drifted. I waved again, a little bit closer, and by golly, it's nice to be right. The ceiling strobe lights started revolving, a loud bell began ringing, and I was already down the corridor and through the stairwell door. I raced down the first flight of steps, squashing the burning pages against me—I got a singed hand, that'll teach me—and rounded the corner, leaping steps.

Floor fourteen.

The doorknob turned.

You breathe fast when you've been moving, and I had to be quiet. I didn't know for sure what was going to be there. I couldn't look guilty and I couldn't stay here much longer in case the engineers would be using this stairwell to reach the top floor to check the alarm. I hauled myself up, took a deep breath. Took another.

Opened the door.

I expected to see a number of things on floor fourteen. Madrigala Internacional's offices, for one thing—for maybe even the only thing—walls demolished and desks positioned everywhere, in cubicles, perhaps.

What I *wasn't* expecting to see, directly across the corridor from me next to one of the frosted-glass-inset, thick oaken doors that lined the hallway, was the engraved marble placard that read DE LA PEÑA.

# 30

Reilly might have a point. I *do* sometimes take chances. The door was there, I was there, I'd gone to a lot of trouble to get onto this floor.

The plan I'd been forming until then had been simply to wander a little backstage, as it were, get a feel for the show, and then either fade into the wings or stride brazenly stage front and center, wanting Linda Madrigala. If I were discovered. If I needed a reason.

Why was I there? Urgent message for Linda from Mike. How'd I get in? Why, through the stairwell door, of course—it wasn't locked. I'd gotten off at the wrong floor below on the elevator and thought the stairs would be faster.

Something like that. Calmly factual. Sure of myself. *As* myself. The charred pieces of appointment book pages were already shoved deep into my jeans front pocket, undetectable short of a full-scale search.

But I was inches now from a door with a placard that said DE LA PEÑA, on Madrigala Internacional's floor, and that changed everything.

I'd thought that I'd asked Mike if Linda knew De la Peña, if that's how Linda and Sylvia met, and I could have sworn he'd said no.

People get things wrong. Mike had been repeating what Linda had told him, and maybe she'd left off that one little extra. Or maybe they'd all gotten friendly *after* the Free Argentina affair: "You're looking for office space? What a coincidence! We have a suite on our floor that we're wanting to lease out." Things like that happen. It can be a smallish community in a foreign country, where you'd naturally band together to speak your own language, live with what's comfortable. Support each other's endeavors.

Except that these weren't immigrant Vietnamese or border-crossing Mexicans. These weren't people scraping by, with English as their second language if they even had time to *learn* a second language what with running their little mom-and-pop grocery store sixteen or twenty hours a day as a family, making ends meet. Or standing on street corners downtown, hoping for pickup as day laborers in the suburbs, wherever, for a chancy few bucks. These people were Hidalgos. These were the wealthy ranchers back in Argentina—the ruling class. European-educated, many of them, and proud of it.

They might still cluster together, I suppose, in the foreign United States, but they cluster in ghettos like Beverly Hills, Miami, New York City. Places where the sense of wealth is what's comfortably familiar, and the aroma of dinner cooking isn't old sesame oil, fried rice, and fish, but fine French cuisine.

Places like Chaven's.

"*Polite*, tu sais, *as always he is . . .*"

Did Rudolfo have a regular table there?

I hadn't asked.

And I hadn't checked out the menu at all, remiss of me, but then I'd been otherwise occupied both times I'd gone. Did Chaven's have one of those specialty contracts for Argentine beef? Brought to them, perhaps, courtesy of Madrigala Internacional, an import sort of investment-looking firm? I *would* like to know what it was they imported.

And I really wanted to know what was behind that oak door.

No one was visible down the thickly carpeted hallway. I could hear murmured conversation from several of the open-doored offices farther down, but there wasn't a soul standing out at the moment to spot me. I crossed the hall and put my hand on the doorknob. It wasn't locked. It opened.

The room wasn't empty.

"I'm so sorry," I started, launching instantly into Concerned Good

Citizen, "but there's a fire alarm going off upstairs—" The five faces turned towards me, four dark, Latino, as startled as I was, but the blond one was rising at the far end of the room. I saw his boxer's broken nose, the memory-flash of his face from last Friday—the blond "boxair" from Chaven's—and I didn't even hesitate. I slammed the door closed and I ran.

Precipitate impulse.

I hit the stairwell door and was through it, already rounding the curve going down. Panicked flight. Twelve was a locked floor, a goddamn unknown. I passed its door in midair and kept going.

The stairwell door was thrown open above me. Everything echoes in stairwells, each clang amplified, the sound of feet pounding down. You don't think you can go any faster, but with the adrenaline surging, you can. I was leaping down multiple steps at a time. Caromed off a landing wall misjudging the turn, and corrected, rebounding, used the railing for leverage, and swung myself farther down and around. I think I was breathing, I can't say for certain—I was just flat out racing, and the guy behind me was making good time.

Ninth floor.

Eighth.

Thinking ahead.

Damn five was a locked floor.

Not locked at the moment.

Possibly.

He'd catch me before the lobby, I could hear him behind me through my own pounding drums. It was a straight sprint down, around and around, just mechanically turning, and he didn't need any great burst of speed, he could simply wear down the distance and lap me.

Seven.

Starting to flag. I'd lose crucial time stopping at five if the door had relocked.

I'd been on six, though. I knew the corridor layout, the elevator lobby with the two frondy trees.

He might not expect that.

I hit the sixth-floor landing and leaped for the door. Yanked it open with both hands, let the door-return shut it as I flashed down the hall. I'd made it just past the bend when I heard the stairwell door jolt open behind me, the metallic scrape unmistakable as the latch disengaged.

I stopped, frozen, hands up, desperately listening.

Could not hear a sound.

All around me was the electrical hum of the building, the overhead lighting, the faint background noise. My heart beating triple-time. I was breathing openmouthed very slowly, softly, fighting the body's urgent need to gasp, to gulp air, to ease the ache in my lungs.

Predators hear that.

So does the prey.

This guy had been racing, too, you know.

And he didn't know quite where I'd gotten to, which of the several door openings I might have gone through. He had the whole rabbit warren of offices up here to check, unless, of course, he heard me on this bare other side of the corner, breathing or sweating.

I damped down again. Pulled in that aura. Made myself one with the wall.

Finally, faintly, I heard the snick of the stairwell door closing shut. He'd been standing there holding it open, waiting like I was.

Listening.

This guy wasn't simply a muscle man, then, an ex-boxer, a bouncer.

This guy was a tracker. He had instincts. Had moves.

Had he moved in? Or had he moved back into the stairwell and, now, slipping ahead of me, was he heading down?

I strained to hear anything.

Pinched off the urge just to look. It would be so simple to poke a cautious eye out there—one quick blink and I'd know.

So would he.

It's the movement you notice. Movement or sound. Sometimes the smell, but human senses aren't as developed as those of animals are.

I heard a slight scrape down the hall. He was here, then. Coming towards me down the corridor. He'd brushed a wall, or had nudged something testing the doorknobs, looking for doors that would open.

How far away?

I couldn't tell. I started easing myself one cautious ball of a foot at a time towards the stairwell at the end of my hall. I was wishing I'd pushed the elevator call button, anything that would *ding*, that would make a sudden loud noise beside him or behind him, but I righteously hadn't had time. If he'd seen me before I'd made the corner, if he'd even just spotted a hint of my shadow, he would have come straight on down.

There'd have been no cautious anythings then. There'd have been nothing but flight when I was already beaten, or the option of fighting him there in the hall.

In Century City.

In an office building with who-knew-how-many workers who might know him, returning from lunch in time to call Security for him or to jump in and help him subdue me.

With charred pages in my pocket.

With a questionable building fire alarm, and four other people, Hidalgos, who'd seen me on their normally locked floor when I'd burst through an office door into their meeting and then took off running.

Fighting this guy wasn't much of an option.

Evading him was.

There was a loud *ding* from around the bend in the hall. It was a case of listening so hard for a particular sound that it took me a second to know what it was. An elevator arriving. That meant people, and this guy would be having to deal with the noise of them down the hall.

I was running then, silently, stretching out for the stairwell door. I tried to turn the handle surreptitiously, but hell if you can, everything always clangs, or it seems to—resonates, jars you. Jarred me for sure. I shoved that door open and flew down the stairs.

Five was locked. I didn't even try it. They *had* to have reset the electronics by now.

Four was coming up, but three sounded better, especially because the door had just banged open above me. I put on my last burst of speed, hit the landing, dragged down on the handle, and pulled desperately to open three's door. It came clanking and screeching wide open, but I was still moving, flitting like a dancer, a damn ballerina, down the next flight of stairs. I made the next landing, made the turn.

Froze.

The stairwell door on three was just groaning shut.

Thud.

And the guy above me was coming fast and furiously, I could feel the steps vibrate as he hurtled down. He hit three's landing and grabbed for the handle, hauled on the door.

Stopped.

Listening.

I didn't breathe.

He'd played this game before and this time he was pissed. He wasn't standing so still, he was angrily breathing. A whole nother floor lay in front of him, with its hallways and doors. Where could I be? Rabbiting away again like I thought it would help me—was I finding a hole? Scurrying back to the opposite stairwell?

Calling an elevator?

He slammed his hand against the doorframe and took a quick step to the stairs. I saw his shadow peering over the railing, looking down, trying angles, but I was a wisp against the wall underneath him and I wasn't breathing, I was just there. He'd have to come farther down into the stairwell in order to see me and I might already be laughing my way down the hall.

I willed him to think so.

Pulled in my horns.

The shadow straightened abruptly and I could hear the door open again.

Heard it close.

I didn't breathe, didn't move. One one thousand, two one thousand, three one thousand, four.

I heard the slight scrape of a shoe.

It wasn't mine.

How many spooks can you fit in a stairwell?

Finally, I heard him open the door again, felt him go through it. I waited anyway because I'm just like that until I thought I could put one foot in front of the other without shaking, and then I tiptoed my way down the last flight of stairs.

These were the stairs I'd originally gone up, kind of a while ago. They didn't go down to the parking garage, they stopped at the first floor. I exited through the door right next to the telephone alcove, down that corridor off the building lobby where my friendly guard sat.

I had no way of knowing where the boxer had gone—upstairs, downstairs, still combing the third floor? And I didn't know his position here at the building. A visitor? A valued employee of an international firm that was prompt with its rent and concerned for security, and that everyone therefore would be eager to please? Guards could be looking for me.

They probably weren't, but it always depends, and all things considered, I didn't want to be crossing that wide-open lobby with its guard and glass windows.

I still had to get to the parking garage and retrieve Reilly's ElCo. Get myself gone.

And I'm normally very law-abiding, or at least I like to think so, but I looked at the other door at the end of that hallway. It was marked EMERGENCY EXIT—ALARM WILL SOUND in the same choice of three languages, only this time I thought, what the hay? I needed an exit, it was a clear-cut emergency, so I pushed my way through it and batted like hell away from the building with the bell going crazy, because the thing about doors is they might be alarmed, but no way was this door as alarmed as *I* was.

# 37

I went back to Chaven's.

Where the hell else was I going to go?

The path intersected *there* Friday night—Chaven's, Rudolfo, the blond guy, and me.

I spent a half hour skulking around Century City first, working my way back on foot to the building's parking garage and Reilly's damn El Camino. I don't know if anyone saw me. Nobody stopped me. It was a little bit tense waiting in the underground line for the ticket-booth man to examine my ticket, punch-clock it in, and decide what to charge me. At times like that it's real tempting to think about throwing a twenty and a quick "Keep the change," but they don't hurry the gate up any faster, I've found, and the bonus confuses them, makes them more likely to remember you later, which isn't the point then at all.

I was using the ElCo's mirrors to see what was around me. Nobody was approaching me sideways on foot, there was nobody blond in the car right behind me. The ticket guy looked kind of bored. I thanked him briefly and drove out.

Chaven's.

There wasn't anyplace else.

I needed to know who this blond guy was. I needed a name, a starting point, something substantial. Going back by myself to Madrigala

Internacional and just simply asking was out of the question, and Chaven's was the only other link that I had.

The maître d' had recognized the blond-guy-the-boxer as a business friend of Rudolfo's, so it seemed likely that the blond guy had been at Chaven's before, with or without De la Peña. Somebody working the bar or the restaurant might know his name. I wasn't anxious to see the maître d' again, so soon after our little heart-to-heart in his office last night, but it was the middle of the afternoon, a weekday, so he might not be there, might only work evenings and weekends. It was a fair-enough chance.

What else did I have?

I could have postponed it, I guess. Could have killed time, had some soda and a lunch roll or something, and waited for Mike. I won't even say that it didn't occur to me.

Mike was worrying about Sylvia, though. As it should be. As it was. He was going to be driving around places all afternoon, looking for her. By the time I waited and called him at five, Linda would be at the bungalow, too, home from her office.

And I *still* didn't know that her office wasn't on the fourteenth floor of the building in Century City, that she wasn't part of Madrigala Internacional. She might know quite a bit more than I did about De la Peña and this blond guy, even about Free Argentina. She'd been at the fund-raiser.

I didn't want to sit, doing nothing, till five.

I was a little bit hungry, now that I'd thought of it. Lunch sounded good. And last time I'd been there, Chaven's had had food. Hell, this way I could look at a menu and order up a specialty steak if they had them. See what the fuss was.

It seemed like a good plan to me.

Hazards?

Well, yes, it was back in Beverly Hills.

BHPD might be there.

The maître d' might be there.

It might be a meeting place for Argentine gangsters. You can go on forever, you know? Talking yourself into or out of a thing. It saps your resolve. I put the ElCo into drive and headed back up to Santa Monica Boulevard, took the right with the light, and went on into town.

It was two o'clock, more or less. Rodeo Drive is the heart of Beverly Hills' shopping and eatery area, a popular place. There weren't any street parking spots open, but I didn't want parking structures and waiting in line. I had three hours before I had to call Mike—I could afford to be patient. I pokeyed around the block several times, turning corners, and eventually found a BMW nosing out from a meter, so I let it have room, snugged in behind it, and adopted the space. It still had time on the meter.

Sign from God.

Chaven's looked a lot more imposing than it had last Friday, or even last night. Something to do with the costume, I guess. I wasn't wearing one now.

Going in as myself.

Or it might have been that memory-flash of the blond guy. I *had* seen him there Friday night when I was talking to Artie. He'd been raising a drink with his back to the bar, scanning the crowd. It had registered at the time, but as nothing—a lone wolf dove-hunting—until I saw him again across the office in Century City. Those startled heads turning. Him rising, surprise giving way to something quite else. Determination and fury.

Rage.

Very personal rage.

I turned and went back to the El Camino, ignoring a gal in a Buick who paused, expectant, hoping to see me drive away from the space. I sat in the front seat with the doors locked securely and pulled Reilly's cellphone out of my bag.

The pager was in there, too. It wasn't vibrating at me, so no one had paged me, trying to find me. Not Mike. Not Reilly.

That was okay. I have trouble remembering the number myself.

I fished out the little card I had for the Brentwood Motel and called Susan Abbott again. The courteous desk guy still sounded efficient, was still very willing to take a message for Susan once we'd established that she wasn't in. He switched me to voice mail this time, though. My own voice, recording whatever I wanted. Fifty whole seconds' worth.

"Susan," I said, "or Reilly—whoever—this is Meg Gillis." God, it sounded like Last Will and Testament time. "It's two-fifteen, Tuesday. I'm going into Chaven's to get a name, if I can, for a blond guy: mid-thirties, short-haired, stocky, five-ten or eleven, two hundred pounds in very good shape. His nose is crooked, like it's been broken a couple of times. He's possibly a boxer, possibly a bodyguard. He met with De la Peña Friday night at Chaven's after I served the divorce papers and I just saw him again at Madrigala Internacional in Century City in De la Peña's office with four other guys. He came after me, so I want to know who he is, and Chaven's is the only other place where I know that he's been. The maître d' there is the one who told me about him meeting De la Peña last Friday."

I couldn't, for the life of me, think what else to say, what else to leave Reilly, and I'd be out of time soon.

"Mike," I said hastily. "Mike's going to be at Linda Madrigala's bungalow sometime around five. You can reach him at—" and I read off the phone number from the back of my paper, the scrap I'd brought with me from Reilly's. I still had half a second.

"I'm really sorry," I started, and the recording line shut off.

Okay.

That was that, then.

Time to move on.

I restowed the pager and the phone in my bag, and stripped back the leather flap for the Colt. I knew the condition the Colt was in, you bet I did, cocked-and-locked, but if you have the time, why wouldn't you check? I had plenty of time.

It was right.

Press-check. Index by feel, cartridge in the chamber. Magazine full. Safety back on.

All systems Go, Captain, ready when you are.

I climbed out of the ElCo and locked it back up. Brushed my hand against the clip on the Spyderco knife in my pocket, my right front jeans pocket. Unobtrusively handy. The touch reminded me of the charred appointment book pages still wadded up in there. I slipped them into one of the sidewalk trash cans as I walked by.

Got to Chaven's.

You pull open the door and go in. It's not hard to do. I didn't even have to expend that much effort, because two people were leaving, the door swinging towards me as I reached for the handle. I sidestepped to let them get out of the doorway and blocked the door on the back-swing.

No maître d' at the podium.

No one immediately there that I recognized.

I went on in.

It was just past the lunch hour, small groups milling in various corners, putting on suit coats and gathering up packages. It was still a trendy, business-type atmosphere, heady with movers and shakers and high-powered lunches, but lightened a bit, halfway between Monday night's work-ethic feeling and Friday night's aura of ultrachic watering hole.

I walked past the several small groups to the podium, with its discreet velvet rope.

"Table for one, mademoiselle?"

It wasn't my French maître d', it was a short lady, bird-size, sweeping in from my left. She had menus and an inquisitive air, eyebrows raised, looking me over. I wasn't dressed like a mover and shaker, but she'd have seen tourists before.

"Yes, thank you," I said.

She escorted me around the podium, unclipping the rope from its post, reclipping behind me, and led me towards the back of the sanctum sanctorum, with its gleaming white-linened tables, its silvery ware.

There's no point in worrying about something if opening your mouth will get you the answer.

"The maître d'," I said, "the one who was here Friday night—he isn't working today?"

"Monsieur Abregard?" She was reappraising again, a touch cooler.

"It might have been Abregard, I can't quite remember. A very dignified gentleman?"

"Oh, yes, he is. Yes. Very dignified." Not nearly as dignified as this little lady. She was ice now, personified. "He won't be in until sometime tomorrow."

"Well, I was just wondering," I said. We were at the table, my table, a smallish one suitable for a single diner like me, or perhaps a close couple. It was in the far corner, on a line with the archway that led to the kitchens and the manager's office with that sometimes-locked door. "I was hoping to ask him about a blond gentleman who was here Friday night."

"A blond gentleman?"

"He was mostly at the bar," I said, watching her. "A gentleman in his thirties, I'd guess, with very short hair. He's a business associate, if I'm remembering correctly, of Rudolfo de la Peña. Looks like a boxer, very capable and fit. A broken nose."

She knew who he was. The menu she was holding out to me wavered ever so slightly. I took it.

"I'm sorry, I don't have any idea," she said. "Perhaps you could check back tomorrow."

"He's a tracker," I said, moving a chair out and sitting. "Or maybe a bouncer? Some sort of security, I think."

"I don't know."

She did.

This man had chased me down twelve flights of stairs and she knew who he was.

"He might have hurt someone," I said.

She was very still. Fragile under all of her sophistication. She was staring at the white expanse of the tablecloth, and you have to let things develop, you can't press too soon. Finally, there was a whisper of sound.

"Are you police?"

"Private."

"Who—" She couldn't get the words out. Tried again. "Who did—?"

"A woman," I said.

She might have been thirty, she might have been forty-five. I had no way of knowing. People preserve well these days and makeup conceals things. I'd just had the impression of older till now. Until now when she was torn and perturbed with emotion, a vestige of fear.

We were all children once.

"I only want his name," I said quietly, looking at the tablecloth myself. "A little bit of background. He won't know where it came from."

"He will—"

"No, he won't," I said. "Not from me."

You can hear the truth sometimes, if you're able to listen. Sometimes you're even able to say it. She was very tautly controlled.

"Gunter Heinreichs. He works at Madrigala Internacional."

It was enough. It was something. Maybe all that I could get, or *would* get, if I tried to compel her.

"Thank you."

She looked at me, startled, started walking away. Two steps, a third, and then she turned back again. A thin husk. A reed.

"He uses a knife," she said.

# 32

I didn't waste a lot of time leaving Chaven's. I settled into my chair, thanked the busboy for water, and looked at the menu I had in my hand for a couple of minutes to give the maîtresse d' time to get back to the front unremarkably, and also to see if they specialized in Argentine beef. There was steak on the menu, in varying cuts and sizes, but "Iowa corn-fed" was the description. Most everything else was *tournadoes of boeuf* or something like that. I'm not big on beef whirling around.

About the time that a waiter was finally approaching, I had my pager out, and Reilly's cellphone, and I was busily making a Very Important Call. I motioned the guy to hold on while I said into the cellphone, "But I was just having lunch—this can't wait?" like a person who knew darned good and well that the call could have waited if only the imbeciles back at the office were anything competent. I listened with obvious annoyance to the dead air on my phone and finally cut it off with "Fine. Tell him I'll be right back, okay?" Punched off the Power button and said to the waiter, "I'm so sorry. I guess I'll have to skip the tornadoes today. These goddamn people."

Oh, he understood, yes, he did—perhaps something to go?

"Thanks," I said, "but I just don't have time—the *big* boss is in, and he's going to fire the office if I don't get right back there. I'm really sorry for the trouble."

No trouble at all.

Another nice man.

The maîtresse d' was nowhere in sight at the podium. I thought about asking if she was all right, but how could I? Why would I? My whole little scene with the waiter had been so that no one would link her, so I kept on going, pushed through the door, emerged into sunlight and a street full of people. Shoppers. Tourists.

Oblivious folk.

I brushed my forearm against the hilt of the blade in my pocket. Felt the weight of the Colt.

*"He uses a knife."*

Welcome to the world.

I reached Reilly's truck without incident. Slid into the front seat, relocked the doors. I still had time on the meter, not a surprise, because what had that taken—twenty minutes?—and I'd put in change for an hour, so I dragged out Reilly's cellphone one more time and punched in the numbers for the Brentwood Motel while I sat at the curb.

"Yes, hello, it's Susan Abbott," I said. "Do I have any messages?"

I had three.

The first and the third ones I knew because I was the person who'd left them.

The one in the middle was Mike.

"Meg," he'd said on the voice mail, sounding stoked and on fire the way only Mike can, "it's urgent, okay? It's really, really important. You've got to meet me at your motel room as soon as you can get there. I'm leaving now and I'll be sitting outside. It's, um, jeez, one-thirty."

Goddammit.

Dammit to hell.

I hadn't checked it before because I hadn't been thinking. I'd *told* him to leave me a message if there was a problem, but I'd thought he'd call later—if five o'clock wouldn't work, say. I hadn't thought he'd have news right away. He hadn't paged me at all, but then he'd have been driving, phoneless, not waiting at Tovarsen's or a place I could reach. Not to mention that I hadn't been so responsive, lately, to pages.

225

Figure one-thirty to two, more or less, for the drive.

He'd been sitting half an hour already, then. Forty-five minutes by the time I could get there.

Mike's not the most patient guy.

I threw the ElCo into gear, and slid out of the space. Did the quick double-check with the mirrors and made a few extra turns on my way out of Beverly, but as far as I could tell I didn't have a shadow. I took the south roads to Brentwood, a different approach, and turned north on Bundy Drive.

Went past the motel.

Mike's Camaro was there in the parking lot, with him there, too, visibly inside it. He was listening to music or reading a magazine. I turned at the corner and made my way back, pulled in right beside him, on his passenger side.

"Hey, Michael," I said, and I'm not the most careful girl going after all, because I was focused on Mike climbing out of his car, I was busy getting myself out to meet him, and it was just the peripheral half-glimpse that warned me, the slightest of movements in the doorway behind.

Someone was there.

In the office doorway.

Watching.

I turned, eye-to-eye, and it was Reilly.


"I had to, babe," Mike was saying. He had my arm in a vise grip and was shaking it hard. "I had to get you in. Are you listening?"

I was listening.

He'd conspired with Reilly. Guys will do that, it's a pack kind of thing.

I just hadn't thought Mike would.

"Leave it," Reilly said. "She doesn't want to hear you." He had a twist in his voice, an edgy disgust. Disgusted with me?

Probably.

"I'm okay," I said coolly. "But I don't want to stand out here talking about it. Are you both coming in?"

It didn't look a lot like anyone wanted to, which was all right with me. I disengaged Mike from my arm and got out my keys. And they were, by God, exchanging aggravated glances, fed-up-male kind of glances.

"Meg," Mike said forcefully, "it isn't Ernesto Ayala who's out there."

"I know," I said, "it's the blond guy. His name's Gunter Heinreichs. Are you sure you don't want to come in?"

I do like turning tables.

I had the room key by then, but Reilly was in my way, had moved in, looking down at me, and face-to-face with him, I couldn't quite carry it off. He took the key from me, right out of my hand, nodded rather grimly when he saw that I'd let him, and went over himself to open the door. Checked out the room. He didn't take very long. Mike was keeping me silent company but he clearly was waiting for Reilly to reappear in the doorway and give the okay.

Reilly did.

It was nice to know that there wasn't a bogeyman under the bed. I locked up Reilly's El Camino before I went in. Left Mike to lock up his own.

I was maybe simmering more than a little, wasn't maybe my best self. It had been a long day. I took the defensive position at the back of the room, not quite looking at Reilly, and waited for Mike to come in. He ranged himself next to Reilly, both of them there by the window.

"So this is a switch," I said, "the two of you bonding. What brought this on?"

"You want to knock it off?" Reilly said, but I couldn't. I don't know what was driving me. Mike was cranked and distinctly put out, me chewing at him in front of Reilly, and normally I handle things better than this.

"Look, babe," Mike said aggressively, "I called the station, and that was *your* idea, remember? To give 'em the description of the guy I saw at Sylvia's this morning?"

Yeah, I remembered.

"But they already had him. They'd pulled him in off the street, driving around, and they've got him sitting in a cell while I'm calling. I don't mind telling you that made me feel better. I didn't like you going off on your own, anyway—we talked about that."

He was fixing me with a disapproving eye before Reilly, and yeah, okay, we had. We didn't need to dwell on that particular subject or get into the details.

"And then Reilly tells me that Ernesto can't be the guy on your tape because they already had him then, right? At the time you would have been calling the house, Reilly had Ernesto out talking on the street."

*Reilly* had him talking? I looked over at Reilly, and his face was expressionless. Deadpan. He'd been out when I'd paged him, away from the station. I remembered him saying, "He was at Sylvia's house?" "Fifteen minutes ago," I'd said, and he had to have known right then that it wasn't the beach guy. Wasn't Ernesto Ayala.

"You didn't want to just tell me?" I said, and Reilly wasn't budging, wasn't giving any quarter, drawling it out like a finely honed insult.

"Think you hung up on me."

Dammit.

Dammit to hell.

"Did he tell you 'Gunter'?"

He nodded.

"So you effing *knew* that already?"

"Yeah, I did," he said.

God.

I could have saved my whole damn adventure then, the twisting and turning, the chasing down stairs. Reilly'd had people just handing it to him.

"How'd you find him?"

"I put the vehicle information out with Patrol when I called in this morning," he said, "just in case."

In case Ernesto was coming to Beverly Hills, he meant, stalking me, since Valley Division had reported his car gone from the house in Van Nuys and nobody knew what it was he was up to. In case he was hanging out by my office or something, Beverly's Patrol could be looking. As they had been. So they'd found him.

"Where was he?"

"About a block south of Sylvia's."

They'd have detained him there while they radioed in to the station so that Reilly could go out to chat if he wanted, at least write up a Field Interview card, see identification. Talk about bumper stickers.

Group affiliations.

And then I'd paged him to tell him about the Spanish guy answering the phone at Sylvia's, told him I'd taped the guy saying he hit her, so Reilly had had something else to discuss with Ernesto—like who all had been at the house that morning, and does this voice sound familiar.

Which was the reason he'd been able to come up with Gunter.

I was glad to have been of some service, I guess.

I don't know why it felt so much instead like I'd lost it, the little bit of leverage I'd had.

"Did he talk about Free Argentina?"

"Yeah."

Reilly wasn't going to tell me, though. I hadn't behaved. And he had the upper hand here, so why should he?

Because even worms turn.

"You could have just said 'Gunter Heinreichs,'" I said sideways to Mike, "on the message you left me."

"I didn't think you'd know who he was."

"Then you could have said that it wasn't Ernesto, that Beverly had him."

"Meg, how could I do that?" Mike was annoyed, exasperated. "You would have thought you were safe."

I never think that I'm safe.

Rarely.

Mike knows that. He was looking at me. "I *had* to get you in, babe," he said softly, wanting me to understand it, not to hold it against him.

And the problem was that I did understand it. He was the one who'd drawn me into this, in his view of things, set the whole train in motion. He's the one with his lines in the sand, his own code of conduct—that ethic that gets us both by. It wouldn't have taken much working from Reilly for Mike to start feeling guilty, responsible, underprotective.

I should have called the damn station myself.

"I thought you were just going to talk to Jacoby."

"Yeah, I was, babe, but he wasn't there."

I looked at him sourly, still in my mood. Feeling put-upon and betrayed and not willing to give it up—"packing a hoon," as my mother would say. Mike knows at least five other people at Beverly PD, and he could have passed the description through any or all of them. Tell me it was accidental him getting to Reilly. And the thing is, too, Mike likes to believe that he's clever. "Jacoby's not in? Well, hell, give me Reilly. I can outwit that son-of-a-gun."

It might not have been only ego, though.

There was Sylvia missing.

Mike would have wanted to talk to someone who knew about her, who might have gotten some word, and since Jacoby was out, Reilly was the logical choice. Mike's other contacts could only give him rumor or hearsay if they even knew anything, and with Sylvia lost and her batterer roaming, Mike would have gone to the source. I couldn't really blame him for that.

I couldn't blame Reilly, either, although God knows I was trying.

He knew I wouldn't come in for him after I hung up this morning, but he thought that I'd do it for Mike. He wanted me in, so he took it.

Not hard to follow.

It just left me with no one convenient to blame but myself, and I was tired of that.

"I haven't had lunch yet," I said. "Maybe that's most of the problem. You guys want some pizza?"

Reilly was looking at me like I'd grown visible horns, but Mike is used to me switching. He had a half-relieved grin.

"Not if it's pineapple," he said.

Reilly was slower.

"Are we ordering in?"

I looked at him carefully.

"Yeah," I said. "I'm sure someone delivers. I don't want to go get it."

He thought about it. Nodded.

That was all right, then. Food would get us moving, get us off our positions. We'd have to look it up in the room's phone book, decide whom to call, what to order. Consort a little. Sweep this accused and accusing stuff out of the way, act more like adults.

Or not.

I don't know.

Maturity bites.

# 33

We ordered the pizza—pepperoni and sausage. Mike used the time to make a flurry of phone calls while we were sitting around waiting for it to arrive. He used my room phone, not a problem, calling people he knew at emergency rooms. CHP. Homeless shelters. Still no news of Sylvia.

I stopped him when he was digging the card out for Linda. "Let me see that," I said, and Linda's office was sure enough on that same fourteenth floor. I fingered the edge of the card. "Not much point in calling her, huh? We don't really have anything to say."

"But she might have heard."

I was pretty sure that she would have. Reilly was studying my face and I didn't want to get into it just at the moment—I wanted food inside me first and maybe a Coke. Sugared courage. I was glad to see the pizza guy's car pulling in about then, hear the knock at the door.

The pizza was good, really hot, better than *tournadoes* at Chaven's, and the company would have been fine if it weren't for the fact that Mike was still making phone calls and Reilly was being too quiet. Mike didn't call Linda.

"How'd you come up with Gunter?" Reilly said finally.

I suppose it was fair. We were in a lull between calls while Michael was eating, and I'd finished my third or fourth slice. Reilly had been watching me chew it and swallow it, so he knew I was done.

"The maître d' at Chaven's mentioned a blond guy last night." I met

Reilly's eyes kind of quickly, looked away. We hadn't talked about Chaven's last night or this morning, we'd been working our way towards it, a little bit of a truce, and then life interfered. I'd guess, though, from the glance at his face that he was thinking I should have told him regardless, so the next piece of information was going to sit *really* well. "The guy talked with De la Peña in the bar Friday night right after I left, but apparently he'd been there the whole time. The maître d' described him as a business associate—someone he'd seen with De la Peña before. Said he looked like a boxer. He didn't volunteer the guy's name, and I didn't want to make too much of it, so I left it at that. I'd been thinking anyway on Friday that De la Peña might be coming in with a bodyguard, so this guy fit the bill. I just hadn't spotted him already in place."

Reilly was looking sardonic as hell.

I've never said I was perfect, but that wouldn't matter—it was a different kind of grudge he was holding. It had to do with people who weren't careful because they thought they were good, who wouldn't therefore listen when he was giving advice out and who ended up tripping all over their egos. "I told you so" couldn't have been any plainer.

"And does he drive a black Ford Torino?" Reilly said.

I didn't know what Gunter drove.

Mike was looking blankly unclear, so Reilly got to fill him in on the car in our office parking lot Friday night, and then they both were united again. One front.

"Goddamn, Meg—"

"It wasn't a big deal," I said.

"You should have told me."

Yeah, well, he should have told me a bunch more about Linda.

"He didn't *follow* me there," I said very pointedly to Reilly, "and why the hell would he go and sit on the office anyway?"

"Looking for Sylvia."

"So why wouldn't he go sit on Mike's place?" but I already knew the answer to that one—Mike hadn't been home. I hadn't been home, either, but my car had been parked right out at the office, under the light there for anyone to see. I guess you could figure that's where I might be.

Or where I might be coming back to . . .

I'd been sitting at the desk in the darkness with the radio on, the miniblinds half-open. Headlights blinding through. It was a dark Ford Torino, parked back in the overhang corner, no visible shadow inside, just a blackness, a feeling.

Something moved, shimmered in the dark behind the windshield—a scope, a barrel catching light?

*"He uses a knife."*

It wasn't quite right.

There'd been that crash in the back, though. Something hitting the wall, as if someone standing on one of the cans in the alley had reached up to the storeroom window, overbalanced, and fallen.

Two people—one front and one back?

Positioning on me.

"Gunter's a tracker," I said, "very cold with it, methodical. I can't see him taking off running just because you drove in. What's Ernesto like?"

Reilly was watching me, considering.

"He's fairly excitable."

"Did he have a knife on him?"

Reilly quite slow.

"Yeah."

Ernesto in the front, then, maybe as a diversion. Gunter coming in through the storeroom with a knife of his own.

"You might want to ask him," I said, "about the Torino."

"Yeah, I do."

There was an odd note in his voice, something harsh, not quite finished. I looked up at him, questioning.

"And I want to know how *you* know that Gunter's a tracker," he said.

\* \* \*

It was just about ugly. It was pretty damned bad. I had to start with the part about Gunter paging me while I was leaving the station, and Reilly was sitting that little bit straighter as if it was news.

Oh, hell.

"You didn't tell him?" I said.

"No, I didn't," and now *Mike* was offended. "I told you I wouldn't."

Well, yeah, but—I looked over at Reilly. He was looking coolly back at me, which meant anything and nothing. Divide 'em and conquer? I was trying to work this one through.

"Why'd you think that you had to get me in, Mike?"

Mike thought it was obvious. "Babe, Gunter's bad news."

"Did Reilly tell you that?"

"Yeah, I did," Reilly said. "You think he isn't?"

No, I was really sure that he was.

Reilly read it. Nodded. He was compressed in the chair, hunkered down.

"Mike didn't tell me whatever it is," he said. "So you tell me now."

I didn't even have the chance to.

"He threatened to cut her," Mike said. "He called her back at the office after she taped him."

Alliances.

Shifting sands.

I couldn't really blame Mike, but I'd have given a lot to have stifled him then. Reilly was putting the whole thing together.

"*Before* you came in to the station."

It wasn't a question. He was assessing it, weighing it, linking it with Mike's pissed-off "I told you I wouldn't" and making it fit: I'd told Mike about Gunter threatening me, but I hadn't told him. Had told Mike not to tell him.

"Reilly—"

His eyes flicked at me. Hostility, tightly contained. Things always seem like they ought to be easy, but they just never are when you throw in emotion.

"How'd he get your pager number?"

I had to answer him, said mechanically, "It was on the machine. He'd checked into us, I think, for Rudolfo." Which didn't make sense anymore because Mike *hadn't* been seeing Sylvia on the sly, and Gunter was the one who'd beaten her up.

*"You think I don't find you, bring you back home?"*

That so-gentle voice.

*"Mi esposo . . ."*

*"Puta."*

"Wait," I said, "just a minute." They were both watching me, but I was focused on Mike, couldn't get the thought clear. "Did you see Sylvia more than that once at the Beverly Center?"

Mike was disturbed, a little defensive.

"We had dinner a couple of weeks ago."

"That's it?"

"Yeah."

That couldn't be all. Could it? Two simple encounters?

"De la Peña was at another meeting or something?"

"Well, yeah." Mike saw me looking at him. "He was out of town. For, like, a week."

Ah.

"She called *you*?"

Defensive again. "Yeah, she did. So?"

So somebody'd obviously found out. Hadn't liked it.

"She called the office?"

"Yeah."

That was one way someone could have gotten our office number. You just push that redial feature to check it, although then you'd have to have access to the phone. And De la Peña had been away. Mike wasn't seeing it, was starting to bristle, but I kept on.

"Did she ever call you at home, Mike?"

"No. I'm telling you—"

Okay.

236

"So you haven't been having a phone thing going? You both calling back and forth, chatting or anything?"

It was none of my business, but, sort of, it was.

"No," he said.

Strange.

"Only the two dinners? The couple of weeks apart?"

"Yeah."

Not much to get hold of, there. Not much to fuel an explosion. I was trying to see it.

"Did you pick her up at the house that night, or did you meet her at the restaurant?"

"I met her," he said.

"She kiss you?"

"Meg—"

"I'm just saying," I said, "'glad to see you,' or whatever—old friend, you know?"

*"What was that man, then . . . the 'old friend' where you stay?"*

"Yeah, I guess she might have."

"She stay over?"

"Meg."

Mike was flaring, defending the honor, and I'd forgotten again that she wasn't like that. I waved it aside.

"She didn't stay over?"

"No."

"But she hugged you, right? That's a natural thing. When you met and when you left, probably. At the restaurant?"

"Yeah," he said, "I guess she did, I don't know. I mean, it's a hug."

It could look like more than that, though, if you were of a jealous frame of mind. People animated, laughing. Warm.

I was staring at Reilly, not really quite seeing him, but trying to, trying hard to connect it.

Jealous of Mike, but not of Rudolfo?

Well, he was an old guy, a has-been, if you looked at him that way.

Past his prime. Not a threat. He *used* to be someone? "Babe, look at these muscles. What desirable female wouldn't rather be servicing me?" He might have some money, some power, but we all understand that. Sugar daddies. The price of the eggs. No hearts involved.

Mike, on the other hand—

Mike *wasn't* old. Mike was an old friend, someone we'd known. Has a fair set of muscles in his own right—attractive ones, too.

"When'd you have that dinner?"

Mike had to think. "A week, week and a half ago."

Today was Tuesday. That made it not last week, but the week before, maybe Friday. Nobody'd gone beating her up until Thursday this past week, though. You'd think it would be more immediate, although some people simmer. They dwell.

"Rudolfo was out of town, you said, when she called you up. Why'd she do that? She was lonesome?"

Mike had the "you're not my mother" look narrowing his eyes. "She just wanted to talk, Meg," and I wish, really, that guys could get over that.

"Right," I said, "but talk about what? Was she planning to leave him?"

"No. Well—" He started thinking it through. Reilly had been very quiet this whole time, sitting mum in his chair, letting me take it. I met his eyes again and he was regarding me dead-eyed, the way you'd look at a jailer, someone who could hurt you.

I wasn't.

Didn't want to be.

"Mike?" I said.

"I don't know." He was trying to replay it, the way you do, but it had been ten days or more. Nothing major then, probably, to make it stand out.

"You know, I think she was," he said suddenly. "I mean, she didn't come out and say so, she just was talking a lot about UCLA and Argentina. How idealistic you are when you're younger, a kid, how you can get into things that you don't really want. Have to make harder choices."

238

"She didn't say what kind of choices, though?"

"No. She . . ." Mike was thinking and then shook his head. "I don't know. I mean, yeah, I did think that she was talking about her marriage. An older, busy guy, everything not quite what she'd thought. And I had the impression that she was going to do something about it—stand up for herself some." He looked at me bleakly then, torn up by the subsequent events, and feeling more guilty, responsible. "I encouraged her, Meg. I didn't figure divorce, maybe go back to school or have a career, something like that. Make a difference. And then when she called—"

Then he saw the bruises. He didn't have to finish the sentence. I was still trying to picture it myself, understand the dimensions.

"So when you went to dinner that week-ago Friday, Rudolfo had just gone? He was going to be out of town for a while?"

"Nah, he was coming back the next day. They were going to some opera. She was making jokes about it, not bad ones or like she hated him. That's why I didn't think it was anything big."

So she'd left Michael that Friday in a pretty good mood, maybe buoyed and determined, going to set things straight with her man. But it took her five days to bring it up? Saturday till Thursday?

Christ, maybe so—I had no way of knowing. She could have changed her mind, put it off. Or she could have tackled him right away and they could have discussed it all week.

Well, actually.

Yes, really, they could have.

Rudolfo was expecting the divorce papers. He'd stuffed them into his pocket and invited me to stay for a drink.

*"Those are divorce papers."*

*"Yes."*

He didn't seem to care deeply.

"You had her followed, anyway," I'd said, and he'd answered simply, "To know."

To know what?

But see, I hadn't asked that particular question. I'd thought that I knew what, I was sure that I did—that Sylvia was fooling around—and so I didn't ask any more. Perhaps, really, he'd meant "To know *who*."

The who might have mattered.

Mike was acceptable enough if you checked up on him—a decent guy, ex-cop with a reasonable business and income—an old friend from her schooldays, maybe even an old love.

*"She was battered all over."*

*"You cannot think I—"*

Clearly, I did.

*"This changes everything."*

But what did it change? A previously worked-out agreement? A gracious and civilized parting?

*"Mr. de la Peña, she's saying it's you. She got Mike to take pictures."*

So what would that make you, then—not a chivalrous Latin philosopher who's gallantly giving way for true love, but just another sad old man who was foolish, who got taken in? And to find out that, even given her freedom, she's spreading falsehoods about you.

*"So I am a monster."*

Would you look, then, "more small"?

"Weren't they Catholic, Mike?"

"Jeez, I don't know," he said. "I think so. She is."

That rang right. *"She, you know, went to school in a convent or something."*

"And she was willing to get a divorce?"

"Huh?"

"Catholic," I said dryly. "Divorce is against the religion."

Stuff like that doesn't matter to Mike.

"Yeah, well, she could get it annulled, I think, later. For cause or whatever. They can do that, you know."

Yeah.

Sometimes.

Would battery be cause? Was *that* behind it? Gunter's beating her up as sort of a distorted favor? I had a case like that once.

But she refused to go to the cops.

*"De la Peña's got pull, back in Argentina."*

"She wasn't worried that he'd fight it, Mike? The annulment, I mean?"

"Well . . ."

Apparently not. Not that Mike knew or that anybody'd talked about at his lunch with Linda and Sylvia last Friday. But of course, Mike had taken the pictures of Sylvia by then. Those might buy an annulment if De la Peña wasn't willing to go along with requesting one after a civil divorce. Adverse publicity.

"Did you have your camera there with you, Mike?"

"No," he said. "Linda had the camera. Why?"

And Linda still had the film and the prints.

"It wasn't Sylvia's idea?"

"She wasn't exactly with it, Meg," he said tartly. "She was pretty totally falling apart."

So it was Linda's notion. Not Sylvia's, not really Mike's.

Linda had the camera. Linda had the film. Linda was sort of the engine. It seemed like it, anyway, but then I didn't like her. Had my prejudice working. Linda the attorney who'd gotten the divorce papers.

"Are we going anywhere with this?" Reilly said.

"What?"

He had a bite to his tone. "This excursion of yours."

I looked up at him blankly, and he stared pointedly back.

"I still haven't heard anything more about Gunter."

He thought I was avoiding the "tracker" explanation—taking us elsewhere.

Maybe I was.

There'd been something almost clear to me in all of that, though.

Only now, it was gone.

# 34

I told them the gist of it then. Reilly was getting progressively grimmer while I was describing my trek up through the stairwells, and Mike wasn't much better, so I didn't go into a whole lot of detail about the flight down. It was enough that they knew that De la Peña had an office on the same floor as Linda's, that I'd surprised Gunter and the four Latinos in there having a meeting, that Gunter had felt impelled to pursue me downstairs.

I didn't mention going back to Chaven's. Reilly didn't specifically ask me how I'd gotten Gunter's name and I might have given the impression that I'd overheard it or had talked to the guard in the lobby or something.

Mike wasn't liking the part about the office on Linda's floor.

"Yeah," I said, "I'm real sure."

"It was 'De la Peña'?"

It was, you know.

Carved in stone.

Well—

I mean, I could get placards made up to put on our office door, too, I suppose. JOHN GILL CORPORATION right above REILLY AND SONS. Would you know it was hogwash if nobody'd told you?

There was no "De la Peña" on the building directory.

I saw it then. It had been staring right at me, and I was an effing blind idiot. Too many trees.

"He was at the house this morning," I said. "Gunter was. At De la Peña's, answering the phone as Rudolfo. He identified himself very specifically that way, because I asked him twice—but he wasn't doing it for me. He didn't know it was me on the line."

"Yeah?" Reilly, half-following me, Mike not at all.

"That's the key," I said, "that he didn't know who it was. I wasn't expecting him, either, a Spanish-speaking guy, so I said the first thing that came into my head. I don't know why, the sound of his accent or the association, whatever, from calling the house, but I came out with 'Rudolfo?' I said it like I knew him, okay? Not like I didn't—'Oh, excuse me, is Mr. de la Peña there?' Just 'Rudolfo?,' like that. So why did Gunter say yes and stick to it? Because the thing is, I came back at him then like I wasn't quite sure, was kind of confused, which God knows I was, so I said it again, 'Rudolfo de la *Peña*?'—and he answered, '*Sí*, De la Peña.' Absolutely claiming it, and he still didn't know who I was. He started asking me then."

Reilly shifted. Point of clarification. "He didn't say, '*Rudolfo* de la Peña,' though, right? Only said, '*Sí*, De la Peña'?"

Oh, Christ, give me grief. "He isn't a long-lost twin brother, Reilly, if that's what you're getting at."

"Just checking," he said mildly. There might have been something, an undercurrent, amused, but he had his head turning, glancing down at his watch, and when he looked up, he was business again. "What's the point of not knowing it was you?"

"Well, what was he doing there?"

"Looking for Sylvia," Mike said.

"He had Ernesto for that. Didn't he?" I aimed that at Reilly, who'd had the pleasure of discussing life and occupations out on the street with Ernesto, and who, so far, had been less than forthcoming about the substance of those conversations.

"Yeah," he said.

"Ernesto's the odd-job guy?"

"Yeah."

The man with the hammer and the several available cars. A little surveillance, a little fixing. Whatever needed doing.

"He used to be a boxer?"

"He's been a lot of things," Reilly said. Seemed to think about it for a second, whether to include us or not, and then went on very smoothly, "Doesn't look to have done any jail time here but he has some interesting reactions to cops."

Well, we all do. I could forgive him that, and, anyway, I was focused on Reilly.

"Here? He's Argentine?"

"Yeah," Reilly said. The end of his sharing streak, I guess. The blabbermouth stage. "So what was the point of '*Sí*, De la Peña'?"

"I think that *was* the point," I said. "Gunter wasn't there on the off chance, waiting for Sylvia, he'd gone there to answer the phone." Both Reilly and Mike were looking less than convinced, but I knew I was right, it just shimmered. "It's like this," I said. "If I've beaten you up and you've gone missing, so I'm waiting surreptitiously there at your house for you to come home, am I going to be answering your phone, no matter how much it's ringing?" I waved off Mike's objections. "Okay, maybe so. I'd answer it as myself, though, right? In case it's you calling in, and I want to try the 'Sweetie-pie, honey, I'll never do it again' routine. Or in case it's the cops trying to reach you or maybe even me for some reason. Or if not, then I flat wouldn't say who I was, I'd find out who was calling, and I'd take a message or I'd hang up, according to whim. What I'm damn sure *not* going to do is to go masquerading around as your dead husband for anyone who happens to call."

"Not *my* dead husband," Reilly said. He was nodding thoughtfully while he contemplated a spot across the room, outwardly placid, but there was that damned little glint that gives him away. I wished Mike wasn't there. I wished I could just launch myself at him, bowl him over, wrap myself around him. Overwhelm both of our defense systems.

His eyes came up to mine. Held.

"It doesn't make sense," Mike said.

He was in his own study at the end of the bed, staring at the carpet and frowning, oblivious to the hormones in the room. I hoped he was anyway. He's usually got an animal instinct for things like that. Reilly was still looking at me and I could feel myself turning red.

"What doesn't?" I said.

"Gunter saying he's De la Peña. What does it do? The guy's dead."

"Well, the world doesn't know that," I said fairly sharply.

"Yeah, they do. They don't know all of it, maybe, but it was in the paper today."

Mike had a point. I didn't like it, but it was still there.

"That was local papers," I said.

"Meg, the guy's a celebrity. Not to us, maybe, because I don't give a rat's hey about soccer, but you don't think this was on all the wire services?"

Maybe. Probably. Not the suicide part because the Argentine consul would be keeping the lid on that for at least a while, had sent some attachés in right away to see the Chief, Reilly'd said. Bugging Jacoby.

Except that the Argentine consul wasn't the be-all and end-all of everything. Things have a way of getting out, and the world loves to gossip. Hell, the maître d' at Chaven's had known it last night, so most of Beverly Hills did, I'd bet you, today. And Michael was right, Rudolfo was a celebrity, an Argentine Flame. Millions of fans worldwide had watched that team win the World Cup, had stomped and cheered and rooted them on. It would be news, all right. Tabloid fodder, as soon as the journals got a whiff of the scandal: "Old Flame in Beverly Hills Love Triangle." It was probably all over the Internet by now.

But it hadn't been last night.

I was sitting up, cold.

Hadn't been this morning.

I was staring at Reilly while I tried to be certain.

"What is it?" he said.

"I ran the search engines this morning, on your computer. I typed in 'De la Peña' and it didn't come up. Wouldn't the search engines link to the news stuff?"

"They ought to, yeah." He thought about it for a moment. "Might not pick up everything."

"But there wasn't *anything* about him this morning. I had to go in through the Argentine *fútbol* page just to see an old picture."

"He was only found yesterday," Reilly said. "It might take longer than that to get into the mainstream."

"Yeah, that's what I'm saying—if the word hadn't spread very far yet, and there was something Gunter needed Rudolfo alive for, at least on the phone."

"Meg—"

I can get fairly stubborn. "He *said* he was De la Peña."

And then shortly after that, less than two hours, in fact, he was up in a fourteenth-floor office with four male Latinos, their faces turning, surprised, when I came through the door. The door with the placard that read DE LA PEÑA.

"Gunter sounds Argentine," I said to both Mike and Reilly. "I mean, the flavor, the accent, as best I can tell. I don't know how he is with Spanish or the Argentine lingo, but he sure speaks English in the same sort of pattern Rudolfo did. Is he Argentine?"

"I don't know." Reilly'd gotten his field notebook out of his pocket, was writing, making chicken-track notes, things to remember.

"You wouldn't think so," I said. "Gunter Heinreich's a German name, and he's definitely blond, but that's not to say that he didn't grow up there. His parents emigrated, maybe? After the war?" A number of Germans made their way to South America then. Latin America. Wherever.

"Something to check," Reilly said.

He could do that. He had all the connections, could get through to Ernesto back at the jail. Find out, at least, what else Ernesto might know.

"It has to be something to do with Free Argentina. That was really what set him off, when he called me back."

"When he made the 'cutting you' threats?"

I ignored the slight edge, was thinking it through. "Yeah. Before that, it was all about Sylvia, was a personal thing. 'You bitch, you record me?!'— like that. Even his calling back with 'I know who you are'—that was just him wanting the upper hand, wanting to scare me because I'd rattled him by doing the taping, and he wasn't going to lose face to a female. But I didn't fold like he was expecting. I told him 'Yeah? I know who you are, too,' and he said, 'You know nothing,' very full of himself, snide, so then I came back with the big gun, 'Free Argentina. Asociación del República Argentina por la Libertad.' That's when he broke. It has to be that." Reilly was looking at me critically, so I made a quick face, conceding. "Okay, so the fact that I thought he was Ernesto the whole time happened to work out."

"Yeah," he said. "Happened to."

Judgmental again.

"It was on the phone," I said. "Pretty damned safe."

"People don't stay on the phone, Meg." He knew that I knew it, was dropping it, glancing over at Mike. "What d'you think?"

"Yeah, it could be," Mike said. "It adds up. It's just the damn notion of Linda being involved." He rubbed angrily at his ear, and it was stupid of me, because she *had* to be, but I always have to work my way through things.

"We don't know how much she's involved."

"Meg—"

"Well, we don't." God, I was taking her part. "Maybe Gunter's been using her. Maybe he finagled the office somehow without her knowing. Christ, Mike, she's been hiding Sylvia at her bungalow since Friday morning, with you hanging around the whole time as protection. Why would she do that? It doesn't make sense. And if she's mixed in with Gunter and whatever he's doing, then he and Ernesto sure didn't need to come after me Friday night to find out where Sylvia was—Linda would have told them already. I mean, look at it—she had Sylvia call you to deliver the papers. What sense would that make, if she's in it? Why involve you at all?"

Mike looked fairly struck.

"She didn't know that Sylvia'd called me," he said.

"She what?"

"She didn't, Meg. She'd just gotten back with the papers, and she wasn't expecting me at the door. I didn't think about it at the time."

Because he'd been fretting about Sylvia then—anxious to get past Linda and see for himself that Sylvia was okay.

Okay.

Well.

That did make a difference.

"So Linda didn't ask you to deliver the papers," I said. "Sylvia did?"

"No." Mike was troubled and drawn. "I just took 'em. Sylvia wanted me to stay with her, she got a little upset about it, but I thought she'd be safe enough with Linda if they kept everything locked. Linda said she had a service she was going to use for the papers, but I told her, no, I had a friend with Francine's service who owed me a favor and this way we'd be sure that it got done that night." He glanced up at Reilly and then at me, that slightly ashamed, caught-at-it look on his face. "I was going to have a few words with De la Peña."

Yeah, I'd thought that he was. He knew that I'd thought so, had known it on Friday when I'd bullied him there at the office into letting me do it.

And it still was better that I'd done it, even the way this whole thing had gone. Mike would have been arrested or harmed, maybe, at Chaven's.

Gunter had been there.

*"What was that man, then, huh? The 'old friend' where you stay?"*

And the taut whisper, *"He uses a knife."*

It would have been legitimate, possibly, even—Gunter in position as bodyguard, Mike starting a fight. Self-defense, pure and simple.

I felt really cold, really thankful that I'm an idiot and follow my instincts. Mike's a big part of my life.

"Okay," I said. Shivered. Shrugged it off. "So Linda wasn't expecting you, you copped the papers, and then I snagged them from you. You show up at her house again that night, ready to guard things—what's she going to say? I can see that. It still doesn't explain why Free Argentina was camped on our office, but maybe Ernesto knows?" That was aimed more at Reilly.

"Yeah, I figure to ask him," he said. "I'm going to call Jacoby in a minute."

"He's back at the station?"

Reilly threw me a look. "I don't know if he's still there," he said pointedly, "but he's been wanting to talk to you."

To me?

Oh, yeah, about the answering machine and the tape I'd recorded. I'd sort of forgotten. It seemed like a long time ago, but it was only this morning, and they'd be wanting a statement, a deposition from me. Background and a history for it, that kind of thing. You can't just leave items off at a police station and think that's enough.

And, also, I suppose, they might want me to take a look at Ernesto, to identify him as the guy who was following me yesterday. Mine wasn't a police case, but they might want to know personally that they had the right guy.

God, I was tired all of a sudden. The caffeine and the pizza ought to have helped, and maybe, given a little less tension, they would have. As it was, I could feel myself cycling down. Whirling. I didn't want to be worrying. Didn't want to be fighting. Just wanted to keep us all safe there forever.

"Meg."

Reilly, grating and hard. Reality calling.

"I'm sorry," I said. I'm always saying that to him.

He leveled cynical eyes.

Makes it harder to talk, you know? To be open. "I just wasn't thinking, okay?"

He let that one go.

I needed to peel myself away from the head of the bed was the problem. I was propped against the headboard, pillows in the small of my back and under my shoulder blades, spine crunching down. I'd claimed the spot when Mike gave up the phone. He'd moved out to get his pizza and then settled onto the foot of the bed, and I hadn't wanted to sit at the table with Reilly, or be looking too chummy, shoulder to shoulder, on the bed there next to Mike.

I didn't want to be pushing any subliminal jealousy buttons, although, really, why was it *my* problem? I had a half-second's flash of what it would be like always to be guessing—"Will that set him off? Will this?" And what the hell was that, then? What kind of life? The voice on the phone so impossibly gentle. Coaxing.

*"Where you are, Sylvia? Where is it you hide now? You think I don't find you, bring you back home?"*

"Oh, my God," I said.

"What?"

That was Reilly, but I wasn't focused on him, I was looking at Mike.

"You were there the whole weekend?"

"Well, yeah."

"But not yesterday."

"Hell, no, not yesterday," he said. "Are you nuts? We were down at the station."

Because they'd found Rudolfo by then. I'd been kind of in shock, you know, when it was my turn in the hot seat up there with Jacoby. I hadn't thought even to ask.

"Who found the body?"

Reilly knew that answer. I could see him thinking about whether he should tell me, but it wasn't a secret.

"The housekeeper," he said. "When she let herself in."

"What time?"

"Six o'clock in the morning."

"She called the PD right away?"

"Yeah."

The units would have gotten there fairly quickly and secured everything. Put in the call to Jacoby. He'd have called the coroner and then gone in with the lab guys, measured and poked around, all of that stuff. Talked for a bit to the housekeeper. Things looking open and shut.

"What time did Jacoby call Sylvia in to the station?"

"He didn't," Reilly said. "He went over to the bungalow with one of the units. He was already out, and it isn't that far."

And he'd want to surprise her, at breakfast or whatever, so he could see how she took the news. Badly, by all accounts. Falling apart.

Except that, hold on—"How'd he know where she was?" Because Sylvia'd gone running away Friday morning, I thought, left no notes and no traces.

"The housekeeper told him."

I looked straight at Reilly. He shrugged.

"She knew," he said.

God damn.

I'm not ever having anybody cleaning my house.

 Mike had the easy answer to that one, though. "Linda called her over the weekend," he said. "To see if she'd bring Sylvia some clothes after she went in on Monday."

"*Linda* called her?"

"She was trying to take care of things," Mike said. "You know, look ahead through the week."

Yeah.

Very organized, that Linda.

Versatile, too.

"I'd like to have a little chat with her," I said, "about anything else she was taking care of."

Reilly didn't even bother to answer. Jacoby would be talking to Linda, if anyone did—it was Beverly's case. I understood that, I was just talking out loud, but at least for the moment, I had Reilly and Mike, and they could tell me some things. I needed to be sure.

"Do you know what time Jacoby went over there on Monday?"

Reilly'd read over the paperwork for me, but that hadn't been a critical fact. "Eight?"

"What were you doing at eight?" I said to Mike.

"God, Meg, I went home to change. I had to come in to the office, you know. Why?"

As in "What's it to you?"

Not such a lot, really, but I like to know the sequence of things. So Mike had gone home Monday morning, kind of early. Showered and changed. Came in to the office to find my black dress on the floor of the storeroom, and then he'd hung around to torment me.

"Were you going back to the bungalow yesterday?" I said. "Was that the plan? If they hadn't discovered the body?"

"Well, I was going to see what was doing at the office," he said, "but, yeah, after a while. Sylvia had the number if she needed to reach me."

Sylvia'd had the office phone number.

And Linda'd had it, of course.

"But you were at the bungalow the whole weekend, right? You brought a bag of clothes and stuff when you went back Friday night, and you didn't leave till Monday morning?"

"Yeah, that's right," he said. "Why?"

"Because Gunter said 'Where you hide *now*?' in that phone call this morning. Sylvia ran away Friday morning but she didn't go missing from Linda's till Monday afternoon. Doesn't that sound like he'd found her in the meantime?"

"I don't see it," Mike said, but Reilly was with me.

"Got in to her after Mike left Monday morning?"

"It could be," I said. "I'm trying to figure it. I'd say Gunter didn't know where she was Friday night—that's the best explanation for the

Torino hanging around at our office. Even if he did find out later, from Linda or however, then there was still no way he could get to Sylvia at the bungalow with Mike settled in for the weekend. And what was Linda going to say when Mike showed up unexpectedly with an overnight bag Friday night? 'No, you can't stay and guard her'?"

"She said it wasn't proper," Mike said. "That's the word she used. 'Proper.' I thought it was a Spanish thing, you know? She moved into the bungalow Friday night, too, as sort of a chaperone. A *dueña*, she said."

It was indescribable, the look on his face—the realization. Mike is a heck of a guy and he'd had no designs on Sylvia or her virtue, so he'd thought that Linda'd moved in to be closer to him. Had liked the thought. We all have our notions.

"She stayed at the bungalow the whole weekend, too, then?"

"Yeah."

Keeping things proper. "So you weren't ever alone with Sylvia," I said.

"Well, she was sleeping most of the time anyway. The doctor had her on something."

Somebody did.

"Okay," I said. "So Jacoby went to the bungalow and talked to Sylvia Monday morning before he had someone call Mike and then me to come in to the station. What time did you go home to change, Mike?"

"Seven, seven-fifteen. Something like that."

He wasn't gone very long before Jacoby got there, if Reilly was right about it being eight o'clock. Forty-five minutes, maybe an hour. Gunter could have come in then, I guess, during that time, but he'd have had to have been hanging around somewhere close, waiting for the moment, that hour. He was a tracker who prided himself, so he might not have minded—but sitting out the whole night? The whole weekend? It seemed really unlikely. I remembered that hand in the stairwell above me, smacking the doorframe in frustration.

And the thing is that even though Michael was gone, Linda would still have been there. She'd moved into the bungalow for the weekend.

Oh, my.

Yes, she had.

"Proper," she'd said. Like a *dueña*, a chaperone.

Not just to satisfy Latino conventions, or to make sure that Sylvia couldn't be talking to Mike, or even as a ploy to keep Mike under her thumb, but to make herself part of the block on the door against Gunter, too?

Only if she had some power he'd recognize.

Well, Madrigala Internacional was his employer.

Possibly. It would depend very much on what the rewards were for Gunter, and I couldn't see a regular paycheck doing it for him. A guy like that doesn't play for small change. He'll cut himself a new deal if he doesn't quite like the old one.

That's one of the reasons, I think, that so many of the Eastern disciplines, the "warrior religions," emphasize honor and restraint along with the building of physical prowess. Once a man's trained to a killing level, what's to prevent him from taking *you* out? Who's guarding the guards?

Linda hadn't left that to chance or to honor. She'd had Mike there with a weapon. Physical backup, if she should need it. Very organized, that lady. Quick-thinking, too. Taking advantage of Mike to keep Gunter at bay.

"Did Linda encourage you to stay for the weekend?" I said over to Mike.

"Well, I don't know about 'encourage,'" he said. It wasn't a topic he was liking, a little bit of a remembered affront to his ego. "She didn't at first, but then she switched and said it was a good idea. She made up the couch for me."

That's encouragement. His charm clearly working on her.

"What's all this getting to?" That was Reilly again, wanting to move us along, and I do sometimes get sidetracked.

"Tell me if I'm wrong," I said. "See what I'm missing. Gunter beat Sylvia up Thursday night, right? Where was Rudolfo? Why didn't he know about it? Because he didn't, Friday night. I'm the one who told him."

"He was in Oakland," Reilly said. I looked at him. He quirked a calm eyebrow back. "Housekeeper. Jacoby called her again yesterday after talking to you."

Double-checking the stories.

Because I'd been so adamant that Rudolfo wasn't despondent, that he'd denied that he hit her. It had done that much good, then, my saying it—had at least raised the question. I felt actually some better.

"So it's proof that he couldn't have done it, Reilly. He wasn't even home."

Reilly was shaking his head. "It was an overnight trip, according to the housekeeper. He was supposed to leave Thursday, late afternoon on the shuttle out of Burbank, get back sometime Friday. She didn't see Sylvia at all, not unusual, apparently, so De la Peña could have attacked her before he left. Still be consistent with hitting her Thursday."

I couldn't argue it. I would have liked to, but there was no point in wasting the time. I had the other string going, and it still made sense to me, this particular sequence.

Gunter was the one who'd beaten Sylvia up Thursday night. *I* knew that, even if nobody else did. I'd heard him. I believed it. *"You deserved it—puta."* Very personal. Entitled. Because of what he thought she'd been up to with Mike?

Mike had had dinner with her almost a whole week before. Nobody'd touched her during that time that we knew of, but then again, Rudolfo was getting home the next day. Had he stayed home all week—an equally effective block on the door? No opportunities that presented themselves until he left L.A. on Thursday? And then what had happened? A confrontation by Gunter? Sylvia denying in vain that Mike was a lover?

Or Sylvia changing her mind altogether?

" . . . she just was talking a lot about UCLA and Argentina," Mike had said. "How idealistic you are when you're younger, a kid, how you can get into things that you don't really want. Have to make harder choices. . . . I had the impression that she was going to do something about it—stand up for herself some."

*"You don't behave."*

*Hola.*

"Gunter's involved with Free Argentina," I said. "So's Linda."

Linda, the attorney, who'd handled the divorce papers. Who'd befriended Miss Sylvia at a fund-raiser last year for Free Argentina, where Sylvia was alone and didn't know many people.

They'd hit it right off.

Linda Madrigala of Madrigala Internacional and Madrigala-dot-com, whose offices were up on that same fourteenth floor as the one marked "De la Peña."

It didn't have to be a fake placard and it didn't have to be Rudolfo's office. There were *two* De la Peñas.

One wanting to be more important, perhaps, in her busy husband's world. Or to change the world, somehow, if Michael was right. Free Argentina. How idealistic we are when we're younger.

What do you get when you marry a rich man?

Sometimes access to money.

Sometimes access to power.

Was Sylvia equipped to deal with the predators that having either one brings?

Not according to Mike.

And not, perhaps, to Rudolfo.

*"I only want to know where Sylvia is."*

Saddened, resigned.

And, *"Sylvia told you?"*

Simple pride. The womenfolk naturally talking about him.

Or maybe it was simply his fondness for her.

*"She was making jokes about it, not bad ones or like she hated him."*

Her fondness for him.

"Is she innocent, Mike?"

It was an odd question to ask him, but he knew what I meant. He said strongly from the end of the bed, "Yeah, Meggie, she is. It's what I told you—she's like a kid."

I just have such a hard time with that one.

"You looked really thoroughly last night? You and Linda?"

"Yeah." His anxiety surging again at my tone. "We walked all over, for blocks around. Knocked on doors, talked to the neighbors, anyone who was home. I even checked through the house and under the bushes. Everywhere, babe."

Sylvia in a nightgown, wandering Bel Air. No shoes. No cash. Where could she go that nobody would have seen her?

One answer was nowhere.

"Did you look under the bed, Mike?"

"Huh?"

*"What was that man, then, the 'old friend' where you stay?"*

Mike was the old friend. She hadn't been staying with him, he was with *her*, where she was staying this weekend.

And "What was that man . . . ?" could mean "What's his name?" or it could mean "What good is he?" as in "I got to you already, he's not worth very much."

If Gunter got to her Monday, it would almost have to have been after Jacoby came to say that Rudolfo was dead, a suicide. That would be pretty shattering news, but Sylvia hadn't reached right away for the comfort of Michael. It wasn't until noon that she'd called Mike at the office, hysterically crying. Linda'd gotten on the phone then, had told Mike that Sylvia was blaming herself for the suicide, was incoherent from drugs. She'd even hired a nurse to stay with her, to dose her.

But somehow, in spite of that, Sylvia was gone.

They hadn't found her last night because Mike and Linda had been looking for a drugged, confused, wandering Sylvia, possibly even a kidnapped Sylvia—not for a Sylvia who was vaguely aware and deliberately hiding.

"Kids hide under beds when their world's falling apart, Mike. When daddies are gone and bad people have hurt them. She might have been there all along, might still *be* there," I said. "Linda hasn't been home."

# 35

Reilly called the station first and talked briefly with Jacoby. The notion seemed to be, as best I overheard it, that we were going to swing by the bungalow on our way to delivering me back to the station.

There wasn't precisely a case here, you know? Yes, Jacoby was within his range, investigating a death, but there wasn't any obvious malfeasance involved. Everything pointed to Rudolfo's being a suicide. I couldn't even argue differently anymore, because I didn't know. People despair. Things set them off.

Someone had undeniably beaten up Sylvia, as far as that went, but she hadn't been willing to press charges or even to make a report at the time—and where domestic violence might be concerned, that legislated mandatory reporting of spousal abuse—well, the spouse she'd said was involved was now tidily deceased.

It's true that I'd been followed back from the beach, but so what? A guy can't try to catch up with a girl? When's that a crime?

I had Gunter on tape admitting he'd hit Sylvia. Sort of. Not really. It was an illegal tape, anyway—interesting, but nowhere admissible. Good for background, a little bit of psychological mind games if the cops were so inclined, but not much else.

He'd threatened to cut me. No witnesses. My word against his.

He'd claimed to be Rudolfo, and that was still bugging me, niggling, because why had he done it, gone to the trouble, but again—what could I possibly prove? That he'd broken into and then entered Sylvia's home in order to answer her phone? Not hardly. Who else had seen him? That he was illegally using her or Rudolfo's fourteenth-floor office? I didn't know whose office it was—there might be fifty De la Peñas on staff with Madrigala. He might have permission. He worked there, didn't he? At least according to the maîtresse d' at Chaven's, whom I couldn't involve.

Linda was heavily shady, too, the way I viewed her, but what had she done, really? She'd taken in her battered friend and helped to protect her. She'd even housed her friend's male friend all weekend, had moved in with them herself to preserve her friend's reputation and so that she would feel safer. Had gotten a doctor to see to her. Hired a nurse.

We had to find Sylvia.

I was hoping to God in the strongest of ways that she *was* there under that bed. Safe, somehow, still.

If Rudolfo had cared for her.

"You ready?" Reilly said, and I was.

Mike was finishing washing his hands, Reilly was hanging up the phone. I'd gotten my bag slung, and I had the motel key out, was standing by the door, ready to lock things. Had Reilly's El Camino key in my hand. He still had the one for my 'Ru buried somewhere.

"I'll drive," Reilly said smoothly to me, moving in to take the truck key, and he didn't have to muscle me because what was I going to say— "Wait, Mike, I'll go with *you*"? We were all adults here. He didn't have to make me look small.

"Fine."

I let us all through. Locked up the door. It was at most a ten-minute drive, and the thing was to get there. I thought we could manage. Reilly wasn't likely to open any worm cans on the ride over. Our unfinished business would take longer than that to work out, and from what I knew of him, he wouldn't want to short change it.

It was starting to be dark out, lights coming on. Mike was taking his Camaro, didn't want to be part of our ménage, I would say, and he pulled out ahead of us, turning right onto Sunset. His taillights looked very bright.

"You all right?" Reilly said.

I was fine. I guess it was nice of him to ask.

"There's been a lot going on," he said, then, very slowly and, God, he *was* opening worms.

"I can't deal with anything right now," I said, "okay? I just want to see if Sylvia's there at the bungalow."

He was very damned silent.

I snuck a look and he was focused on driving, each little precision movement. It was an uncomfortably long ten-minute drive, and yes, I *should* have talked to him, should have been more responsive but sometimes the defenses are all automatic, sometimes I can't sort them out.

Linda's house was at the front of her property. Mike turned into the driveway, went past the side of the house into a sort of paved parking circle at the back. We pulled in behind him and stopped. The house was quite dark looming beside us. There were just the few miniature lights on here and there in the backyard, the kind that turn on automatically at dusk. Decorative more than useful, but anything helps. The bungalow was dark, too, ringed with bushes and shrubbery.

Nobody home.

Mike was climbing out of the Camaro, coming back to us.

"What d'you think?"

I thought we should knock. We'd come all this way, and I just had Jacoby to look forward to, otherwise—and Reilly. He was a sergeant in the seat there beside me. I guess we couldn't break in.

"You cover me," I said to them both as I opened the truck door. "I'll ring the bell."

Got out.

Did it.

Nothing.

No answer.

Tried it again.

It wasn't a bell so much as a buzzer. I could hear it echoing faintly through the bungalow like a maddened bee. *Bzzzzt. Bzzzzt.*

Swat.

We could use a damn SWAT team. I don't know why people have bushes in their yards. It's not safe. Too much concealment, and nothing like cover.

And those decorative lights only give you weird shadows. They don't illuminate really, because there's not enough wattage. I like floodlights myself. Arcs.

I tried the door handle. It didn't turn. It had a cheap lock, easy enough to pick, but, of course, I wouldn't do that.

Couldn't.

Reilly was there.

Mike, too. I don't mean to put it on Reilly all the time. I was eyeing the windows along the front of the bungalow. They had wooden frames. I reached over and I could touch one, barely, but I'd have to move off the doorstep into the grass, push myself waist-deep through the hedges, the bushes under the window frame, to get enough leverage to open it.

Linda didn't have this damned place alarmed? Bel Air Security coming any second? I'd be glad enough of Reilly's badge then, I guess.

Always ungrateful.

He was coming up behind me on the thought, Mike with him, like a phalanx, a flying wedge. I was aware of them, the way you would be, but I kept myself focused on the bungalow, its several windows, the bushes in the backyard, and the dark house beyond.

"I wasn't going to break in," I said.

"Yeah."

Reilly, that was, responding under his breath, gullible as a grass-green child.

Mike was moving onto the lawn to the right, crossing the yard to the side of the bungalow, heading for the back. I followed him, angling, with Reilly trailing to the rear.

It was, I don't know, creepy back there. There were some sort of fruit-tree-bush things planted in clumps that were probably lovely in daylight, but in the half-dark, the dusk, they obscured the frame of the building and bunched oddly out. Swollen. Misshapen.

The windows along the back were shaded and drawn. Blank. No sign whatsoever of human habitation. A very faint path ran through the grass, more of an indention than a designated walkway. It led to a door midway down the rear wall of the bungalow.

Mike went to knock.

I stayed back with Reilly.

There are only so many things that your senses can cover, and for me, it's harder to be with a partner, because I'm too aware of him moving beside me, inside my circle—the danger, the strike zone. All of my alarms going off, but the conscious mind saying "Stop."

Easy to say. Much harder to do.

I stepped a little away. Sideways, not much, I just shifted the half-step. Another. Reilly reached out a hand.

He was homed in on Mike, too, the same way that I was, on the door and the building, but his radar had detected me slipping away. That peripheral vision. You *un*focus, actually, widen your eyes.

Mike knocked again.

I hovered next to Reilly, unable to go or completely to stay.

Something was jangling my nerves, agitating, setting them screaming, but I didn't know what. The situation, undoubtedly—no one was answering. No one was home.

Where the hell was the girl, then, if she wasn't here?

Mike was turning around towards us, shrugging, his back to the bungalow, and you don't ever do that, you can't leave it unknown behind you—except, of course, we were watching, Reilly and I were, looking out for him, guarding.

I took another step right.

"Meg."

I couldn't listen to Reilly, couldn't explain. I had my hand on the

Colt in the bag, and it was just me being spooky, needing my space. So like a girl.

There were too many bushes.

"What d'you think?" Mike, calling over to us, and he'd said that already, that same thing, out front by the main house. Me, I thought we should break in, slim the door, but there wasn't probable cause. We couldn't just do it.

Reilly was moving my way again. He was a little in front now, between me and the building.

"Try one more time."

Mike turned back to do it, and I saw the flicker, the hairsbreadth of movement of one of the shades.

"Window," I said very softly. "Farthest one to the left."

"Yeah."

Christ.

Michael was knocking, standing wide to the door. There was no way to call him, nothing to say that would warn him without warning whoever.

Please God it was Sylvia. Please let it be her.

I had the Colt out and ready, automatic response, and beside me was Reilly with his Smith, holding low.

I took another step right, diagonally away, and he was going to have to deal with that fact himself, all those impulses conflicting, because I needed the clearance.

I didn't have time.

"I can hear her," Mike said very suddenly, "she's in there—Sylvia! Babe, it's Mike, you okay?"

She wasn't okay.

He was trying the door now, ratcheting the handle, shoving it, pounding hard on the frame.

"Don't," I said, "Mike," and he turned on me, fierce.

"She's crying, Meg—she's in there, goddammit."

Somebody was.

"Call her again." That was Reilly in command mode, steady and calm. "Tell her to come out to you, Mike. Get her to open the door."

He saw it then, Mike did, saw us positioned, saw what it might be—the worst-case scenario—but what can you do? He was the point man, the closest.

The goat.

He turned back to the door. At least he had the sense now to stand to the side of it. He wasn't drawing his weapon—what good would it do?

"Sylvia, come on, baby, hey, can you hear me? Sylvia, it's me, it's just Mike . . ." Coaxing, soothing, the way you'd talk to a child. No more bad nightmares, honey, open the door. Open your eyes, sugar-pie-lamby, it's me. Only me. You can come out now . . .

I was looking at bushes, at windows, at shadows in the night, splitting my attention between the yard and the building, trying hard not to listen. Mike was saying what he needed to say that might reach her—that was *if* she was reachable, if she was in and could hear him, could somehow respond. His job was to lure her. Mine was to guard.

I could feel Reilly doing the same.

Something scrabbled at the door. Mike raised his right hand abruptly, a signal, and then I could hear it. Somebody inside was fumbling. Sobbing. "It's all right," Mike was saying, "Sylvia, come on."

God, let it be.

I was focused and sighted, and you have to work not to narrow, that tunnel snaring your vision, zooming you down to the front sight, while vaguely beyond is the center of mass, point of impact. Index finger to the trigger, taking the slack.

If she was a hostage, there wouldn't be time.

The door opened a crack, just a little—two inches or three. Mike was still to the side at least, using his head, calling her softly. "Hey, baby, c'mon."

Darkness inside.

The white strip of face peered out at us blindly. Didn't move, didn't blink. Agonizingly slow.

The dark eyes.

I couldn't make out what was behind her, if anything was, a shadow, a shape, some other damn thing, but she was moving finally, drawing the door inward, and then she came through it all in a rush. Came tumbling out, tripping, incoherently sobbing, stumbling to Mike. He gathered her in to him, tucking protectively.

I kept my eyes on the door.

There was nothing else there—nothing visible anyway, but something was gnawing me.

The damn chase through the stairwell.

Frozen in place.

"You all right?" Reilly said. We were still both focusing there on the doorway, eight feet apart, and it was something elusive—a smell?

A feeling.

Too many times hunted.

Mike was relaxing, bringing Sylvia towards us, out of the range of the door. He turned his head to say something to her, "It's okay now, you're safe," but it wasn't, we weren't, because something was wrong, it was terribly wrong, and I couldn't think what—

*What* came leaping at me out of the darkness behind me, chopping down at the Colt in my hand.

"Reilly," I screamed.

Ducked with it.

Whirled.

It was all I had time for, a warning.

A knife lays you open clean to the bone, numbs the limb, but he wasn't going for me, he was going for Reilly. You take the big one out first, and I was just nothing, the small one, the female. Easily prey.

*God*—Reilly—

I dove after him then, not thinking, not able to think, purely instinct. He was on Reilly already. He slashed.

And Reilly went down.

# 36

There's no second-guessing it.

You do what you have to because there's no time.

Gunter was on top of us, eight feet and closing, very, very fast. He'd sliced *me* coming down. Crossed the distance in less than a tenth of a second, gashed Reilly with the return upward sweep of the blade, had shoved off with his left hand, spun with the motion, was moving for Mike.

I had a glimpse of Mike thrusting Sylvia behind him, starting to come, but she was clutching at him, clinging—he'd never make it in time, they'd be nothing but meat, and I was already launched.

I hit the guy dead-on sideways, torso going upwards, my full body force rising. Used my legs as the springboard and I drove up under his knife arm, his right arm, ramming it straight up over his head with the bulk of my shoulder so that my head and my body could snug-in behind him.

I had no feeling in my right forearm, the hand, no operative movement, but I'd by God swung it up and over his far shoulder as I hit him full-force with my body weight flying—used the torque, the momentum, to fling it. I reached up his back with my left hand, scrabbling frantically, groping, trying to snag my right wrist with the hand, and Gunter was flailing around, moving. I couldn't hold him, wouldn't be able to—he was working himself free, he was goddammit strong and he had an effing sharp knife there above me, my right arm starting to slide back off him unfettered, a dead weight, slick with blood. I made one last effort and lunged upwards against him, barely caught my right wrist as it slid back past his head. I clamped on to it with my left hand, made the triangle, and then I locked down, constricting his neck and the knife arm, still upthrust and trapped in between.

You don't give up. You don't ever give up. Out of each little victory, something is born.

I was working to take out his knee at the same time, do him some damage, but he was shifting, absorbing it. Whipping around to get me off balance.

Knife-fighter agile.

A bladesman.

He, of course, had a second knife. I knew that he would. Most bladesmen do. He had it in his left pocket, a flick-knife, a folder. He pulled it free with his left hand, flipped it open, one-handed, and swept it immediately down and behind him, jabbing the point where my face would have been except that I'd tucked it, burrowed into his back when I felt his arm moving, and that's what the skull's for, all that hard bone.

He was working the angles, the odds. He thrust back in front of him again with the knife on the upswing, ready to whittle me, carve off more parts of my arm if that's all he could reach, anything to make me let go. You get the blade on the arm and you saw, and there was hell I could do about it except take the cuts, try to swing him around and knock him off balance if only a little, because I had to hold on, had to keep him restricted to only one knife and the limited movement, or we were all dead.

I kneed him again viciously, bit into his back. No dojo rules. My teeth were there anyway and it gave him a new source of pain for distraction.

Mike came in then and hit us solidly, bam, on the left side, knocked us both backwards a couple of steps. He'd tackled low, had his hands out, I guess, to grab Gunter's knifehand before he could finish the change-up to slash me, but I couldn't tell that, couldn't see a damn thing. I was buried in Gunter's spine, hanging on. I just knew we were moving and that there were more arms, that Gunter was kicking, someone else punching back.

And while we were stumbling there in the backyard on the uneven ground, confusion in the darkness, the three of us writhing and fighting, another force hit from behind me, *whoomp*, out of the night. It lifted us all off the ground like a fullback, threw the whole boiling mess of us down.

Oh, my God, we'd never checked the bushes, never had the time—"Asociación" stands for more than one person.

I was rolling with it, frantic, trying to hang on to Gunter's shoulders, to keep the blade trapped and above me, but the angles were wrong. The forearm wasn't numb anymore, it was screaming blue murder, and it was bending or breaking, I just couldn't tell.

I kicked out, connected. Somebody grunted.

I couldn't see anything, see who had me, but there was an arm around my waist then and an absolute hand on my fingers, dislodging me, peeling me up and off Gunter's body. Gunter was surging up, too, fighting, and the somebody threw me. Picked me up regardless and chucked me off to the right.

I landed.

Rolled.

Tried to gather.

It was a black shifting mass, indistinguishable there on the ground, grappling, but the mountain that had moved me had to be Reilly.

Reilly and Mike.

Both of them in there battling this guy.

I had to do something—I couldn't just lie there—I had to come up with a plan. Sylvia was a wisp at the side of the bungalow. She should have been running and screaming, attracting attention, getting us help, but she was useless there, stunned, a glimmer of white nightgown that huddled and rocked, softly keening, and Gunter was heaving up against Reilly and Mike, making headway.

He was agile and tricky, strong, and God, they were cops, all that goddammit training. They were working on him, trying to contain him as if he were a suspect—wrestle him down, get those pain holds, overpower him, and he was a madman, an animal, didn't care about pain. He was fighting for life, or, if not, to destroy them.

He had two knives at least, maybe more.

I saw a glint for an instant in his left hand, and then he was punching that hand up at Mike.

"Mike," I shrieked. "Knife."

I don't know if he heard me. I saw the hand connect, saw Mike's body retract from the blow, but they were pitching and tossing, everything blurred. Reilly, I thought, reaching out blindly, grabbing. I had my knife from my pocket coming out automatically, my Spyderco, and I can use it left-handed, but I wouldn't help them much now by crawling back in. My job was to find my damn gun. Bigger, better power. A stopper if we needed it, if Gunter got loose.

I went scrabbling with the thought then, pushing one-handed around in the bushes, trying to locate the Colt. It had to be somewhere nearby there. Had to be.

I touched it.

The tip of my fingers, there in the grass.

I shook my head, trying to clear it and see, to grip the gun, draw it in to me, but it wasn't the Colt. It was only my bag, half-open and scattered, pens, papers.

Useless.

I could feel myself losing it, the darkness wavering, everything starting to fade.

Charlie was yelling at me then, and my dad—how many times?—like a chorus, a constant: *"You gonna give up, girl? You don't ever give up. You don't let them beat you. There's always something else you can do—"*

My pager.

Reilly's cellphone.

If I couldn't get help, I could at least leave a trail.

I clawed it to me somehow, jabbed the Power button down with my thumb. I couldn't hold the thing one-handed and work it, I had to leave it there on the ground. I tried to raise my head and peer over it to look at the fighting, to know what was happening, but I couldn't. Couldn't see. It was too dark, and God, getting darker, but the numbers lit up then in front of me, so I drew in my focus, left the conflict, concentrated on making my index finger push buttons.

Nine-one-one.

You have to hit Send.

It wasn't a landline. No automatic location would come up on the dispatcher's screen, I knew that, so I had to talk, had to manage or they'd never get there.

I was shivering, shaking.

"*Shock*," Charlie said. He was saying it loudly, insistently, "*loss of blood, Meg, you're losing it, you've got to do something*," so I got angry at him, pissed, because how was *he* helping? It's effing easy to stand to the side.

I took that upsurge of energy, used it to say the address into the cellphone, said it twice so they'd hear me, have it clearly on tape. Officers down—plainclothes. Need help now, in back of the bungalow. I said that, said Mike's name and Reilly's, a Beverly sergeant, send an ambulance—hurry.

I did it correctly, I think, tried to, because I could feel myself going, was fogging again.

Useless. So useless.

I should be giving descriptions, Gunter's name, leading them in more precisely. I just lay there with my head on the grass, lips next to the cellphone. She'd sent the units already, I knew that she would have, but they have to ask questions, keep you talking, the dispatchers do, it's a part of their job, and please, God, please, Daddy, I didn't want to be dying on the phone for this gal, have her always have that to remember.

"It's all right," I said to her hazily, tried to say so she'd hear me, "you did the best that you could."

Someone was coming at me out of the darkness.

I had the Spyderco knife out, trying, but the someone was wrapping me, holding me down so that I couldn't use it, and it was, I think, Reilly.

# 37

I woke up in a hospital bed.

I had that garlicky taste in my mouth so I'd had anesthesia. Surgery, probably. Didn't want to open my eyes a whole lot because then everything spun, and it was pretty glaringly bright.

"How ya doing, 'Gie?"

That was Mike, asking.

Michael was okay, then.

"Feel like hell," I said, slurring. "How's Reilly?"

Mike didn't answer.

Panic like a bubble in my throat, rising and choking me. *"Mike?"*

He wasn't there.

I opened my eyes then in spite of the glare, in spite of the massive sick headache that moving much gave me. Found the call button. Pressed it. I couldn't use my right arm, it was bandaged and strapped down, locked down. The left arm had tubes taped all over it with needles undoubtedly in me, the tubes hooked to bags on a fluid stand, but I made them stretch far enough across me anyway to push the damn button.

Nurse-person arrived.

"The guys who came in with me—?"

She didn't know.

"Two of them," I said, tried to say through my dry mouth, "knife wounds?"

She thought I should rest. Was patting me, resetting the button, adjusting the flow of the fluids beside me. "Don't worry now, hon, it's okay."

It *wasn't* okay.

I tried to find words, had to tell her, because this was wrong, it was terribly wrong, and I couldn't think what—

Swirled back down into darkness. Desperate darkness. Recycling and dredging, trying to swim.

Crying.

*"Over nothing, Mary Margaret, don't tell your father."*

"I won't, Ma," I said, "no, I won't," because I had to protect her but I was too small. Ferociously asking—

*"You won't stay for dinner?"*

"I can't," I said, but I never had told him that I didn't want to.

*"He wanted me to stay."*

Reilly very still in the seat there beside me, where Mike had been sitting.

*"Did you want to?"*

God, I didn't know.

He was wrapping me then, holding me aggressively still with his hands and I don't know why I respond when he's hard like this and angry, but I do—he knows I do.

*"You like dressing up?"*

*"Hey, baby, c'mon."*

"I like you," I said, and pressed into him, clung.

I woke up heaving-sick to my stomach, but that's what the pans are for, those kidney-shaped dishes.

"Well, that ought to make you feel better," Mike said. He was sitting again in a chair by the side of the bed, reaching awkwardly to pour me some water so I could wash out my mouth.

"Oh, you damn man." I took the cup, rinsed and spit, all those elegant things you like to have company for. It made him real, though— not a ghost or a figment. The cup felt solid, the water, wet. The tissue I was wiping my mouth off with tore.

Reality signs.

"Where's Reilly?" I said.

"Downstairs." Mike didn't seem to know I'd been worried, was being very casual about it. "He's trying to figure out the paperwork for getting you out of here. I was thinking we should just book down the back stairway, but he wouldn't go for it."

No.

No, he wouldn't.

I was kind of smiling at Mike, feeling, God, a lot better suddenly. Rinsed my mouth again. Looked at the tubes in my arm. I wouldn't have nearly the headache if those things came out.

"How long have I been here?"

"Most of the day. Most of last night, too, of course."

Well, yeah.

"What happened?" I said.

He got a little bit grimmer. "Linda's dead. Gunter took her off at the house before we got there."

Oh, hell.

I didn't know her at all, but Mike had spent the weekend, had liked her. The question was "Why did he do her?" but that could wait for a minute. I sent a small prayer.

"Where's Gunter now?" I said carefully. "LAPD have him?"

"Coroner."

Ah.

Mike was expressionless. "Self-defense. He came up through me with the one blade and was going for Reilly, so Reilly gutted him with the knife Gunter had in his other hand. Twisted his arm around, took him out."

A poetic kind of justice. I didn't mind it at all. I'm a reflexive person—God, a reactionary—so I did my automatic quick prayer for the good Gunter might have had in him, wished it well, a swift journey and a better life next time.

"He got you?"

Mike touched his chest. "Got the ribs," he said.

Thank God for bone.

And Reilly was downstairs now, trying to spring me, so that was okay.

"Why'd Gunter kill Linda?"

Mike would know something about it.

LAPD would have shipped me off in the ambulance right away, me being pretty much out of it, needing surgical help, but Mike and Reilly were mobile last night, not, I guess, as hurt as I'd thought. They'd have been treated by the paramedics at the scene and kept for a while—first separately, to explain themselves and the crime scene while calls were being made to check out their bona fides, and then, once that panned out, they'd have been kept to identify things. It was entirely possible even, cop stuff working this way, that with Reilly there being a sergeant, and Beverly Hills having an interest if not quite a case, they'd have been tactfully allowed to hang around if they liked, to see what else LAPD was discovering.

Linda's body, for instance, up at the house.

Mike would have stayed then, if he could have, to get more information.

"Why'd he do her?" I said again, because Mike wasn't answering.

"Money." He was staring rather moodily at the foot of my bed. "De la Peña's money," he said finally. "Through Sylvia. She'd been sleeping with him, Meg."

No doubt who the "she" was—or the "him," I guess, really.

I asked it anyway.

"Sylvia and Gunter?"

"Yeah."

Those saints keep getting harder to come by, but it made sense, it did. It was just, you know, that she wasn't an impossible saint anymore, she was a little lost rocking figure in a too big white nightgown.

"Did she say so?"

"Meg." He was looking at me, exasperated, because I was the one who'd been saying so all along. I was the one who'd made fun of him— "She have another boyfriend, Mike?"—when he'd been sticking up for her, being an idiot.

I can be wrong.

"Did she say so, Mike?"

He flung up his hands then—goddamn irrational women.

"No."

"So how do you know?"

"Ernesto's been talking," he said irritably. "I went over with Reilly last night after we got done, and we watched through the mirror while Jacoby went through it."

A mirrored interview room with Detective Jacoby. At BHPD.

"Did Jacoby go up to the scene, too?"

"Oh, yeah, he did," Mike said. "As soon as they called the station, checking on Reilly. Well, he'd been sitting around anyway, waiting for us to come in."

Because we were only going to be stopping at the bungalow for a couple of minutes on the off chance that Sylvia was there before heading in to the station to explain my involvement to him. Those couple of minutes would have stretched to an hour, at least, from the time we left the motel until LAPD had come in and contained everything. They'd have set up the perimeter, gotten their Homicide team in and gotten the stories while they had someone checking us out. That someone would have called the Watch Commander first at BHPD to verify Reilly's status and to get the name and a reachable phone number of Reilly's supervisor so they could discuss it directly with him.

Reilly's supervisor is Abbott. Lieutenant Abbott.

Oh, well.

"Nobody's talking to Sylvia?"

"She's down the hall here," Mike said. "They shipped her out right after you. She's not doing real well."

"Hurt?"

"Shock. I guess the consulate's coming in pretty strong, too."

"Don't bother our national." Yeah, I could see it. They currently had two down and dead in America—three if you counted Rudolfo.

"They protecting Ernesto?"

"Not so much."

Well, he wasn't a Hidalgo.

"What was he telling Jacoby?"

"That she was having a thing with Gunter. Said it was an open secret, everybody knew about it. Whenever De la Peña went out of town, there was Gunter moving on in."

So Sylvia might have been tempted. She might even have been thinking about it. It didn't have to mean that she'd taken him on.

"Everybody doesn't know everything," I said. "Gunter was a bodyguard, security or whatever. That was his job. De la Peña knew him, obviously, had had him do stuff before, because they'd been together at Chaven's often enough for the maître d' to recognize him—so what was *that* connection? Ernesto know that one?"

"It was the Free Argentina stuff," Mike said, "Linda's pet cause. She and Sylvia got together at one of the rallies, and then got De la Peña to donate money, use his connections to do some fund-raising for them. And Gunter wasn't a bodyguard, he was head of security for Madrigala, came over with Linda from Argentina, so he'd hire locals like Ernesto to help keep order at the rallies, protect the celebrities. They all knew each other that way."

"There you go, then," I said. "'Hey, old buddy, I'm going out of town, can you keep an eye on the wife for me?' You know how guys are. Even if Gunter had notions, it doesn't mean that Sylvia did."

"Yeah, well, he wasn't just keeping an eye, according to Ernesto. He waited outside a number of times with the car while Gunter went in. Made it very plain. You know this whole thing with *me*—when Sylvia and I went out for dinner that last time?"

I nodded.

"Ernesto was following her that week for De la Peña, Meg. He says Gunter had called him in privately the week before, asked him to check out what she was doing for *el jefe*, the 'big boss,' while De la Peña and Gunter were fund-raising in Florida. He didn't seem too concerned about it then, but Ernesto says Gunter just went white, *furioso*, when he got back and saw the pictures he'd taken."

Pictures of Sylvia and Mike.

Hugging outside a restaurant.

Old friends.

When Gunter had pretty well thought there'd be nothing to show *el jefe* because he himself was away that week, traveling with him. It would have upset all kinds of his plans, personal and otherwise.

If he'd decided to annex the property, for instance—exercise eminent domain, let's say, or that even-more-ancient droit du seigneur. Take over the pretty young wife. Get the fortune one way or another.

And then, gosh, the pretty young wife appeared to have other ideas, was actually playing *him* false.

Okay, I could see it. An affront to Gunter's ego all the way around, and no way to vent it with De la Peña back home. He'd have had to wait, stewing, until Thursday to confront Sylvia when *el jefe* left for Oakland. He'd found her, perhaps, saying, "No, I won't sleep with you," and also, perhaps, "I'm making some changes."

*Furioso* wouldn't quite cover it.

Sylvia hadn't known, probably, what she was dealing with. Linda did, though. Seemed like. She'd kept Mike at the bungalow all weekend.

"But I don't see why he did Linda, Mike. He had to go back to the house for her and I wouldn't think it was worth it."

"I don't know," Mike said. "Why'd he come at us? Felt everything closing in? Didn't want to leave any witnesses? It still looks like for money. There was a duffel bag full of cash by the side door with some bankbooks stuffed in there, ready to go. Linda had it in her safe, they figure, because that was opened and empty. LAPD found it when they went in." He sort of looked over at me. "She was right by it."

So she could have been fixing to run and he tracked her. Or he was lying in wait until she got home and then he forced her to open the safe and give him the cash. The bankbooks.

"Foreign accounts?"

"Yeah, apparently. LAPD's looking into it."

So he got the money and then he just sliced her?

It always seems like there ought to be more of a reason, but you never know. He'd come over with Linda from Argentina, and she appeared to know what he was, had used Mike as a defense, so they had some sort of history. Maybe she knew things about him he didn't want public. Ex-lovers? An uneasy alliance, working together for the greater good of a free Argentina?

Maybe.

Gunter was a mercenary if ever I saw one, every man for himself, but I guess it depends on the cause—maybe Free Argentina was going to finance the revolution.

By fund-raising.

Or investments.

Holy Moly and Mother-Be-Good.

Four Latino guys in an office that was marked "De la Peña."

Gunter on the phone at the house, saying, "*Sí*, De la Peña."

What had Mike just said? "Used his connections to do fund-raising for them."

Well, yeah, sure.

In Florida, for instance, or in Oakland, near San Francisco, where there was an Argentine presence, a community.

Here in Hollywood and Beverly Hills. Where else would you find liberal people with more cash than sense? Yes, dearest darlings, let's help rescue the poor, the downtrodden, the depressed. And for the ones who *had* sense, well, Argentina was encouraging foreign investments these days. If you didn't want to donate, you could invest. Big returns for your dollar. Where better to go than to an established firm like Madrigala Internacional, with plush offices in Century City and a Web site that boasted alternate addresses in Tokyo and Buenos Aires?

They'd had no links on that Web site.

Cheesy sort of outfit.

What does it cost to put up a Web site these days?

Not much, I'd think. I haven't paid particular attention, but a college kid could write up the program for you, find you a Web provider to host it. A Web site adds a certain cachet, an authenticity, a stamp of electronic approval in today's world, and nobody polices what you choose to put up there. Mike and I could be John Gill Security Corporation with offices listed in London and Rome, for example. John Gill International. Who's going to say it's not so?

You'd need something more than a Web site, posh offices, and a glib lawyer's tongue to pull in the big bucks, though. It would be very handy to have a celebrity Argentine Flame.

I couldn't picture Rudolfo doing it on purpose, defrauding investors, but if *he'd* been misled by his wife's good friend, Linda . . .

"*Sí*, De la Peña."

A money transfer, or an investment meeting, that they'd needed Rudolfo alive for?

Yesterday.

*Big* bucks.

And he'd killed himself Friday after talking to me.

Did he know then? Was it something I said? Or was it something from Gunter, who'd talked to him after I did and left him "more small"?

"They should check the bank records back and forth," I said, "between Free Argentina and Madrigala Internacional. And, I guess, De la Peña."

"Yeah," Reilly said from the doorway. "LAPD's doing that."

# 38

Reilly listens at doorways before he comes in. It's an annoying thing, really—antisocial. Very bad manners but effective as hell. I found myself grinning at him.

"How are you?"

He just nodded, looking me over. Flicked at Mike sitting next to me.

"She's got to be checked by the doctor again first," he said. "They won't let her go, otherwise."

"Jeez."

"Hospital rules."

"There's always that back stairway," I offered. "They probably don't have it guarded."

Reilly just scratched at an eyebrow and stayed where he was. Happened to be blocking the door. "They're trying to locate the doctor."

"Well, I can get dressed while we're waiting." I only had the one working hand, which, of course, wasn't the useful one, it was the same hand as the tubes, but I was already peeling at the tape on my arm with my teeth. If you don't think that hurt, let me tell you—hurts like hell, especially when it's pulling the little bitty hairs from your forearm. Reilly wasn't coming in to assist me. "Michael?"

He had two hands free, but he was looking at Reilly.

"They're not going to keep me here," I said nicely. "I'm good enough and they need the hospital room. I've had a day's worth of antibiotics and tetanus and whatever else they thought of to put in the tubes. I'm fine."

"Yeah," Reilly said. "When the doctor gets here, we'll see."

Charlie would have been helping me change.

Mike cleared his throat diplomatically, pushed the chair back, and stood up to stretch. Easy grace. "Well, I think I'll take off for a while," he said. "I want to go see Sylvia before they transfer her out."

Going to look after her even if she *wasn't* a saint. That's what I like about Mike, really. He's a great guy and you don't have to be perfect.

"She's just down the hall?"

"Yeah."

"Can I come along?"

He was glancing at me, questioning, but I did want to see her, see for myself what she was. And I didn't want to sit here with Reilly, who was looking reserved and enigmatic, but, yes, a little bit blaming, standing there by the doorway, not coming in. He still had his grudge on, even after last night?

"This fluid-stand thing rolls," I said, "and I'll just have to hang on to the hospital gown, right? Keep it wrapped around me, unless you wanted to get me my jeans."

"'Gie, I don't know if you should be walking."

This was the guy who was going to help me escape down the back stairs, and now wouldn't even rip a piece of tape from my arm.

"I can walk," I said tartly.

I pushed the covers aside, swung my legs over the left side of the bed to prove it, and sat all the way up. So things got a little dizzy for a second or two—it happens, you know? If I didn't have the damn tubes in my arm, I wouldn't have the damn headache, and, anyway, the metal fluid-stand thing provided support. I shoved off the bed and I stood there, holding on to it.

"What room is she in?"

Mike was looking over at Reilly again, and it's natural, okay? but it was ticking me off. The truth is, though, I guess, if they weren't either one caring, it would be a bad thing.

"Meg—"

"I won't know what I can do if I don't try," I said. The weight of my arm was pulling me really a long way down, the splint and the wrappings lopsiding me, and I'm not sure how long I could have stood there if Reilly hadn't come in then, mouth pressed and tight, and gotten me into a chair.

"You want to get a wheelchair?" he said to Mike.

Mike vanished.

I'd forgotten about Gunter stabbing my head until I was leaning over, holding it up with my good hand, and I felt all the bandages. Maybe that was the headache. Reilly was hunkered down beside me, not saying anything, just being there, but radiating disapproval, coming off him like a heat wave.

"I thought he got you," I said thickly. "Slashed you right up the middle and you with no time."

He was silent for a second or two.

"I heard you yell," he said. "He only got my jacket and some of the skin."

"You went down," I said. Saw it again.

"I was going to take the head shot."

I looked at him.

"What?"

"The head shot. I went down to shoot him so I wouldn't hit Mike. Only then you went in and got in the way."

Bullets go through things. People.

Entry and exit wounds.

Sometimes they lodge, but you just can't be sure. Mike and Sylvia were part of the backstop for bullets at the angle Reilly'd had, they were right behind Gunter, and there was no way he'd risk it. So he'd been reacting but reasoning, quick awareness of chances, and he'd made it look natural so Gunter wouldn't suspect anything as he went down.

And then I'd been in there.

Reilly, scrabbling around on his back on the uneven ground in the darkness—time running, the target moving, aiming up for the head shot so he wouldn't hit anyone but Gunter in the uncertain lighting—and then there was me in the way.

"I didn't know," I said numbly.

"Well, what were you *thinking*?" Every last little bit of repressed anger and anguish in the world in his voice. "Goddammit, Meg, he had a knife."

Hacking at me. The knife jabbing back at my face.

He'd had to watch that while he lay there and weighed off the risks of taking a head shot, with us whipping around and Mike rushing in.

"I thought you were dead," I said, "dead or dying." My voice broke then, my own shell cracking, and I was crying like an idiot at him, but I didn't care. "I didn't know you had a bitching great plan. I was just doing whatever I could to buy us some time."

"*Time*? Meg—"

"Mike was there," I said fiercely, "reinforcements, but not if Gunter got to him first. I wasn't out there *alone*, Reilly. I wasn't playing MachoBabe Wannabe, if that's what you're thinking. We've worked together, Mike and I have, we've trained. I knew he'd come in. I knew I could count on it. There were guys when I was working who wouldn't, and that's just one of the things that you deal with, but Mike would always be there. It's never mattered, the circumstances or the odds—if I barreled in, he'd go in swinging beside me—and me for him, too, Reilly. That's how it works. So if I can tie up the one knife, and Mike gets the other, then maybe between us we could get this guy down. Otherwise, we're all lunch, don't you see? What're a few cuts next to that?"

He'd been shaking his head stubbornly when I started, not wanting to hear it, not wanting to give up the anger because anger's a barrier, a fortification. The strong part of fear. He'd heard me anyway, though—he had to, because I wasn't stopping. When the barriers break, you have to rush in.

Or rush out.

Whichever it is.

We build those walls for protection, stone upon stone, but they also enclose, block us in.

He was rubbing at his forehead, tired, while he thought about what I'd been saying, put it into a different perspective. Not just me being foolhardy, risking myself. "All right," he said finally.

Was it?

He had a gash down his cheekbone and some patched-up skin, I'd guess, under his shirt. He'd have had a really long night, not much sleep after the intense physical output of fighting. He'd have been answering LAPD's questions for hours about killing Gunter, telling them whatever he knew about Linda. Been over at her house with them, looking at her body and the stuff in the safe, gathering what details he could. He'd been talking to his own people, too, because Mike had said they'd gone back to the station to listen in on Jacoby in an interview room there quizzing Ernesto. Reilly'd undoubtedly been quizzed some himself.

And meanwhile, he'd had to worry about me.

"I'm sorry," I whispered, and he hates when I say that, a reflex, a jerk. Came up off his heels.

"Yeah?"

I *was* sorry. I'd been able to see parts of it coming, repercussions, but I hadn't been able to do the right things to stop it. "You can disown me, Reilly."

"What are you talking about?"

"At your department," I said. "For Jacoby and Abbott."

He moved impatiently above me. "You're not making sense, Meg."

I was trying to. Wiping the damn tears away with my left hand, but they just kept on falling.

"Mike's a witness," I said. "So's the desk guy at the motel, and the cops who were with you when I hung up on you yesterday. You weren't a part of what I was doing, you didn't know. If Abbott comes asking."

He was getting it then, and he was, if anything, white—absolutely incensed. Said disbelieving, each word distinct, "This had better be the drugs talking."

He couldn't even be sensible.

"It isn't a lie, Reilly. We *were* fighting. I'm a twit who wouldn't listen, I hung up on you. It's in place now, it's established—God, I took a *motel* room so that you couldn't find me. It's to use if you have to," and I had to make him see it. "It's your life," I said. "It's your job."

"Is that how you and Mike do it?"

I looked up at him then, his face hard as stone.

"You tell me," he said. Said it straight and unyielding. "Is that how you and Mike work?"

"No."

He nodded grimly, succinctly.

"You think I'd want less?"

Loyalty.

Faith.

God, he wanted more.

"Mike isn't going to lose his job for helping me," I said.

"I'm not, either." He was crisply determined, leaning in, both hands on the chair arms. "And I'm not having half my department thinking I'm losing my grip. What that means is that you're going to accept that I know what I'm doing, and we're going to start doing things the right way."

*His* way.

Ultimatum.

"You want me to sit home and knit?"

"Knitting's fine," he said curtly. "I don't care what you do. But you aren't leading me on this kind of chase again."

I don't normally lead people on chases. I normally go to work and back home again, jiggety-jog. Reilly'd had no sleep to speak of for the last day or so, and he'd been thoroughly strained, as anxious about me, I think, as I'd been about him. Maybe we'd neither of us been sure how this whole thing would end, if we'd end up together or not. He wasn't saying it nicely, but he was saying he wanted "together."

I guess I wanted "together," too.

We could work out the details.

"Okay," I said.

# 39

Mike came in with the wheelchair. His timing was great, so you have to consider that he's another one of those guys who hang around outside doorways and listen. Occupational hazard. Cops tend to do that.

Or maybe it's just the kind of cops I know.

We got me into the wheelchair, got me rolling down the hall with the fluid-stand thing coming right along, although, really, by that time, I could have pulled out the tubes. I didn't want to do it with Reilly watching, though, so I left it alone.

Jacoby was in Sylvia's room, apparently just finishing up talking to her. Getting her story, I guess, such as it was. He had an eye on me, a nod for Reilly, and the two of them sort of met by the doorway, faded back into the hall unobtrusively, while Mike wheeled me in, over by Sylvia's bed. She was sitting up against pillows, looking very pale, very battered. Her eyes were slightly foggy under the bruises, but Mike was moving on in to her, taking her hand.

"How you doing, babe?" all concerned.

She clutched sort of convulsively.

"It's okay, baby," he said. Had his other hand stroking. "You going back to the consulate for a while? Let them take care of you?"

She nodded and started to cry, great silent tears. He looked at me helplessly, and she *was* just a little wisp of a girl, not much bigger than

Josh. I wheeled the chair in more and Michael got out of the way. He left me her hand, so I took it.

"Hi, Sylvia," I said. "I'm Mike's partner, Meg. I just came in to visit. They're going to let me go home today, too."

She cried harder, sobbing.

I'd said "home."

I'm an idiot, really.

"It'll be all right," I said softly. "It doesn't seem like it now, it doesn't maybe seem worth it, but you have to hold on, okay? Just walk through the days until it gets better."

She was shaking her head.

"It will," I said. "I promise you, Sylvia."

Her lips formed "Rudolfo," a fragment of sound.

"He loved you," I said.

Her head was shaking again, because how *could* he have loved her? He'd left her alone.

"People take their own roads," I said. "We can't always see what it is, can't take the blame. Maybe he thought he was saving you somehow, keeping you free of his problems. I don't know. It was something to do with Free Argentina, I think, more than you."

I was meaning financial ruin or public disclosure, exposure, but she tightened on me, frantically.

"Despair . . ." she said.

No.

*Not* despair.

I couldn't, I wouldn't accept that, was shaking my own head, but she said it again, the word forming and breaking.

"Despair . . ."

"You see?" That was Jacoby behind me. He and Reilly were back inside the door. He wasn't unkind, wasn't meaning to be. He was simply being matter-of-fact, and maybe he even was right. Maybe I *was* just blaming myself, didn't want to believe, but I was looking at Sylvia, so small on the pillows. She was struggling to say it again, to get the word out—and it was Argentina that we had as the background. Hidalgos and money. Internal strife.

Free Argentina.

And, God, then I saw it.

The word she was saying wasn't "despair."

"'Desaparecidos?'" I said softly. "The 'Disappeared Ones,' Sylvia?"

She was nodding, easing. Intent on my face. The Disappeared Ones that I'd read about up on the Internet—the thousands of people who'd vanished into interrogation centers during the Argentine turmoil, the civil unrest of the seventies and eighties. While Rudolfo was busy being a celebrity lion, a pampered idol, a Flame, safe in the worldview, the public eye, on the *fútbol* fields of other countries.

"His first wife," Sylvia husked out. "My family, too."

Rudolfo, at Chaven's, *"I should have stayed with my first wife,"* and Mike saying of Sylvia, *"She, you know, went to school in a convent or something."*

A bond.

*"When someone comes, so interested and alive, and they remind you, too well, of what you were, what you could be . . ."*

I'd thought of lost glory, thought of lost love.

I hadn't thought of lost lives.

"Oh, little honey," I said, "what was Free Argentina?"

"To track down, to investigate. A monument to them. But Gunter—" She winced away from the memory. "Linda—"

"They were taking the money?" I said.

She nodded bleakly.

"Rudolfo was raising it? You were?"

"'Dolfo." She smiled at me weakly. "People knew him, you see."

Yes, I could see it. And I didn't want to ask her, but I needed to know. "What was the divorce?"

The smile slipped sideways. "I don't know," she said. "I don't know why he wanted it."

"*He* wanted it?"

"Well, I said . . . I have been so confused. It seemed like the best thing, and 'Dolfo agreed." She was crying again, wiping helplessly at the tears. "But I changed my mind. I told Gunter that, that I wouldn't leave Rudolfo, and he said—he just hit me, kept hitting me because I wouldn't give in."

"Gunter did?"

She nodded.

I said, very gently, "Had you been with him, Sylvia?"

"No."

"Never?"

Sylvia was agonized, biting her lip.

"No, I didn't, I swear it. He wanted to, and I was tempted, I admit that I was. He had been so nice until then, and attentive."

Attentive while Rudolfo was gone, raising money for Free Argentina—the fund that Gunter was helping to raid. Quite a bonus for him to win the girl, too, and Sylvia would have looked easy, desirable, the young wife of *el jefe*.

"It was Thursday night when he hit you?"

"Yes, 'Dolfo was gone. Gunter came and he was already quite angry. He was calling me 'whore.'"

*Puta.* Because he'd seen the pictures Ernesto had taken of Sylvia with Mike. And Sylvia was telling him that she wasn't divorcing.

"So you went to Linda's?" The scorpion's nest.

"I didn't know where else to go. He said he was watching, that he'd hurt Rudolfo. I thought Linda would know what to do."

Linda the attorney.

"Why did you tell Mike it was Rudolfo who hit you?"

"She said . . ." Sylvia was sobbing. "Linda said it was best. That we should deliver the papers and hide for the weekend, so that Gunter would think I was doing what he said. It was only till Tuesday, till the money came in from Florida, and then she would persuade him to go.

She would threaten him, you see? Mike had the pictures of me and so he would have to go away or be put into jail. And that way, with the money, he wouldn't hurt Rudolfo. Only, then . . . then—" She broke down again.

Then Rudolfo was dead.

A suicide.

"Rudolfo was trying to protect you," I said, and if it wasn't the real truth, I didn't care. Truth is always subjective, one person's version, and that day in the hospital, my version was as good as anyone else's. I said it to her strongly so that she could believe. "I told him Friday night that you'd been harmed."

She was looking at me, caught, with her hope in her eyes.

"I thought that *he* hit you, Sylvia, but he knew that he hadn't, that someone else had. I found out at Chaven's that he talked to Gunter there later that night. He must have confronted him about it, must have been told, as you were, that Gunter was waiting for Tuesday, for the money to come. Linda got your cooperation by the threat to Rudolfo's safety, and Rudolfo must have been threatened with yours. He didn't know where you were Friday night because I wouldn't tell him, so there wasn't anything there he could do."

The lion, looking "more small."

"He must have gone home and concluded that the only way to stop Linda and Gunter for good was to bring everything into the open and make the whole thing public. His death would do that. It would focus attention, start an investigation, maybe, into Free Argentina. At the very least, without him there'd be no money transfer on Tuesday. I'd told him Mike was with you, so he could be sure that was keeping Gunter away—and he must have thought they'd find his body on Saturday, that Mike or the Argentine consul would take you in then and keep you safe. He was protecting you, Sylvia."

It was truth enough for her—it might even have been so. She didn't need to know that he thought she'd betrayed him, that he'd doubted her love or her loyalty. That he'd taken her, perhaps, too lightly, had been looking at me. There was money involved and egos, prestige. There are all kinds of reasons that a man takes his life, but this one did some good for the people surviving, and certainly between us, Sylvia and I could believe. She was stroking my bad hand with her other hand, lightly touching the bandages. Trembling.

"You stopped him," she said, "Gunter," but that wasn't true.

"Reilly got him," I said. "I just delayed him a little."

"He was coming for me."

"Maybe," I said, although, really, I thought Gunter had thought we were on to him, there in the house as he was, doing Linda.

"Yes," she said simply. "It's why Gunter was so angry—why he hit me, kept hitting me. *Estoy embarazada.*"

She was embarrassed?

"It's why I had to decide to stay with Rudolfo. For the new beginning for us, to give back to the families. The doctors, they say I am fine."

*Embarazada?*

Oh, my God.

"You're pregnant?" I said.

She was nodding.

I looked over at Mike and at Reilly. Jacoby was standing there, too, and they all had the same look on their faces. I might have had it, myself. Cops have the hardest time sometimes believing.

Gunter's child?

She'd said no. She'd denied it.

A child for Rudolfo.

"He couldn't have known," I said numbly, my own faith kind of shaken, because the man I'd encountered on Friday, the man I'd just exalted to Sylvia, would never have blown himself to oblivion with something like that to fight for.

"No," Sylvia said. "He didn't know. I was going to tell him Friday night when he came home. It is why I had said I would meet him at Chaven's."

At Chaven's. Not for a parting, but a celebration.

It's life, that's all. It's the waste and the promise. If she just had told him or if he'd just held on. There are always more choices than you can imagine. I'd met him by then. We would have helped him.

"You take care of that baby," I said to her, and Reilly was coming in to remove me, because, yes, I was worn-out, and, yes, I was crying. I spend a lot of my time these days doing that, but I held on to her hand for another few seconds.

"You take care of yourself," I said, "too."

# 40

"How're you doing?" Reilly said.

I was fine. Had the window rolled down. He'd gotten me out of the hospital after I'd gone back to my room and cleaned up, satisfied all the doctors, and he was driving me home in the ElCo. Mike was getting my things from the motel, which probably meant I'd have to go over and find stuff later, but all that could wait.

"Taking you to my place," Reilly said. "That's okay?" He was being very casual about it. Was flicking a glance, though.

"I'll have to borrow one of your shirts to wear."

"Not a problem."

No?

"I guess that's a better answer than 'I have a drawer full of negligees.'"

He threw me a real look.

"None of them fit me," he said, and okay, I laughed at him.

"I meant for your guests."

"I make 'em bring their own stuff," he said. "Usually." He was raising his eyebrow at me, waiting for a comeback, but I didn't have any, I was just loving him. His face kind of gentled and sobered.

"Let's get it right," he said.

Yeah.

I nodded at him without speaking. Had my left hand already touching his thigh, was resting it there, stroking a little the way that you do, and his right hand came over, covered my kneecap.

We drove like that for a while.

"You going to heal up quick?" he said.

I usually do. I nodded a yes.

"They want me to do therapy, though, in a couple of weeks."

He quirked that damn eyebrow again.

"*Physical* therapy," I said.

"Ah." His face very innocent. "You had me worried for a second."

I wish.

"I'll make you chicken soup," he said. "That's healthy, right?"

I guess it is, yeah. It depends what you put in it. Me, I don't like soup much because it reminds me of hospital food.

"You can just stop somewhere and get me a burger."

"Can't," he said, shaking his head. "I'm saving up for when you get better. We're supposed to go out to eat, remember? We made a date."

We had. I'd forgotten. It seemed like a long time ago.

We were coming up on a stoplight turning red, and he was slowing down, stopping. Well, actually, he was pulling us over to the curb some ways ahead of the light.

"Don't know where I can take you, though," he said very easily. "Because, I guess, Chaven's is out."

And he'd parked the damn truck with the sentence, had both arms coming around me, was holding my left hand down so that I couldn't smack him while he was closing in. Paused for a second, looking straight at me, meaningfully.

"If I ever see that black dress again——"

He tucked in and kissed me very thoroughly then and somewhere in there he let go of my hand so that he could use his own hand to touch me, so that I could touch him.

"You okay, Meg?" He was breathing a little bit harder. Sounded concerned, halfway between a laugh and a groan. "You all right?"

I was really quite fine. Just bemused as I always am by the way he can read me, can reach me—that chemistry thing.

He was settling me back into the seat very firmly, buckling my seat belt protectively in. "I'm taking you home," he said, "and I'm putting you to bed by yourself till you're better, but I didn't want you to forget that I'm waiting."

I wasn't forgetting.

"You're going to sleep on the couch?"

He shook his head.

"On the floor next to you," he said, swinging the truck into motion. Looked over at me. "That way I can be sure that you'll stay there."

I'd stay.

"It's only my head and my hand that are hurt," I said. "I might be willing to sacrifice, put myself out a little."

"Yeah?" He laughed wickedly at me and I felt my vital signs surging. "You're going to lie there thinking of England?"

Not England, no.

And not Argentina.

Because, really, for me, there's no place like home.

# *Acknowledgments*

I wanted to say thanks once again to my Fine Family unit of Red and the kids, C. and R. (yes, honeys, *you*), for their faith and their patience. "My mom only microwaves but that's 'cause she's a writer. . . ."—She chops up a mean apple, too.

Thanks also go to my folks, Barb and Cliff, who thought having six kids would be an adventure (and boy, did they get *that* one right). There's Kathy (and Frank, with their two, D. and M.); Paul (and Vesna, contented with cats); Cassandra (and Allen); Erich (and Carmen, with M. and C.E.—should have had an "I" in the middle there, bro); and Tam (who's playing her current cards close to her chest). Thanks, guys! I couldn't have grown as I did without all of you. (Well, you helped me learn very early how to duck and to run!!!:)

Susanne Kirk is my great Scribner editor, who's made this publishing voyage so very easy. Thank you, Sus—you're absolutely the best! Deborah Tuttle is another person at Scribner who's been just terrific, so, thanks very much, Debbie. You have what I call "the listening ear." I miss Elizabeth Barden and Hope Breeman, who helped me so much last year, but I wish them well and I wouldn't hold them back for the world. And I want particularly to say thank you to Laura Wise and Angella Baker, fine copy editors, who've done yeo-woman work for me on *Bait* and on *Hook*. Thank you, ladies, I really appreciate it!

Evan Marshall is my agent and now a published writer in his own right, which was a wonderful thing to discover about him this year. Thanks, Evan, for all your hard work!—And since we know that it's really Nancy Bandel who runs everything there in New Jersey, I'm thanking her, too—thanks, Nancy!:)

I cherish my girl gang: Debi; Leesa; Vickie; Jana; Katie; Cheryl; Corey; and Lillian. (Tracy from Florida; Lynn K. from Massachusetts; Gail S.; Lisa McM.; Trish S.; and Vivian T.; all count very highly as honorary members. . . .) We started—how many years ago?—when the kids were in kindergarten, and it means such a lot to have people to share with. (So Deb, when are we getting the dang logo and T-shirts???)

# *Acknowledgments*

Thanks go out from my heart to the RavenFold—an opinionated and contentious bunch, but very informed and informative—There's Obi-Wan; Shimizu-San; Bearman; TOB; Rosco; Ken S.; Barrett T.; the GHOst; and my SoCal contingent (Fred M., .John B., Ron W., and Jim D.). Jerri and Ralph S. Mouse are right up there, but there's also Friar Frog, of course, and cofounder Barry; Greg L.; Pete G.; Guntactics; dvcnra; thegunny; Erik G.; marciano curmudgeon; bubbas45; and tmgoethe; as well as Vern and his lovely wife, Barb-I-Mean-"Gloria." I don't want to leave out Sue Mog; Leslie A.; MIKEY; Dave Broadsword; Irv Bigsfish; Alvin;WHH "Billy" Hayes; Chingesh; Ian; weltyblair; or my conscience, Jmatej. There are a HOST of others (who'll undoubtedly come up to smack me), but you're the ones I've known longest and best. DVC from CJ.:), the Valkyrie Babe.

I've met so many wonderful and funny people this year—publishing *does* open doors! Top of the list is my dear Sandie Herron (of a Novel Idea fame) and her best husband Bill; along with Sparkle, Gub, Cluelass and the rest of the AOL WoMbats; not to mention the AOL Mystery RELMs (Sherrill, Erma, Pat, Jacquelynn, Secret—you know who you are!) There's Kelly Caldwell, my first Internet interviewer; Shelly McArthur and Richard Brewer of Mysterious Bookshop; Barbara Peters (Poisoned Pen); Joan Wunsch (Coffee, Tea and Mystery); Ed and Pat Thomas (Book Carnival); Donna Boutelle (who's a UCLB fan); Lou Boxer (an MO-PA fan); the inimitable Anne Poe and her husband John Lehr (touting themselves as Poe's Cousin . . . hmmm); Kate of Kate's Books; Willetta Heising (Detecting Women); Wm. Kent Kreuger; Paul Bishop; and Marty J. Smith.

The SinC clan has been great—local, national, AND Internet Chapter—a thousand thanks to Barbara Paul and the hardworking others of SinC-IC. And I want to say a personal thank you to Diane Bouchard; Kris Neri; and Jamie Wallace; who've been scrambling to handle SinC/LA. An excellent job, ladies, very well done.

It wouldn't be life without the DotLers—ANOTHER contentious bunch —do I see a pattern?:) Chief among them are Diane Kovacs and Kara Robinson *(patientiae scintillae);* the infamous D. L. Browne; J. Alec West; THE Lev Raphael; Joescarp; Bob with one O; Doris Ann the 2000-year-old librarian;

## Acknowledgments

Judi M.; Judith H.; J. Wendel; Sophie J., Chaisegirl; Gail L.; Elena Santangelo; Meg C.; and Annie Underwood Grant. What a crew! (Sometimes a *wrecking* crew, but . . . :)

On a more serious note, I want to say a special thank you to Louis Awerbuck and Leigh Lambert—I appreciate the time and the training, but more than that, the friendship. *Mi casa es su casa*, as the Latinos would say. . . . And a thank you to Harry and Catherine Humphries, who, along with Ernie Emerson and Lowell Anderson, kept an unobtrusively protective eye out for me at GSGI. I'm glad for all of us that I didn't need it (and, uh, sorry again about your jaw, Ernie!:)

My Glendale guys have always been great—Bill Halvorsen and Mario Marchman up at the range; Big Bob MacLeod and Ron Allison (no, Beth, I didn't forget you); Randy Petersen (can we puhleeze get that dang trophy NEXT year?:); Randy Robbins, who made things right with the Chief; and our good friends, Jerry and Carolyn Roberts (with a litttle prayer included for Jenny). Jim Lowry did us a big favor (thank you, Jim:); and we love to play with Steve Rupp and Dave Olson. Thanks, too, to friends from our past, Russ Pierce; Skip Fitzgerald; Wayne Williams; Roger Brown; and J.P. (Jim Peterson); as well as that hotspur guy, Jerry "Maurice" Bunzey. (I didn't mean to omit you all last time, exactly, so put those weapons away!:)

There are a couple of people at BHPD that I'd like to thank, and hope that it isn't something against them. I appreciated the objective interest of Frank Naumann, who took the trouble to find out who I was without making assumptions—the mark of a good cop, and somewhat of a rarity these days—and also the warm efficiency of Helen Elliott, the Volunteer Coordinator there. Those two are golden for public relations, but the chief at BHPD seems like a smart man, so I expect that he knows that already.

And, finally, I really have to thank God for the wolf at my door, who made me, perhaps, that touch more determined because he doubted me so thoroughly.

*A chara!*
*CJS :)*

## *About the Author*

C. J. Songer worked for several years with the Glendale, California, Police Department and is married to a former Robbery/Homicide investigator for the same department. Versed in weapons and self-defense, she's taken courses at Gunsite, "the Harvard of shooting schools," in Arizona; Thunder Ranch in Texas; and FrontSight in California. She's had training with current and ex–Navy SEALs, and has shot, by invitation, at tactical matches where street survival skills are measured. Her first novel in the Meg Gillis series was *Bait*, published by Scribner in 1998. She lives in southern California.